FALL OF A SCRIBE

Ancient Egypt Mysteries
Book Two

Keith Moray

SAPERE
BOOKS

FALL OF A SCRIBE

Published by Sapere Books.

24 Trafalgar Road, Ilkley, LS29 8HH

saperebooks.com

ISBN: 978-0-85495-093-5

Keith Moray is represented by Isabel Atherton at Creative Authors.

For my granddaughter, Martha, who just seems to know many things about ancient Egypt.

A tomb now suffices him for whom the world was not enough
Epitaph on the tomb of Alexander the Great

As a saviour of the Greeks, this watchman of Pharos, O lord Proteus,
was set up by Sostratus, son of Dexiphanes, from Cnidus.
For in Egypt there are no look-out posts on a mountain, as in the
islands,
but low lies the breakwater where ships take harbour.
Therefore this tower, in a straight and upright line,
appears to cleave the sky from countless furlongs away
during the day, but throughout the night quickly a sailor on the waves
will see a great fire blazing from its summit.
And he may even run to the Bull's Horn, and not miss
Zeus the Saviour, O Proteus, whoever sails this way.

Epigrams, Posidippus of Pella (310–240 BC)

ACKNOWLEDGEMENTS

With thanks to my professors and lecturers at the University of Dundee medical school, who taught me how to scribble quickly, and to respect the human body in both life and death, much as the ancient Egyptians did.

Thanks to Ahmed Elsayed, my Egyptologist friend and guide, who gave me much valuable information and showed me several plundered tombs in the Saqqara necropolis, as well as the iconic statue of the 'Cairo Scribe' in the old Egyptian Museum of Cairo. Those together with the several minutes I was able to spend entirely alone with the red granite sarcophagus in the King's Chamber of the Great Pyramid on the Giza plateau inspired me to write this novel.

As ever, my grateful thanks to Isabel Atherton, my wonderful agent, and to Amy Durant and all the fabulous people at Sapere Books.

And finally, thanks to my lovely wife Rachel for all the support she gives to this humble scribe.

PROLOGUE

Crocodilopolis, Nile Delta
276 BC

The day had been hot and oppressive, but now Ra was beginning his slow descent from his highest point. It was not a good time to face the crocodile.

A crowd had assembled outside the temple of the crocodile-headed god Sobek, eager to see the great spectacle. Men, women and children had come from all parts of the city and from other towns on the Nile and its Delta. Nobles, officials and representatives from the many different priesthoods had been brought to the temple on litters or on palanquins raised upon the shoulders of slaves. Tradesmen and artisans had made their way there either on the backs of animals or on their own legs, as had the labourers in the fields and the watermen from the river.

The young man whose body had been found in the reeds by the Nile with his throat slit had been a popular young constable.

Hanufer, the captain of the Medjay police, was only a few years older than the victim, and he had felt the death keenly, as had the other men under his command. Tracking down the two murderers had not been easy, and they might have been free even now had they not been overconfident in their ability to lie. Many of the locals lived in fear of them and had been reluctant to talk to the Medjay.

The dead man, young Constable Sinue, had disobeyed Hanufer's orders and investigated some suspected murderers and robbers on his own, taking with him two of the trained baboons that the Medjay used to chase down and intimidate criminals. The young constable had not expected an ambush, during which bows and arrows had been used to take down the baboons. He was captured, tortured and brutally slain. His body and those of the two baboons were discovered by a Nile police patrol boat two days after he went missing.

Hanufer had interrogated both men suspected of Sinue's murder along with a dozen others and found that their stories had matched rather too well. When he talked to them a second time, he was able to spot a kink in their accounts. With the permission of the city governor, he had them bound and had their feet beaten with rods. It did not take long to elicit their confessions. Their bows and arrows were found, along with the weapon the elder one had used to slit the constable's throat.

At their trial, they admitted that they had been robbers for many years, but Hanufer suspected that neither had the leadership nor organising skills to operate on anything greater than a local level. He had secretly determined that when time allowed, he would find out if there was a chain of command leading to bigger fish than these.

There had been much to do in supporting the family of Sinue. The young constable's body was being mummified, along with the two baboons whom the Medjay planned to have entombed with him, with the permission of his family.

Trumpets were sounded from within, and the temple gates were swung open to allow the gathered crowd to slowly enter the temple enclosure. Hanufer stood at the base of the dais upon which the city governor sat with several shaven-headed priests of Sobek standing on one side of him, and two members of Sinue's family on the other. As a noble, the governor wore a wig and a Greek-style chlamys.

Some of the arriving nobles had their palanquins turned and set down so that they could watch the proceedings. Twenty Medjay constables stood to attention in two lines, each wearing metal and leather chest pieces and heavy *cothurnus* boots. They had sheathed short swords hanging from their waists and batons dangling from their wrists. Four corporals also stood to attention, with spears held upright at their sides.

'People of Crocodilopolis,' called out Meritites, the city governor, 'you all know why we are here today. It is thanks to Captain Hanufer and his men that two heinous robbers who have murdered one of the Medjay will be punished. This is by direct order of the pharaoh's vizier, Admiral Patroclus. Here in the sacred temple of Great Sobek, you may watch, respect and know why the law must be obeyed. Bring forth the two criminals, Mesedsure and Pa-neck.'

He nodded to Hanufer, who took a deep breath and adjusted his own wig before issuing an order to Sergeant Sabu. Hanufer wore a simple chiton tunic, while the shaven-headed Sabu wore a chest piece like his constables.

Sabu clapped his hands, and two of his corporals disappeared into a building to the side of the temple. They returned some moments later with two men, who wore shackles on their ankles and had their hands bound behind their backs. Both men looked utterly terrified. As they approached a walled enclosure, they started to pull back but were roughly shoved on by the corporals.

Again, Sabu clapped his hands, and four constables joined the corporals, much to the two prisoners' horror.

Angry murmurs rose from the assembled crowd as the two convicted men were manhandled up the steps that had been placed against the walls of the enclosure. Two large, sharpened stakes the height of a man could be seen protruding above the enclosed walls, which surrounded a great pool. The two stakes had been planted into one of two small artificial islands within the pool. From the walls a temporary bridge had been positioned, so that the criminals could reach the island in the middle of the pool.

The two screaming men were half-carried across this, then each was raised by one corporal and two constables and held high above the stakes.

Hanufer swallowed hard, trying to suppress the wave of nausea that threatened to overcome him. He looked at the governor, who nodded emphatically.

'Turn them both,' Hanufer said, indicating that they should be rotated so that their bellies were above the points of the stakes.

The crowd began chanting the names they had been given upon being found guilty: Mesedsure, meaning 'hated of Ra', and Pa-neck, 'the serpent'.

'Now, lower them for the impalement.'

There were shouts of horror and anger from the crowd, but most of the people gathered were urging them to make haste and do the deed.

The two prisoners let out blood-curdling shrieks as the points penetrated their flesh, so that they writhed in agony, screaming louder than the whole of the crowd. With their hands bound behind their backs, they were unable do anything to stop their downward progress.

Hanufer tasted bile in his throat, but steadfastly watched as the officers released the limbs of the prisoners and retreated back over the bridge.

'Let the embodiment of the great god Sobek be released!' called out Meritites, as he held out a hand to the elderly priest standing next to him.

Hanufer knew Shemey, the head priest of Sobek well. He was now some sixty years of age and had served the temple since he was a boy of ten. In that time, he had looked after three of the great Nile crocodiles that were kept and worshipped in the temple pool. As a young priest he had lost half of his right hand to Sobek-Ammit, as the sacred creature under his care was called. Shemey never resented that and had told Hanufer that because the creature had consumed some of his body, he believed that he was forever linked with whatever sacred crocodile was cared for in the temple. It was for this reason that whenever the Sobek-Ammit lost a tooth or a toe, he kept them or had them fashioned into rings or amulets to distribute to those who had done the temple some special service.

Hanufer watched Shemey lead his priests down towards the innermost enclosure where Sobek-Ammit had been basking in the heat of the day. Under Shemey's instructions, the priests pulled chains that raised a great metal shutter. The crowd watched as the temple's sacred, aged crocodile, the length of three men and with the girth to match, crawled out and slithered into the pool, seemingly unconcerned by the crowd of spectators. The gold chains and jewels that bedecked the creature glittered in the sun, making the crowd gasp. Some pointed at a large red stone that had been embedded in the right eye socket after some disease had rotted its eye. With a strange grace, it glided towards the island.

The two impaled prisoners were now emitting groans of agony, presumably having discovered that the more they screamed, the greater the pain. Despite this, upon seeing and hearing the crocodile, they began screaming again.

It smells the blood already dripping down the poles, Hanufer thought to himself. His thumbs automatically rubbed the rings he wore on each forefinger. One was carved from a tooth that had fallen from the lower jaw of the sacred crocodile and bore an image of the god Sobek. It had been given to him on the orders of Shemey after he had solved a particularly unpleasant crime committed within the temple three years before. Sobek was the god of his home city of Sumenu, which the Greeks had called Crocodilopolis until recently; Pharaoh Ptolemy the second, whom they called Philadelphus, had had the city's name changed to Arsinoe, in honour of his sister-wife.

The other ring was made of silver and moulded with the image of Maat, the goddess of truth, who wore the sacred feather in her hair. Hanufer revered both and touched the rings when he needed help with solving a problem, or if he needed to know that he was on the right path.

He wanted to close his eyes, but it was his duty to watch and show no weakness. Many eyes would be on him, whenever they tore their attention from the scene that would soon be played out before them.

It was inevitable: the men would either die from the impalement, or in the jaws of the crocodile when their bodies slipped far enough down the stakes to be reached. If Sobek-Ammit felt hungry and energetic enough, he could launch himself upwards to hasten the process. For now, it seemed as if he was content to crawl onto the edge of the island and wait.

Everyone in the crowd and upon the dais watched intently — all except one.

Hanufer was not aware that among the crowd, there was a pair of tear-filled eyes that glared at him with hate.

CHAPTER 1

Alexandria, 275 BC

Hanufer awoke suddenly, covered in a patina of cold perspiration. He felt his heart pounding inside his chest, and in the darkness that surrounded him he wondered if the creatures were still chasing him. He fancied he could hear the splash of their powerful feet in the mud as they came out of the water, dragging their huge bodies and tails after them. The stench of blood and torn flesh brought with it a wave of nausea, and he shot upright and swung his legs over the side of his bed to stand up.

The feel of the rush mat beneath his feet was immediately comforting, and he realised he was in his own chamber. The urge to vomit disappeared, replaced by a sudden need to feel fresh air on his face.

It was just a dream, he chided himself as he ran a hand over his shaven head and crossed the chamber to push open the shutters.

It was still the middle of the night. The moon shone over the sea and the bright beams from the great lighthouse on the nearby Island of Pharos illuminated the tops of the Royal Palaces and the higher buildings of Alexandria. The sky above was filled with a myriad of stars, so many of them gods and goddesses or the souls of past pharaohs. Soon it would be the Wepet Renpet Festival, which marked the start of the New Year when the star Sothis, which the Greeks called Sirius, would rise above the horizon alongside Ra after it had last been seen at sundown in the east. Within days the Nile would begin to flood, and the land would become fertile once more.

Standing naked by the window he filled his lungs with air, relishing the smell of the sea and the blossoms in the garden below. He was a tall and fit man who had rarely been troubled by illness, or by fears or black moods, so these dreams that had started to plague him annoyed and unsettled him.

He touched his rings for comfort, for they represented the deities he considered the most important in his life and whom he believed looked after him: Maat and Sobek.

Hanufer thought that since the dreams were of crocodile monsters, Sobek, the crocodile-headed god would have dispelled them, but in his wisdom the god had not done so. Either that or he had considered it a matter for a lesser deity. Therefore, on the advice of old Hessi, one of the Egyptian physicians who practised in Rhakotis, Hanufer had taken to placing a statuette of Bes and Tutu on either side of his bed.

Turning, he looked at them in the moonlight. The goddess Tutu, daughter of the exalted goddess Neith, had the head of a beautiful woman and the body of a striding, winged lion, with the smaller heads of hawks, crocodiles and other creatures of the Nile marshlands protruding from it. She was the goddess protector against demons, and he had placed an offering of figs in front of her before he had retired.

On the other side was a figurine of Bes, a short god with a huge head, bulging eyes and bowed legs. A household deity and protector against evil, he too had received an offering, but in his case it was a plate of dried duck flesh and a goblet of beer.

'My lovely Nefrit would not approve of either of you,' he told the figurines, shaking his head. 'When she graces my bed with her presence, the wings of Isis must enfold us, for these dreams of shadow monsters do not bother me at all.'

Then, fearing that he might have offended the gods, he bowed to them and smacked his head seven times with the heel of his hand.

But thinking of his beloved Nefrit, the High Priestess of Isis whom he was soon to wed, he felt more at ease, his mind switching momentarily from the demonic to the carnal.

'Yet why cannot I see the monsters as I sleep, only their shadows?'

The dreams had troubled him for several weeks after he had overseen the impalements and sacrifice to the crocodile of two criminals. Back then, he had been captain of the Medjay, and the executions had taken place in his home city. However, the dreams had disappeared when he had been appointed the *Archiphylakites*, the Overseer of the Alexandrian police by Pharaoh Ptolemy Philadelphus himself. Then, a month previously, for no reason at all the shadow monsters had returned.

It was as if they were a sign of evil to come. Evil that lurked in the shadows.

Cario, the young Greek *demosios*, a public slave attached to the police headquarters, was a wiry, good-looking fellow of a little over twenty years, who had been born and bred in Gortyn in Crete. His master Apollinaris had brought him to Alexandria when he had taken up an appointment as a scholar in the Musaeum. He had educated Cario himself, teaching him to read and write in Greek, as well as the rudiments of rhetoric and logic. Everyone at the Musaeum had thought that Cario was his son, which Cario himself suspected to be the case, and he had dreamed of manumission, when he would be made a

19

freed slave before Apollinaris died. Unfortunately for Cario, his master had been addicted to wine and other vices and had fallen into debt, resulting in a serious illness and sudden death. Since Cario was legally considered a mere chattel, he was sold to become a *demosios*, a public slave to the office of the police. There he was mistreated until Hanufer took up his position as the Overseer of Police.

The police headquarters consisted of an annexe of the *Dikasterion*, the Alexandrian court building, which was surrounded by ornamental groves just off the Emporium, the city's main marketplace.

As usual, the young slave rose before the sun was up and ate some bread and dried fruit in the corner of the kitchen where he lived. Then he tidied the office ready for the arrival of Hanufer and Sergeant Sabu, who had accompanied him from the Medjay and who was now officially recognised as the *Hyparchiphylakites*, the Deputy of Police. Despite Sabu's raised position, he himself felt most comfortable being addressed as Sergeant Sabu, and wore the same chest piece as did his constables, albeit with the insignia of the *Hyparchiphylakites* on his.

Hanufer and Sabu shared a large office, which was dominated by two desks. Hanufer's was larger and higher than his subordinate's. Both desks were covered in baskets containing papyri, clay tablets and ostraca, the shards of pottery used for making rough messages. Cario had carefully prepared the men's writing paraphernalia, along with pots of water to dip the reed pens and brushes into to use with the ink blocks and various coloured paints. Large chests took up space on the floor, and a map of the city of Alexandria was fixed on the wall behind Hanufer's desk.

Two corporals were sitting on a bench at the side of the room, sipping weak beer that Cario had brought for them. Both wore the leather chest pieces and high leather boots of officers of the Alexandrian police. 'The boss isn't going to be happy, Filemon,' said Pylyp, the elder of the two. 'That's the second prostitute to be murdered in the past two weeks.'

Cario frowned. 'As if Lord Hanufer did not have enough to think about with the Wepet Renpet Festival to prepare for, especially if it happens to fall on the day when offerings have to be made on the birthday of divine Alexander.'

Corporal Filemon looked up at the slave, dressed in a simple tunic which exposed the delta brand of a *demosios* slave on his shoulder, and nodded his head. Both corporals had a good relationship with the young slave and were well aware that he had received an education from his former master. His respect for the gods and the memory of Alexander the Great sometimes made him seem more like a novice priest than a slave.

'Yes, the boss has much to think about — not to mention his personal situation,' Filemon replied with a wink.

'This murder may alarm him even more in that case,' said Pylyp.

'Have you seen the body?' asked Cario.

Both men shook their heads. 'Not yet,' said Filemon. 'We only received the reports from the night duty constables. Apparently it's not pretty. The killing, that is, even though the victim was said to be.'

'And as if that isn't enough, there was another death last night,' added Pylyp. 'One of the Necropolis guards was speared by one of the other guards on duty. It went straight through his eye and into his head. The constables have the one who did it locked up, and he's screaming about a ghost.'

'A ghost?' Cario echoed in alarm, almost spilling the pitcher of beer that he had lifted to replenish the corporals' mugs.

At the sound of heavy footsteps in the corridor, the two corporals swiftly gulped back their beer and shoved the empty mugs towards Cario, who placed them under his arm and walked out through the open back door of the office.

Sergeant Sabu entered a few steps ahead of Hanufer. He stopped and eyed the two corporals with suspicion as they stood to attention.

'Trouble overnight?' Sabu snapped. 'We heard you talking as we came in. What's this about a ghost?'

Pylyp and Filemon were both Greeks, who like most of their number had been dubious about the wisdom of appointing Egyptians in positions of authority over them. It had not taken long for Hanufer to demonstrate to everyone from the pharaoh downwards that he was a man of great intelligence and a natural leader. Sergeant Sabu likewise showed that he was not a man to cross or disobey.

The Overseer and his Deputy both wore the typical Greek chitons, since Hanufer felt it was important that the Greek citizens of Alexandria should be able to identify with them. Sabu was about a hand's breadth taller than Hanufer. He had the physique of a warrior and his head and face were shaven. Hanufer wore the traditional Egyptian black shoulder-length wig and kohl around his eyes. He also wore the gold pectoral of office, which had been given to him by Ptolemy Philadelphus himself. At its base was the official seal that he used on all documents and which gave him immediate authority to enter and investigate anywhere.

Cario reappeared with fresh mugs and a replenished pitcher of beer. Hanufer spied it and shook his head, but Sabu took the proffered mug and waited for Cario to fill it.

'We have two deaths to report, my lord,' Pylyp told Hanufer. 'We have not seen the bodies ourselves yet; we just received the news from the night duty guards.'

'Natural deaths?' Sabu asked as he raised his mug to his lips.

'A murder and either an accident or another murder, my lord,' Filemon returned.

'The murder first, then,' said Hanufer, sitting behind his desk and drawing the basket of papyri nearer. The sheets had all been laid out flat in a pile by Cario.

'The victim was a prostitute found in her brothel by the keeper this morning, my lord,' Pylyp said, taking over the report. 'She had her throat slit from ear to ear. There was apparently blood all over the place, and a puddle of it on the floor had flowed under the door. That was what alerted the brothel-keeper this morning.'

'Any disturbance heard by anyone else?'

'Not that we know of, my lord. As I said, we haven't seen the body yet; we thought we should inform you first. We told the constables of the night guard to leave the body where it was found. One of the constables is still there with it.'

'Where is this brothel?' Sabu asked. 'Show us.'

Pylyp went over to the map of the city nailed to the wall behind Hanufer's desk. The overseer pushed his chair back to make room for him. The corporal studied the outline of the city, which was shaped like an unfolded chlamys cloak. Two main roads intersected across the middle of the city, which was divided into five districts, each being designated by a Greek letter. After a moment, Pylyp traced one of the streets in the epsilon district, the area in the southern part of the city above Lake Mareotis.

'Here, sir. On the street of the wine sellers and pleasure houses. The brothel belongs to an old rogue called Gorgias.'

Hanufer nodded. 'And what is this about a ghost?'

Filemon cleared his throat. 'Once more, we only have a brief outline of what happened, my lord. There are three Necropolis guards on duty at the western Necropolis every night. As you know, the Necropolis or the City of the Dead is beyond the prison and the western wall of the city.'

'We have been there,' interrupted Sabu, draining his mug and handing it to Cario. 'It is divided in two, with the Greek cemetery to the seaward side and the Egyptian Necropolis on the Lake Mareotis half.'

'More or less, Sergeant,' Filemon replied. 'There are some citizens who see themselves as both Egyptian and Greek, so you get some Greeks among the Egyptian dead and vice versa.'

Hanufer nodded. 'That is what we thought — although by and large the Egyptians are mummified and buried in rock tombs, and the Greeks mainly favour being cremated and having their ashes placed in urns in vaults.'

'That is just so, my lord. Both also tend to celebrate with funeral feasts and make offerings.'

'And there are still others who also get buried or cremated in the Necropolis,' said Pylyp. 'Some Jews, Nubians and some tribes.'

Hanufer sat back with his fingertips pressed together. 'And in the next few days, when the Wepet Renpet Festival begins, families will flood into the Necropolis to pay their respects and make offerings to their dead relatives.'

Filemon waited for Hanufer to signal for him to continue. 'So, my lord, there were three guards on duty. As usual, each took a sector of the Necropolis to patrol in case of robbers or desecrators.'

'Do they find anything usually?' Hanufer queried.

'Hardly ever, my lord,' replied Filemon. 'I have never known it, until last night. One of the guards said that he saw a ghost and blew his horn to alert his fellows, but this ghost came at him. He said that he threw his spear at it, but it just went straight through it, only to hit the other poor guard in the head as he ran from another part of the Necropolis to help.' He put a hand to his left eye and grimaced. 'It went straight into his eye socket and lodged in his head. His body went into a fit, even though he must have been dead straight away.'

'That can certainly happen,' Sabu said. 'I've seen it in battle, and everyone has seen chickens run about after their heads have been chopped off. It must be their spirits leaving their bodies after such violence.'

'Well, the other guard, who was their sergeant, arrived and arrested the killer,' Filemon went on. 'At first he thought the one who'd thrown the spear was drunk, he was raving so much.'

Hanufer paused before picking up another sheet of papyrus. 'Did the sergeant say anything about this ghost?'

'He says he thought he saw something, sir. But he wasn't sure if it was a trick of the moonlight or from the light of the Pharos lighthouse. He said the shadows at the Necropolis can make you edgy, so that you think you have seen things. He said the guard who threw the spear may have been extra skittish.'

At the mention of shadows, Hanufer felt a tingle shoot up his spine and he thought of the dreams he had been having. He shivered and pushed the thought away.

'Where is the body of the Necropolis guard?' Sabu asked.

'The sergeant guard who arrested the other got two of the prison warders to go and get it. They put it in a cell next to the killer.'

Hanufer looked at Sabu and raised an eyebrow. 'Well, both incidents need to be investigated thoroughly. Sabu, you get the details from the corporals and go and investigate the murder of the prostitute. Pylyp and Filemon, you go and interrogate the Necropolis guards, and then go and examine where the guard was killed.'

A strange throaty noise sounded in the corridor, and Cario went out to see who was there. A moment later, he showed in a Nubian messenger, who was wearing a tunic in the blue and red colours of the vizier.

The messenger, named Tabid, did not say a word. This was not surprising, for Hanufer knew from experience that the man had no tongue. The Overseer of Police took the rolled-up papyrus and read the message.

'It seems to be a morning for urgencies,' he said to Sabu. 'The vizier, Admiral Patroclus, wants to see me immediately at the palace.'

The fact that Patroclus had sent Tabid indicated to Hanufer that it was an urgent matter, for even if this messenger was intercepted and coerced, he would not be able to say anything. The man was like a living shadow — a thought that sent another shiver up Hanufer's spine.

CHAPTER 2

Hanufer usually liked to walk, but since the Royal Palaces were some distance from the police offices, he ordered a horse to be brought for him. It would be quicker to saddle the horse than to arrange a chariot, and the vizier was not a man to be kept waiting.

The Royal Palaces occupied the eastern coastal area of Alexandria and extended out on the spit of land that formed the outer edge of the Great Harbour. Well trained palace guards were beside the outer gates and main doorways of the labyrinth of marble-floored corridors with onyx colonnades that led into the palaces.

Admiral Patroclus, the pharaoh's vizier, was also the High Priest of Alexander. The latter title was more honorary than functional. It meant that he was expected to lead processions and be present at feasts and ceremonies dedicated to the deified Alexander, whom everyone knew as The Great. The emperor of the world himself had begun the process when he had first invaded and conquered Egypt. Always a shrewd man, he had made it his policy to bring Greek culture to the lands he had invaded and subdued, and yet to adopt some of the customs of those people. He had known instinctively that in absorbing some of their religious practices, he would appear to them as a benevolent and enlightened conqueror. Accordingly, one of his first acts was to visit the Oracle at the Siwa Oasis, where three hundred years previously Pharaoh Ahmose the second had built a shrine to the god Amun. There he was duly given a sign by the god, and the priests of Amun immediately proclaimed that Alexander was the actual son of Amun.

When Alexander died in Babylon as he sought to extend his empire, a potential power struggle threatened when the *Diadochi*, the Emperor's five generals, debated who should rule in his stead. Ptolemy Soter, rather than fight for overall control, opted to take over the satrapship of Egypt. Immediately, he declared himself pharaoh, moved the capital from Memphis to Alexandria — the city that Alexander himself had founded — and started a new religion dedicated to the god Serapis, an amalgamation of the Egyptian gods Osiris and Apis and the Grecian gods Hades and Dionysus.

It was a shrewd move by Ptolemy, but even shrewder was his kidnapping of the body of Alexander from General Perdiccas, who had been in the process of transferring the body in a great gold and crystal sarcophagus from Syria back to Aegia in Macedonia. Having abducted the sarcophagus, Ptolemy had it taken first to Memphis, then to Alexandria, where it was entombed deep beneath the Soma, a specially built temple dedicated to Alexander. This act had given Egypt supremacy over the other *Diadochi*, for they held the mortal remains of the son of Amun.

When his son Ptolemy Philadelphus took the throne after a period of co-regency with the first Pharaoh Ptolemy, he completed the deification and ordered that the cult of Alexander the God should be the paramount religion of Egypt, supplanting even the great Serapis cult started by his father.

Pharaoh Ptolemy Philadelphus had honoured Patroclus by making him the first High Priest of Alexander, and as such his position in Egypt was only surpassed by that of the pharaoh, his sister-wife Queen Arsinoe and by their children.

Hanufer, as the *Archiphylakites* — the Overseer of Police — occupied a position of great prestige and was known to all of the palace guards. However, he was aware that as most of them

From inside his chiton, Patroclus drew out a silver ring and slid it across the desk to Hanufer. 'Look at this. I believe it is significant.'

'It is a seal ring, my lord,' Hanufer said, inspecting it closely. 'It is quite beautiful. It has an ivory face and a figure on it. By the size of it, I think it would have adorned a man's finger.'

'What is the figure, Hanufer?'

The overseer bit his lip. 'It is one that looks familiar to me, but I can't say exactly why. It seems to be a seated woman, a goddess, I presume. She has a snake wrapped round her neck and is sitting astride a large dog, and she appears to be holding a lit torch in each hand.'

'Good, and what of the ring itself?'

Hanufer smiled. 'It is made of two pieces, each the shape of a snake. There is a slight gap, so possibly it was originally designed for a woman's hand. It is an intricate piece of jewellery.'

'Very good. You are right: it is a goddess, but not one normally worshipped by the Greeks. She is Hecate, an ancient goddess of the moon, gateways, crossroads and of dark magic. From what I gather, she was worshipped in ancient days by the Carians of Asia Minor. Do you know of her?'

'I do not know any more than you have just told me. We have a goddess called Heqet, who is sometimes associated with childbirth and with the Nile. She has the head of a frog, and is not at all like this Hecate. And we also have a god called Heka, which is our word for magic, but he is a male god. I do not think they are in any way the same, but I will have to make further enquiry from those more knowledgeable.'

'Then I have no doubt you will find out more. You are a discoverer of secrets, after all.'

Hanufer nodded dutifully. From the time of his appointment as *Archiphylakites*, Overseer of Police, Admiral Patroclus had made no secret of his disdain for the pharaoh's policy of placing Egyptians in positions of responsibility. Although Hanufer had proven his ability and gained the pharaoh's approval, Patroclus seemed unable to give more than a grudging acknowledgement, despite the fact that he clearly needed Hanufer's help. It was the attitude of a master to a servant, albeit a servant who had saved his master's life and reputation in the past.

'I don't quite see how this relates to this woman, Artemisia, my lord?'

'It was found on the body of a rich Egyptian official called Usermontu. He was the *Architekton* of Alexandria who built many of the major buildings and villas in the city. He actually designed this new pylon gate I told you that the pharaoh is dedicating outside the Temple of Demeter. He wore this ring and had been a lover of Artemisia. We believe he was poisoned.'

'Poisoned?' Hanufer repeated in surprise. 'You mean he was murdered? But why have I not heard of this?'

'Because Her Majesty and I made no complaint. We had his death attributed to a natural end.'

'How long ago was this, my lord?'

'Two weeks ago.'

Hanufer was too shocked to reply but sat awaiting further explanation. He held the ring out to the vizier.

'Keep it for your investigation,' said Patroclus with a humourless smile. He rose to cross the room to a tray on which there was an amphora of wine and several goblets. He poured two and handed one to Hanufer. 'You will enjoy this wine. I have it specially imported from Athens.'

Hanufer sipped the wine, although he had no wish to drink at this time of the day.

Patroclus smacked his lips appreciatively after taking a gulp. 'Among my many other duties, I am the head of Her Majesty's unofficial secret police. I tell you this now, but you must never reveal it. I will keep out of your way officially, and I expect you to do the same with me — unless I order you otherwise!' He eyed Hanufer over the rim of his goblet, and the glint in his eyes was enough to emphasise the warning behind his words.

'Is there more, my lord?'

'The pharaoh and his queen must be protected at all costs. There must be no recurrence of the danger that surrounded the dead poet Sotades.'

Hanufer ran a fingertip thoughtfully around the rim of his goblet. 'And what exactly is Queen Arsinoe's concern?'

'That should be obvious. Queen Arsinoe is concerned that there is another woman, and you know how she herself became queen. She had her half-brother Ptolemy repudiate Queen Arsinoe, the first of that name. She does not feel entirely secure in her position and does not want to be supplanted herself. Also, she does not wish Pharaoh Ptolemy to be found dead in his bed.'

'Could she not just have Artemisia removed? Not killed, but banished to some remote town or city?'

Patroclus shook his head. 'No, His Majesty has an attachment to her. Not only is Artemisia a *hetaera*, but she has skills in soothsaying and reading dreams. There is a small temple to Hecate in Canopus, more a shrine than an actual temple, which was built for her by wealthy citizens, presumably of Carian descent. She was installed by them as a priestess of that temple. I believe that made her services as a *hetaera* much in demand there. So, if anything happened to her, the pharaoh would demand answers.' He stared meaningfully at Hanufer and added, 'Even of his queen. We cannot have another Sotades situation! I have not the time to deal with this.'

'So, this ring with the sign of Hecate — what do you think, my lord?' Hanufer asked.

'Queen Arsinoe is concerned that Artemisia bewitches men and kills them after taking their favours and much of their money. And if she is a witch, the queen needs to be sure before trying to deal with her. It would mean telling her brother-husband.'

'I understand, now — I think,' replied Hanufer, draining his own goblet.

'It is Artemisia who is being made a basket carrier and a Priestess of Hecate. That is something else you should know: this pylon gate is called a *hecata* because it is dedicated to Hecate.'

Hanufer snapped his fingers, then immediately apologised to the vizier. 'Of course, that is why the figure on the ring is familiar. I believe there is a statue atop the column.'

Patroclus nodded. 'After the dedication, Artemisia will be present at the feast, where she will entertain with her dancing and lyre. And there is added significance to her seeming devotion to the goddess Hecate.'

'Perhaps you could enlighten me, my lord.'

The vizier swallowed some wine and put his goblet on the desk with a gesture of impatience. 'The goddess Demeter is one of the most ancient Greek goddesses. Her daughter was called Persephone, and she was abducted by the god of the underworld, Hades.'

Hanufer nodded. 'This I know. She reappeared, and because of that Demeter and Persephone were both regarded as goddesses of fertility and guardians of the gateway to the underworld.'

'But did you know that Persephone only reappeared because the goddess Hecate saw the abduction and went down to the underworld with her torch in hand and found her? For this reason, Hecate is also known as the goddess of crossroads.'

'I see, my lord.'

'Artemisia has clearly informed His Majesty the pharaoh of this, hence the dedication of this new pylon. It will be at the entrance to the temple of Demeter, which happens to be at the corner where the Street of the Soma and the Canopic Way cross.' Patroclus tapped his fingers on the desk and fixed Hanufer with a penetrating look. 'You can begin your investigations tonight at the feast in the gathering hall of the Temple of Demeter. But since Pharaoh Ptolemy and Queen Arsinoe will be there, you will have to be subtle.'

Several voices could be heard from the corridor outside.

Patroclus sighed. 'It is time for you to go. I have an army and navy to organise.'

'May I have the address of, and some information about, the official, Usermontu, my lord? And also the address where this Artemisia may be found?'

The vizier nodded curtly. 'I will send a messenger to your office with this information.'

Hanufer nodded and stood up. 'And I will retreat into the shadows, my lord. There is much that one can learn from there when your quarry does not know of your presence.'

The two priests Evenius and Kephalos and the scribe Hatensor were waiting outside the door, while another group consisting of an army general and colonel, a naval captain and two officials of the Nile Delta police stood apart in whispered discussion. The four guards stood at attention.

Recognising the senior officer of the Nile Delta police officials as *Archiphylakites* Heri-ib, his opposite number, Hanufer bowed to them all, but also smiled at Heri-ib, who raised a hand in acknowledgement.

He knew that the Nile police were in regular contact with the vizier, for the Nile and its tributaries were the very essence of Egypt, but he had not known that they were in Alexandria at this time. Before he had an opportunity to talk to Heri-ib, the vizier called for them all to enter his office. Hanufer was intrigued as to why the Nile police had been summoned by the vizier. The last time he had seen the other overseer had been at the execution of two criminals in Crocodilopolis the year before, for it was one of their patrol boats that found the body of the murdered constable.

As he was shown out of the palace by guards, Hanufer again had an uneasy feeling. Could Artemisia really be a murderess or a witch? Was she really a threat to Queen Arsinoe, and perhaps even to Pharaoh Ptolemy Philadelphus? He did not have much to go on, and he wondered if he was going to be chasing shadows.

As that thought entered his mind and he passed the papyrus-shaped columns along the corridor, he had an uneasy feeling that he was being watched.

Almost at once they moved forward, asking questions and protesting in alarm. Many of them were weeping. It was clear that even if their keeper was not in mourning, most of them were.

Sabu raised his hands for silence. 'I will speak to each of you before I leave, but first I must see the body of the dead —'

'Ahset!' interrupted a forthright young woman. She stared directly at Sabu, her hands on her hips and her jaw set defiantly. 'Her name was Ahset, and she was a good woman. She was my friend.'

'Pah! Only talk to the officer when you are spoken to,' Gorgias snapped at her.

But Sabu silenced him with a raised hand. He addressed the woman. 'Then I will talk to you first about your friend Ahset once I have seen her body. What is your name?'

'I am Keket, and we were both from Crocodilopolis.'

Sabu raised his eyebrows. 'You are Egyptian? You look —'

'I look how I am told to look and behave,' Keket replied, turning and sweeping her hand at the other women. 'We all do whatever we are told.'

Sabu noted the sly grin that crossed Gorgias's face. He disliked the man even more.

'Take me to see Ahset's body,' he ordered the brothel-keeper.

Sabu was used to violent deaths, but the sight of the young woman lying on the reed mat made him wince. A pool of congealed blood had spread from the wound in her throat and flowed under the door, soaking the bottom of the curtain that covered it.

'You slipped in the blood there?' he asked Gorgias.

45

'I was going to pass water, sir. I often do in the hours before dawn. I almost fell, and I cursed in the dark. I banged on the door but there was no answer, so I let myself in. She was lying like that. The oil lamp was still burning. I almost cried, sir. She was one of my favourites. I love them all, you see. We're like family.'

Sabu was unconvinced by his show of mock affection. He looked about the room, noting the large bed and the wine amphora. There were two goblets and a lute on a table, alongside a variety of instruments of pain and pleasure, including whips, camel hair flyswats, woven reeds and assorted ropes. On another table was a water clock that had run its time.

The sergeant knelt down to take a closer look at the body.

Ahset had been a beautiful young woman. Sabu estimated that she was around twenty years old at most. She had olive skin, pure black hair and full lips, which were now bloodless.

Without moving her clothes, he knew from the odour that on the point of her death, her bowels and bladder had emptied themselves.

Her face was frozen in a startled expression, with her eyes wide and her mouth gaping to reveal her tongue.

'Is this the only door to this room?' he asked Gorgias as he stood up.

'Yes, sir, it is.'

'And the window, is it always closed?'

Gorgias shook his head. 'Often it is open. It gets hot in some of these rooms — especially when the women are busy.' Once again, the ghost of a knowing smirk crossed his face.

'How many customers a day would Ahset have seen?' Sabu asked.

'It varies, sir. She was popular, so it could be anything up to fifteen or so.'

impress the likes of us, whom they see as mere bodies for them to use.'

'Did you see Ahset after she saw him out?'

'No, the last time I saw her was when she took him into her chamber. He looked to have been drinking before he came. He was nervous, I would say, the last few times I saw him. He jumped if there was an unexpected noise.'

'How did she sound?'

'She was happy, as usual, and made a fuss of him. That's what we do. Later, I heard her singing after she showed him out, and I think she was dancing along the corridor, though I didn't see her. I was with a client myself, and my mind was focused on other things.' She raised an eyebrow slightly to allow Sabu to draw his own conclusions.

Sabu cleared his throat. 'When did you find out that Ahset was dead?'

'This morning, when Gorgias found her.'

'Did you weep when you heard of her death?'

'Why would I?' she said with sudden candour. 'Death gave her relief from this life we lead. I envied her that. I felt anger, though, that some bastard snuffed her life out by slitting her throat.'

Sabu was surprised at the vehemence in her voice. 'And what about you? Tell me about yourself.'

Her expression again became flirtatious as she leaned forward. 'Why would you want to know about me, Sergeant Sabu? Do I interest you?'

Sabu felt his face grow hot. 'I am interested only in finding who killed your friend, Ahset.' Her eyes fluttered downward, and she looked profoundly sad. 'I want to bring whoever is responsible to justice,' he added.

It was then that Keket started to weep.

CHAPTER 4

Corporals Pylyp and Filemon knew some of the *desmophylakes*, the guards in the prison near the west wall of the city, since they had been constables before growing too old for the rigorous duties demanded of them. The guards of the Necropolis, on the other hand, were under the authority of the Priests of the Necropolis, and they did not know them at all.

'What do you expect from the undisciplined and untrained dregs that those damned priests employ?' said the grizzled old *desmophylax*, the head warden as he opened the thrice-barred door to let them into the gloomy corridor of the prison, lit by a couple of flickering torches. 'Fighting among themselves like that!'

Another voice from further along in the shadows was quick to interject. 'We aren't dregs, you swine. I'm not, and neither are my friends, Kallisto and Dion, nor any of the Necropolis guards.'

As the corporals' eyes adjusted to the gloom, they saw a tall bearded man dressed in leather boots and a leather tunic walk towards them. His right hand held the pommel of a short sword that hung in a sheath from his thick leather belt.

The old *desmophylax* sneered. 'Then why's one of them lying dead in a cell, and the other's in the cell next to him, nursing a broken head?'

'I don't know exactly, you dog, but I know Kallisto wouldn't have harmed Dion. It was an accident, I'm sure. As for Kallisto's head, I had no choice but to knock him out because he was mad with fear, guilt and panic.'

'Don't call me —' the head warden snarled belligerently, only to be stopped by Pylyp.

'Enough of that, Nikias,' he said, addressing the old man. 'Our boss, *Archiphylakites* Hanufer, sent us to hear what happened, and that's what we mean to do.'

The guards of the Necropolis, the vast City of the Dead beyond the western wall of Alexandria, were generally held in low esteem by the police and prison guards. They had to report to and take orders from the priests of the Temple of Proteus and Harpokrates in Rhakotis. Harpokrates, the god of silence and mysteries, was another of the Egyptian gods who had been adopted by the Greeks. His Egyptian name was Har-pa-khered, which meant the child god Horus, who represented the newborn sun each morning. Also, in keeping with the policy of the first Ptolemy, his cult had been amalgamated with that of Proteus, the home god of the Island of Pharos, who was also associated with silence and prophecy. Thus, several shrines and temples to the two gods had been built across Alexandria. Although neither of these two gods was associated with death or the care of the dead, the mystery of death and the silence of the grave were regarded as sufficient reason for the priests of their cults to be allocated the role of custodians of the Necropolis. Neither the local Greeks nor the Egyptians had ever questioned the matter.

'So, let's begin with you,' Pylyp said, addressing the guard of the Necropolis. 'What's your name, and what can you tell us?'

'I'm Linus, and I was the sergeant of last night's watch. Kallisto and Dion were under my orders. Halfway through our shift, we do a round of both sides of the Necropolis. I took the Greek half on the seaward side, while Kallisto and Dion took the Egyptian half. I heard shouting and then a blood-curdling scream of agony. That was Dion. I ran through the City of the

Dead. Lots of the tombs are cut into the rocks, but there are all sorts of funerary shrines and buildings, with planted trees and bushes, so I couldn't tell what had happened until I came on the scene. Kallisto was trying to yank his spear out of Dion's head. The poor man was on the ground, having a fit, and Kallisto had a foot on his jaw and was pulling. Dion was making a horrible gurgling noise, but I think he was already dead.'

'A death rattle,' Pylyp put in.

'You said he was mad with fear, guilt and panic?' Filemon prompted.

'Of course. He'd thrown his spear and hit his comrade. He was crying out that he didn't mean it and was begging the gods not to let him die.'

'And you knocked him out?' Filemon asked.

'I had to. His eyes showed he was out of control.'

'But I thought he was your comrade, too?' Pylyp asked.

Linus frowned. 'He was. I mean, he is, but as he pulled the spear free, he started waving it about. He was raving about a ghost. I didn't know if he was possessed by a spirit, so I gave him the flat of my sword on the side of his head. Then I tied him up and came here, where I got help to go and bring him back, along with Dion's body.'

Nikias grunted. 'Since they were supposed to be comrades, we gave them neighbouring cells.' He turned and strode off down the corridor. 'Come on then, see what you make of this. I can't say I like the idea of this dead body staying here too long. In this heat it'll soon stink the whole place out, and then I'll have a riot with the other prisoners.'

The body of Dion the Necropolis guard had been laid out on a pallet bed in a windowless cell. The only illumination was from a guttering torch opposite the barred cell door. In the flickering light, the wound in his head looked terrible. There was a gaping hole where his left eye and half his cheek should have been. Clotted blood and grey-pink pulp had oozed from the wound. His other eye had rolled so that only its white was visible, and his mouth was open in a silent scream.

The two corporals looked down at the body in horror.

'It looks as if he took the spear when he was facing the thrower,' said Pylyp.

Linus shrugged. 'I did not see the actual thing, as I told you. I only came on it as Kallisto was trying to pull his spear out. When he did, blood and brain came out.'

'They were good friends, you said?' Filemon queried.

'All three of us are, Corporal,' Linus replied. 'Or we were.'

'What do you make of this ghost your comrade talked about before you knocked him out?'

'I don't know. I didn't see the spear strike, but with all Kallisto's raving about a ghost, I thought I saw something in the corner of my eye. But it was dark except for the moon and the lighthouse light. Maybe it was a ghost, because when I turned it had gone. What other explanation can there be?'

Pylyp and Filemon glanced at each other but said nothing.

Nikias the turnkey sneered. 'As long as I don't find any ghosts in here. You can keep them in the Necropolis.'

At a signal from Pylyp, Nikias took them to the neighbouring cell, which was similarly illuminated by a torch on the opposite wall. Through the bars, they saw Kallisto. He was sitting on his bed, one hand holding his head and the other covering his mouth as he rocked back and forth, emitting a sorrowful moan.

He looked up through red-rimmed eyes as Nikias banged on the barred door. Nikias told him who they were and why they had come.

'I didn't mean it. I wasn't aiming at him,' he volunteered.

'That's what all murderers say,' Nikias snorted.

Linus balled his fists and glowered at him. 'Take care, mongrel.'

Filemon stepped between the two men and shook his head warningly, causing both to back away from each other.

'So how did you manage to hit him?' Pylyp asked.

'I was trying to get the ghost. It was drifting across the ground like smoke.'

'Like smoke?'

'It was white and shiny in the light from the moon and from the lighthouse. I ... I think it was coming for me; it was groaning and thrashing about. I ... I threw my spear, and I think it passed straight through the thing. Only ... only it caught Dion as he was running towards me. I didn't see him, I swear by all the gods.'

'Did you see Sergeant Linus?' Filemon asked.

'I ... I don't know. I was scared out of my wits. I was trying to get my spear out of Dion's head. I thought that maybe if I got it out, he might still be alive. I hated putting my foot on his face, but I didn't know what to do. He was my comrade. When I did get it out, I thought the ghost was coming for me again. Maybe I saw Linus and lashed out, then ... that's all I remember.'

He began to shake uncontrollably, and Pylyp gestured for the others to follow him.

'Linus, you come with us,' he said as they reached the thrice-barred door at the entrance to the prison.

'Are you arresting him, too?' Nikias asked with a cruel grin.

'No. He's going to show us exactly where this all happened.'

'And what about the body in the cell?'

'It stays until our boss decides otherwise,' replied Pylyp.

The Necropolis was a strange, distorted mirror image of the city of Alexandria, in that it had two main avenues at right angles to one another, both lined with palm trees. The tombs were not regularly arranged like the streets of Alexandria, but there was a rough arrangement into unequal sections, the tombs placed according to the lie of the land and the difficulty or otherwise of cutting into rock.

The Egyptian tombs mainly occupied the Lake Mareotis side of the cemetery and the Greeks the seaward side. There were also smaller sectors on both the westernmost and easternmost areas, which were occupied by cemeteries for Jewish people and other communities.

Numerous *exedra* buildings — stone porticos — dotted the Necropolis. As Sergeant Linus had said, olive trees, palms and assorted bushes had also been planted near the tombs.

'Most of the Egyptian tombs are below ground. Passages cut into the rock lead to the burial chambers, or to a *triklinion* — a banqueting hall where the mourners have a feast or make offerings at the funeral,' Linus explained as he led the way through the Necropolis.

'And the Greek graves are on the other side of the Necropolis, you said?' asked Pylyp.

The Necropolis sergeant nodded. 'They also have *exedra* and *triklinions*, but many are buildings on the surface, with vaults for whole families.'

'And most of us Greeks are cremated,' Filemon said.

Linus nodded. 'That is so. Their funerary urns are placed in separate chambers in the vaults. That is good enough for most Greeks, but as you know, important Greeks like generals and admirals and high priests have been embalmed in tombs. Of late, many other Greeks are having their relatives embalmed and buried in sarcophagi like the Egyptians. They are following the lead of the royal family and adopting Egyptian culture.' He showed them the Necropolis guard building where the day duty guards had already started work. Two were manning the guard room, and the others were out in the Necropolis. 'My comrades are unsettled by this accident,' he told Pylyp and Filemon. 'I reported to them after we took Kallisto into custody, as was my duty.' He spat sideways. 'Like me, they know it was an accident, and they are also certain that Kallisto saw a ghost and tried to defend himself.'

'Where are the guards who are out in the Necropolis now?' Pylyp asked.

'They are doing their rounds, but I told them to stay away from where it happened, as I knew you police would want to see it.'

The two corporals nodded approvingly.

Linus looked towards the clear blue sky and the burning sun. Placing a fist over his heart he added, 'May the gods protect us all from those that should remain in their graves.'

They passed a long, single-storey building with columns and a large stela that looked like a temple, but clearly was not. It had high slit windows, from which a strong smell of brine, spices and decay emerged. 'That is the House of Anubis, where the embalmers work. They call themselves the Men of Anubis. At any one time, they have several bodies being prepared to be mummified. Strange fellows, those embalmers. All of them are Egyptian, and they have no humour.'

'Not surprising,' replied Filemon, covering his nose as they passed by.

Linus explained that he was leading them along the route that he had taken the night before. Eventually, they came to a clearing surrounded by boulders and rocks with bushes growing between them. 'There!' he said, pointing. 'That is where Dion was struck. He must have come from over there on your left.'

'And you came on the scene from here,' Filemon said, bending to look at the ground. 'And where was Kallisto?'

'Standing over him, as I told you. He was trying to pull his spear from Dion's head.'

'So where would he have thrown the spear from?' Pylyp asked.

Linus pointed to the right. 'He would have come from there. Through that break in the bushes, I think.'

'And he said that the spear went through the ghost?'

'That's what he said. It was like smoke.'

Filemon looked around. 'The nearest tombs are how far away?'

'Thirty cubits in one direction, maybe fifty in the other.' Linus pointed back and forth. 'Same again the other ways.' He pointed off to the right. 'I told you I saw something in the corner of my eye, but when I turned to look properly, it had gone. It would have been over there.' He pointed to some palm trees and bushes.

Pylyp frowned and walked carefully in the indicated direction. Halfway across, he dropped to his knee and examined the ground. 'Filemon, look at this,' he called after a moment or two.

The other corporal went to him. For a few moments they conversed, both of them looking back at the blood-stained ground and then at the bush. 'I think Overseer Hanufer had better see this,' Filemon said.

'What is the matter?' Linus asked as he approached, but he stopped when Pylyp stood and held up his hand authoritatively. 'No one else must come here until our boss has been,' he commanded. 'He will be interested in this ghost.'

CHAPTER 5

Hanufer had left the Royal Palace and rode along the harbour road towards the Temple of Isis. It was a familiar route to him now and always filled him with joyous expectation, not because it was the temple of one of the most hallowed Egyptian goddesses, but because the high priestess, Nefrit, was his lover. He had decided to visit today on his way back from his meeting with Admiral Patroclus.

He liked the position of the temple on the raised platform between the Small Harbour and the Royal Harbour, with the little Island of Antirhodos creating the impression of a protective godlike hand in the water. He dismounted and gave the reins of his horse to a servant, and then entered the temple grounds. He mounted the steps and passed the twin statues of the goddess by the great door, then walked through the colonnaded court of the *purgatorium*, through which passed the little stream diverted from the Canopic Canal.

The sound of sistrums drifted from the temple, accompanied by the voices of praise singers. He waited in a covered portico until both the music and the singing stopped.

Two temple maids dressed in veils and long gowns greeted him when he entered the *naos*, the great chamber that contained the towering statue of Isis. They bowed from the waist, smiled at him and then demurely stood aside.

'The Lady Nefrit has gone through to her dressing chamber, my lord,' one of them said with a slight smile. Hanufer returned the smile, and after bowing and saying a silent prayer to the great brightly coloured statue of Isis, he went through to the high priestess's private dressing chamber and entered silently.

'Hanufer!' Nefrit exclaimed joyfully as he encircled her waist with his arms. She spun round and looked over his shoulder to ensure that the door was closed behind him. Then her lips met his and they enjoyed a long, passionate kiss.

When they finally broke away, they stood holding each other's hands.

Hanufer thought that Nefrit was the most beautiful woman he had ever met. She only came up to his shoulder, and she had a voluptuous figure that was barely concealed by her long white sheath dress. As an Egyptian from Philae in Upper Egypt, she had been a devout follower of Isis all her life. Her father had been a scribe and her mother a priestess at the Temple of Isis there. Like Hanufer, she wore an oiled black wig that matched her kohl-painted eyes.

With her high cheekbones, her delicately chiselled nose and her ruby-red painted lips, to Hanufer she was the epitome of Egyptian beauty. On her head she wore a small headdress with two ivory cow horns; between them was a silver disc representing the moon.

'This is most unexpected, my love,' she whispered. 'I did not think I would see you until I crept into your bed tonight.'

'Do not rouse such thoughts in me now, Nefrit,' he returned. 'I have to admit that my reason for coming was not so much to steal embraces as to ask for information.'

Nefrit pouted in mock disappointment and crossed the chamber to pour two goblets of palm wine. 'When we marry, we will not have to sneak into each other's company,' she said, handing him a drink. 'The most propitious day to announce our togetherness is still a month hence, according to the prayers I said and the message that the great Lady Isis sent me.

The Opet Festival celebrates the wedding of Amun and Mut, so what better time could there be for our marriage?'

Hanufer did not ask exactly what prayers she had said and what message she had received, for that would be an intrusion into her communication as the high priestess with her goddess. He accepted her assurance that Isis had smiled on their togetherness, and he was grateful that it was perfectly acceptable for a priestess to be wed to another outside the priestly class.

'What information do you need?' Nefrit asked as she dabbed her ruby lips after sipping the wine.

'Unfortunately, this has to do with some unexpected deaths. Since it may involve those in exalted stations, I can say no more.' He thrust out his chin meaningly at the door. Nefrit caught his look and nodded. Although the temple maidens were devoted to her, they might still enjoy having gossip to trade with others of their station. 'I need to know more about the goddess Hecate and her cult.' He knew that Nefrit had a deep knowledge of many religions.

Nefrit looked surprised and wrinkled her nose. 'Ah, the ancient Carian goddess. She is not a favourite deity of mine, for although she has some attributes in common with the great Lady Isis, she has many that are more in keeping with the despicable Seth. She is a goddess of the moon and of magic, as is Isis. But she is also a goddess of the dark, of pathways that cross, of magic, witchcraft, poisons and ghosts.'

Hanufer felt a familiar shiver at the mention of the last three. 'You are sure of that? Of witchcraft, poisons and ghosts?'

Nefrit nodded. 'The Greeks have more interest in this witchcraft than we Egyptians. They are also far more interested in poisons. They say that Alexander himself, who is now a god of this city, was slain by poison.'

Hanufer was silent for a moment, remembering that Patroclus had said that the *Architekton* Usermontu had seemingly been poisoned. 'In what way is she associated with ghosts?'

Nefrit sat down on a low couch and gestured for Hanufer to join her. 'It is said that she can control the spirits of the dead if a witch or magician prays to her and makes suitable offerings. Those offerings usually involve the spilling of blood.'

'And these ghosts that she can control — are they different from our *ka* and *ba*?'

Nefrit nodded. 'They are very different. The Carians had a much simpler idea of what makes up the soul of a person. For them, the ghost is the whole spirit of the dead person detached from the body when the cord of life is severed. It is like the cord that joins a baby to its mother until it is born. But as we know, the soul and the body are important. The body is the house in which the soul lives; it must be preserved so the person is able to pass into the afterlife. Within the body, the heart contains the essence of the person — that which must be weighed against the feather of truth given by Maat in the hall of judgement when one dies.'

Hanufer held out his hand with the ring dedicated to the goddess Maat. 'She rules my life, Nefrit. As an officer of the police, she guides me in my pursuit of truth.'

Nefrit squeezed his hand. 'But the soul is where Egyptians are more knowledgeable than the Greeks. We know that the *ka* is the spirit double of the body, that can walk about the tomb after death, and the *ba* is the bird of life that can flutter around the mummified body. It is the holder of the quirks and ways of thinking that are unique to that person. And then there is the *akh*, the physical body and the spirit form nearest to the gods, the *ren* or name of the person and the *shuyet*, their shadow.'

'The *shuyet*, the shadow,' Hanufer repeated. 'It changes in the sun; it gets bigger and smaller, longer or fatter, and yet it always seeks the shade, where it seems happiest.'

'Indeed, the shadow is a part of us that is unfathomable, but it can reveal much about a person.'

Hanufer grasped her hands. 'And is Hecate a goddess of shadows?'

Nefrit shivered. 'I can feel that you are unsettled, my love, with all this talk of Hecate. Is something troubling you?'

Hanufer shrugged. 'I don't know. But I have a feeling that she may have something to do with an unexplained death. The answer may be in poisons or witchcraft, or in the shadows.'

The constable that Sabu had sent to deliver a message to Hanufer was waiting in the *purgatorium*, flirting with one of the temple handmaids when the Overseer of Police came out. At the sound of his footsteps, the constable immediately stiffened to attention and the handmaid scuttled off with a basket of flowers in her hand.

'How did you know that I would be here?' Hanufer asked.

The constable shuffled. 'Sergeant Sabu said that if I did not find you by the time I reached the Royal Palace, then I was to try here before going back to the police headquarters.'

He handed Hanufer the message from Sabu. The overseer read it, then they walked out of the temple and collected the horse from the waiting temple servant. Hanufer mounted, then gestured for the constable to climb up behind him.

It took some time to ride to the brothel in Rhakotis, where the brothel-keeper Gorgias was eagerly waiting to admit him. The constable tethered the horse then joined his fellow in guarding the door.

'Will you be able to have the body removed straight away, sir?' Gorgias asked. 'If the women don't work, they cannot eat.'

Hanufer eyed him distastefully. 'Whether they work or not is immaterial. It is your duty to see that they are cared for, and that includes feeding them. It is a tragedy that one of your women has lost her life here, and it is only fitting that the house should be in mourning for her.'

Chastened, Gorgias showed Hanufer into the chamber of the dead prostitute where Sabu was waiting and then quickly left.

'Her name was Ahset,' Sabu informed Hanufer as he stood at the door, looking around. He was taking in the scene and constructing a picture of what could have happened.

'So, what do you think happened here, Sabu?' Hanufer asked after a few moments. He bent down to wave aside the small swarm of blowflies that had already accumulated. 'Your message said something is not right.'

Sabu frowned. 'She had her throat cut, my lord, but we have no idea who by. Her last client was a scribe or priest or scholar, who was a little drunk on wine when he left. She was found lying on the floor on this mat with her throat slashed, yet no one heard any noise. The last they heard of her was when she showed that last customer out. She was singing and dancing along the corridor, according to Gorgias and her friend, another prostitute called Keket — they both heard her. Keket was with a … guest at the time.' He swallowed hard. 'And so, sir, I think she was surprised somehow, killed before she had time to scream.'

Hanufer scrutinised Ahset's pretty face, fixed in death. Her scanty peplos dress was soaked in blood, and he was aware of the odour of excrement and urine. Her eyes stared up at the ceiling, and her irises were merely a narrow ring around her dilated pupils.

Hanufer winced at the size of the throat wound. 'I agree with you. If she was facing her murderer, she would have made some noise when the knife or whatever was used appeared. Unless a hand covered her mouth.'

He gestured for Sabu to stand before him. Then suddenly he reached out and put a hand over the sergeant's mouth, at the same time raising his other hand towards his throat.

As expected, Sabu instantly drew his head backwards, and his powerful hands grabbed both of Hanufer's wrists.

'My lord?'

Hanufer smiled. 'Exactly, I cannot imagine that Ahset would have been able to defend herself as quickly or adroitly as you, but she would have darted back and almost certainly screamed.'

'Unless she had her throat slit from behind?' Sabu ventured. He pointed to the table with the amphora and goblets. 'Maybe she was getting her murderer a drink?'

'But her last client had already left.'

'Could it have been someone she knew?' As soon as he said it, Sabu felt a pang of regret. He had no feeling whatsoever for Gorgias the brothel-keeper, but he worried about the women Ahset had worked alongside — Keket in particular.

'It is possible. Unless she did not see her killer at all,' Hanufer said, going over to the window and pushing it open to put his head outside. He saw a narrow alleyway running behind the brothel and the other buildings adjoining it.

'It is not far from the ground. A fit and able person could easily enter here and hide themselves behind the door until Ahset came back in. Then they could have surprised her.'

'And slit her throat!'

'But where is the spray of blood? There is none over the amphora or goblets, none on walls. The blood is all around the body and on the floor. It has run out the door.'

'Which is how Gorgias said he found the body. He slipped in it when he went to relieve himself before dawn.'

'And he had locked the building up himself.'

Sabu nodded.

'I will interview him and all the women, particularly this Keket, since she heard her.'

'She seems a good friend of Ahset's,' Sabu said, conscious that he was too swift to reply.

To his relief, Hanufer merely nodded. He noticed that his superior was fingering both his rings, a habit that told him Hanufer was concentrating.

Once more, he knelt down to examine the body. Holding the head, he gently moved it to the right and then to the left.

'Something is definitely not right here, Sabu. Get one of the constables to fetch a horse and bier to move the body. And send the other to the Medical School of Alexandria. I will write a message to either Herophilus or Erasistratus. I need them to examine this body. We will tell Gorgias that Ahset's family, if she has any, are to be informed.'

Drawing out a sandalwood writing set from inside his chiton, Hanufer settled down in the chair by the amphora of wine and removed a scrap of papyrus to write his missive. He pushed the tray aside and, selecting a reed pen, he used the wine to moisten the tip.

He wrote several lines, reread them, and then leaned forward and took the tip of his pectoral. This held a circular disc of lapis lazuli on which the seal of the *Archiphylakites* was embossed. Pressing it on his ink block and then on the papyrus, he made the message official.

Having finished, he sprinkled a pinch of powder made of ground shells from a small hinged recess in the palette and then blew it across the ink. Giving it a final shake, he rolled it up and handed it to Sabu.

'I believe Ahset was already dead before her throat was cut. I want the anatomists to confirm or refute that.'

Sabu stared at him in disbelief. 'Then you think someone was waiting for her?'

Hanufer nodded. 'And we need to talk to her last client, this scribe or whatever he is. We need to find him.'

CHAPTER 6

Hanufer and Sabu arrived back at the *Dikasterion*, the imposing building just off the Emporium, the main marketplace of Alexandria. It had columns either side of large wooden doors, above which was a statue of *Dike*, the Greek goddess of justice, depicted as a slender woman wearing a laurel wreath and holding a balance scale before her.

In the police office they found Pylyp and Filemon waiting to report to them. As Hanufer sat at his desk and looked at the additional papyri that Cario had laid out for him to see, the corporals told them of their concerns about the death of Dion the Necropolis guard and of their interview with Kallisto, his fellow guard and killer.

'Their sergeant is called Linus. He was adamant that it must have been an accident, sir,' said Pylyp. 'He says the other Necropolis guards would say so too, sir.'

'Kallisto looked distraught, my lord,' Filemon added, 'as if it had been a terrible accident.'

'But it was when Linus showed us the scene of the death that we became alarmed,' Pylyp went on. 'The story Kallisto gave was that he tossed his spear at a ghost, but he says it passed straight through it and hit Dion, who had rushed to the scene from the other direction. The spear went through his left eye and into his brain.'

'Did you see the body?' Hanufer asked.

'Yes, sir,' Filemon replied. 'It was an ugly sight. In pulling out the spear, Kallisto seems to have pulled away half the cheek and some of the brain, the way your Egyptian embalmers do.'

Sabu grunted irritably. 'They do it through the nose, not the eye.'

Hanufer harumphed. 'And where is the body?'

'In the prison, in a cell next to the guard who killed him. We thought you would want to question him personally and also see the body.'

Hanufer looked at the two corporals through narrowed eyes. Both of them had proven to be capable and responsible men, and although they were not highly educated he sensed that they had potential. They knew Alexandria well, and they were liked by the constables below them. It was for these reasons that he kept them attached to his office and trusted them to investigate certain cases on their own.

'And why do you think that I need to see the body and interview Kallisto personally? Why can't Sergeant Sabu, the Deputy of Police, do so?'

Sabu was standing beside the desk. Both corporals were tall men, but Sabu was taller still and had broader shoulders. He folded his arms and stared challengingly at them.

Pylyp and Filemon looked uncertainly at each other, then Pylyp spoke. 'As I said, sir, Linus showed us the scene. It's an open area in the middle ground of the Necropolis. It is surrounded by trees and bushes. We think we know the spot where Kallisto said he saw the ghost and threw his spear. The place where the guard Dion was hit is obvious, as a large amount of blood soaked into the ground.'

'So, of course you looked at the area between where Kallisto threw his spear and where Dion was struck,' Sabu prompted.

'That's right, sir,' replied Filemon. 'Pylyp did exactly that and called me over to see.'

'And?' Hanufer asked, leaning forward with interest.

'Kallisto told us that his spear went through the ghost as if it was smoke. But there was blood, sir, and footprints. Bare footprints. An interesting ghost, my lord. That's why we thought you would want to see the body, the guard and the place where Dion was killed. We left orders with Linus that no one was to go near that part of the Necropolis until you had seen it.'

Kallisto stood to attention when Hanufer and Sabu entered his cell, leaving Nikias the head warden and Pylyp in the corridor. Filemon had gone to meet Linus at the Necropolis to ensure the scene of Dion's death was undisturbed.

In the flickering torchlight, Kallisto's face was haggard and his eyes red-rimmed from weeping. Hanufer gestured for him to sit, and he sank gratefully onto his crude bed. Then the overseer asked him what had happened.

'By all the gods of my parents, I did not mean to kill my comrade,' Kallisto said as he finished his account.

Hanufer was inclined to believe him, yet it was evident that his spear had killed the other guard.

'This ghost, you said it was like smoke. What exactly did it look like?'

Kallisto trembled as he looked up at Hanufer and Sabu. 'It … it was bent and moved like it was going to pounce. It was naked, shining white in the moon and the light from the Pharos lighthouse. It was making horrible snorting noises, like an animal.'

'Snorting? What do you mean?'

Kallisto did his best to reproduce the noise.

'That is like a spluttering sound. Almost a cough.'

Kallisto shrugged. 'Maybe.'

'It was ready to pounce? Do you mean it saw you? That it was coming for you?'

'When I first heard and saw it, I thought it was just a lost spirit. Maybe a new spirit looking for its body, its grave or tomb. It was hunched and making that noise. I called out to it, then it saw me. I could see its eyes gleaming. It was then that Dion appeared from the other side, behind it. He called too, and it looked his way and then at me, as if it didn't know which of us to attack.'

'You're sure it was going to attack?'

'I didn't wait to find out. I threw my spear.'

'Were you good with your spear?' Sabu interjected.

The guard looked at him and nodded emphatically. 'I was a hoplite — I have used my spear in battle. I can hit a target any time.'

'Had you been drinking beer or wine?' Hanufer demanded suddenly.

Kallisto looked startled. He hesitated. 'A ... a few mugs, sir. Not a lot.'

'But maybe enough not to be so accurate. How is your vision?'

The guard's eyes opened wider. 'How did ... I mean, I see as well as any man.'

Hanufer clicked his tongue. 'We shall see. Did this ghost turn to smoke?'

'I ... I think so. It must have, because it seemed to go through him. There was certainly a cloud of smoke about it. It happened so quickly, because Dion cried out and then started screaming as my spear hit him in the head. He went down and I ran to him.'

'What about the ghost? It vanished, you said.'

'I ... I didn't care. I only saw my comrade. He was dying and I ... I —'

'Did you look for the ghost after that?'

'I didn't see it, because I was trying to get the spear out of Dion's head. He was bleeding and thrashing about. It was only when I managed to yank the spear out that I heard noises, like the ghost was coming for me.' He looked up desperately at Hanufer. 'I couldn't see then, sir. My eyes were full of tears and the blood that was spurting from my friend's head. But I heard it and I ... I think I tried to fend it off, and then I felt a blow on my head and nothing else. When I woke, Linus, my sergeant, had bound me up, and he and the prison guards were shouting at me and dragging me to the prison.' He made an anguished noise and covered his eyes with his hands. 'And others were carrying Dion's body.'

After examining the body in the next cell, Hanufer ordered Pylyp to take it to the Medical School along with another hastily written message for the anatomists.

'Pylyp was right,' Hanufer said to Sabu as they left the prison. 'This is a most interesting ghost that bleeds and has caused our second unexpected death this day. Let us see what the City of the Dead can tell us.'

Hanufer and Sabu visited the Necropolis with Sergeant Linus and examined the area around the site where Kallisto had met his death. They saw the blood-soaked ground where the spear had seemed to pass through the ghost and where there were some indistinct footprints. But a more extensive search of the area revealed nothing further.

On Hanufer's whispered instruction, Sabu had gathered handfuls of dirt and sprinkled it over the blood-soaked area and the footprints. In its centre he placed a small rock that he etched with his knife, so that they would be able to identify it again.

'Linus, ensure that this area is not disturbed by your other men,' Hanufer instructed. 'We may need to return later.' He turned to Sabu. 'Now, let us see if the anatomists at the Medical School can help us further.'

The Musaeum and the Great Library of Alexandria were situated in the *beta* region of the city, the northern part nearest the Great Harbour. It was the most affluent area, for it included the Royal Palaces and the homes and villas of the wealthy, both Greek and Egyptian.

The Musaeum had been one of the first building complexes embarked upon by Ptolemy Soter, the father of the current pharaoh. It was actually linked to the Royal Palaces by a *peripatos*, a long, covered walkway. It had been the first Ptolemy's plan to establish a seat of learning such as had never been seen before. He had been inspired to do so by Demetrius of Phalerum, an Athenian peripatetic philosopher and statesman who had stayed at the first Ptolemy's invitation and suggested to him that he should use the model of Aristotle's Lyceum at Athens. Thus, they came up with the concept of the Musaeum, a great institution in the centre of Alexandria, which would become the home of music, poetry, philosophy and learning. The most learned scholars, artists, philosophers and musicians from around the world would be employed at the pharaoh's expense to develop and advance their areas of learning.

A Temple to the Muses with a head priest was at the centre of this institution, and new buildings were added according to the Musaeum's requirements. It had an *exedra*, a large arcade where the *philologoi*, the scholars, could sit and converse, with study rooms, studios and chambers suited to their particular areas of expertise. Attached to it was a large palatial building called the *oikos*, where they lodged and ate.

As the Musaeum rapidly developed, the number of papyri and books had increased until Demetrius suggested that a Great Library should also be constructed to house the products of the *philologoi's* intellectual and artistic pursuits. When Ptolemy Philadelphus was called by his father to share his throne during the first pharaoh's final years, he greatly extended both the scope and aim of the Musaeum and the Library. This included the establishment of a medical school and hospital.

The way to the hospital from the Temple of the Muses was a straight, colonnaded path that was covered by wooden latticework over which vines had been cultivated. It was the way that the *philologoi* went to reach the Medical School. The citizens of Alexandria could reach the hospital by the main doors that opened into the city's busy Emporium.

When Hanufer and Sabu visited the hospital and Medical School to see the anatomists, a young slave was waiting to greet them. They followed the boy through several corridors, passing many chambers where patients in beds were being treated by doctors or tended by assistants. The odour of body fluids and the smell of incense wafted after them.

At last, they arrived at a large wooden door, where the young slave struck a gong at the side and then stepped back.

Sandaled feet could be heard from the other side, then a bolt was slid back and Erasistratus, a man of about thirty with a thick black beard, cautiously opened the door. He was wearing a heavy leather apron over a chiton.

Beyond him Hanufer could see the body of Ahset lying on one of four wooden tables. Two more bodies in various stages of dissection occupied two of the other tables, and upon the last was the body of Dion the Necropolis guard.

'Ah, Hanufer of Crocodilopolis and his good Sergeant Sabu, come in,' Erasistratus said affably, stepping aside to let them pass. The young slave boy tried to look inside, but he was shooed away by the anatomist, who kicked the door shut behind him. He turned to the police officers and clapped his hands.

'Well, I should have been teaching the student physicians at this hour, but I find that you have sent us not one but two intriguing puzzles to solve. The body of the speared guard arrived only a short time before you. My colleague Herophilus passed on his apologies for not being here, but he said that someone had to teach the students.'

'Can you look at the Necropolis guard first?' Hanufer asked.

They moved to the table upon which the body lay. Erasistratus looked it over. 'It is bad, but I saw worse brought in from the battlefields when I was a young surgeon. A spear wound, you said in your message?'

'It caught him straight in the eye,' Sabu volunteered. 'Went into his brain, and he started to have a fit.'

The anatomist fingered the gaping wound. 'The cheekbone and the bones of the orbit have been smashed. Much of the brain has been dragged out.'

Hanufer described what had happened while Erasistratus leaned over the body. He looked up and grinned at the mention of a ghost. 'Are you taking this seriously?'

'The guard responsible claims that his spear went through a ghost as if it was smoke,' Sabu explained. 'But the corporals who investigated the ground found blood in the area that the ghost was seen.'

'Sergeant Sabu and I have just been to the Necropolis,' added Hanufer. 'We found the blood-soaked sand and a few footprints, but then they disappeared as the ground went from sand to rock.'

The anatomist scratched his beard. 'And this blood-soaked ground, was it far from the body? Blood can gush out and splatter from a distance.'

'This would seem too far,' Hanufer replied. 'It was as it was told to us: about halfway between the guard who threw the spear and the place where this poor fellow died.'

Erasistratus nodded and then bent over the body once more to make a more extensive examination. After a few moments, he shook his head. 'This injury is the only one this fellow has. He is not wounded anywhere else.'

'So that rules out it being his blood on the ground,' said Sabu.

'Which makes the ghost a curious one,' said Hanufer. 'One that bleeds and vanishes.' He frowned and moved over to the other table. Erasistratus and Sabu followed.

The anatomist stood looking down at the body of Ahset. 'So, what is it you want to know? The poor woman had her throat cut — you can see the blade went right through her windpipe and halfway through her gullet. She had no chance of surviving.'

'Have you felt her neck?' Hanufer asked.

'Only briefly, to check stiffness. There is some, but it is still only developing.'

'We think she was killed last evening.'

The anatomist shrugged. 'Then the slight stiffening is correct. But it will not last.' He indicated the other bodies. 'This we see in all these dissections.'

'Yet still, I thought that the neck seemed looser than I would have expected.'

Erasistratus smiled. 'Not surprising, considering her neck is cut so deeply.'

'I wondered if she had her neck broken first, then her throat slit while she was lying down.'

The anatomist looked at him suspiciously. 'What makes you think this?'

'There was no splashing of blood,' Sabu volunteered. 'I saw the body first and thought that there was something wrong, but I could not put my finger on what exactly. Overseer Hanufer saw the same things but spotted the absence of blood except on the floor.'

'So, I need you to tell me if her neck was broken,' Hanufer added.

Erasistratus tugged at his beard and nodded to Sabu. 'If you turn her over onto her face, I will get a suitable *macairion* and some fine dissecting tongs. My apologies to this poor woman; I'm going to have to make another slit up the back of her neck.'

First Erasistratus cut a deep line below the base of the skull and then incised another to the middle of the shoulders. Using his *macairion* and the small pincers, he eased the skin from the muscles and then gradually moved the muscles until he was able to insert his fingers into the hole to feel for the bones underneath.

'Yes, you are right, my friend. The vertebral bones are broken.'

'Is that from a blow to the neck?' Sabu asked.

Erasistratus withdrew his hand. Turning to the side table, he dipped and rinsed his fingers in a bowl of already bloody water. 'No, it was from a twisting movement. She had her neck wrung.' He pointed at a skeleton that had been strung together and hung from a hook on the wall. 'I will show you how. The processes of three of the vertebrae have been broken. The cord from her encephalon was almost certainly ruptured. She would have died immediately.' He crossed to the skeleton and pointed to the bones of the neck. 'These processes that stick out are where one bone moves on another. They are not made by the gods to turn all the way, so they break when forced too far. Watch anyone wringing a chicken's neck and you will see what I mean.'

Hanufer grimaced. 'And if she was laid down and had her throat cut, she would still have bled?'

'Certainly. My colleague Herophilus showed how the heart pumps blood along tubes that we call arteries. Together we have shown that with death, the heart stops beating and the bleeding will stop soon after. But cutting through these major vessels in the neck would allow the blood to escape for some time.'

'And if her murderer wanted to make it look as if the slit throat was the cause of her death, could he have increased the flow of blood by pressing on her chest?'

Erasistratus knitted his brows in thought. 'Hmm. An elaborate way of killing her, but yes, that would be possible.' He rubbed his hands on his apron and looked hopefully at Hanufer. 'May we keep the body for teaching and further dissection?'

Hanufer shook his head. 'Not for display. I think this poor woman's body has suffered enough. She is Egyptian, so I think that she should receive a decent mummification.'

'Her friend Keket will want to mourn her, I am sure,' said Sabu. 'As well as some of the other women who worked with her,' he added quickly.

Hanufer nodded. 'I am sure you are right. In any case, we need to contact her relatives if she has any, and her friend will be the place to start. You can make that your next task, Sabu.'

The big sergeant suppressed a smile. 'Yes, of course, sir.'

CHAPTER 7

The late afternoon brought some relief from the oppressive heat. In order to clear his head after the horrors of the day, Hanufer had spent some time visiting the column of the god Sobek in the small public space surrounded by palm trees. It gave him some comfort to spend time alone with the statue of the god of his home city.

His bad dreams had been worrying him. At first he had assumed they were just bad memories of the impalements he had had to oversee back in Crocodilopolis, but memories usually receded into the background until they were forgotten. He thought the passage of time and his busy life would make these dreams fade, but they hadn't. That was when he started wondering if he was being sent a warning by one of the gods. The shadow monster seemed to be crocodilian, so he naturally assumed it had to be the god Sobek. Yet frightening though crocodiles were, he had never feared them as others did, because he was a faithful follower of the god. If it was a warning from Sobek, what did it mean?

It is a pity that I cannot consult with Shemey the High Priest of Sobek, as I would if I was in Crocodilopolis, Hanufer mused.

He sighed and looked up at the statue of Sobek, depicted as a powerfully built man with the head of a crocodile. Touching his rings to his lips, he made a silent prayer before reaching into his chiton and retrieving a small bag, from which he took out a small bunch of sweet dates. He bowed and placed them on the pedestal between the marble feet.

'For you, Great Sobek,' he whispered. Then he poured out some wheat grains from the same bag. 'And I bring these for your wife, Renenutet. If you can help salve these bad dreams, I will be grateful and will make a proper sacrifice next time I visit Crocodilopolis.'

It pained him that there was no statue to the goddess of the harvest, who was also the great protectress of the royal house of the pharaoh. He closed his eyes and tried to picture her standing beside Sobek: the beautiful figure of a woman with the head of a cobra. He was suddenly overcome by a feeling of relief, as if both gods had heard him.

But as soon as he opened his eyes, the uneasy sense of foreboding returned. As he thought about it, a breeze suddenly blew the grains and some of the dates off the pedestal.

'So that is your answer. I must clear away these mysteries,' he whispered. He knelt down and picked up the grains and dates, returning them to the pedestal. With a bow and a silent prayer of thanks, he turned and made his way towards his villa. He would have a rest and see if the dream occurred again. Then, refreshed, he would go to the feast at the Temple of Demeter. The prospect filled him with dread, for Pharaoh Ptolemy and Queen Arsinoe would be there, as Admiral Patroclus had told him. And he had to observe and subtly investigate Artemisia — a woman he knew little about.

The Temple of Demeter was one of the largest in Alexandria. Hanufer walked to it along the Canopic Way — one of the streets of the city that had been built wide enough for a chariot to turn within it. At the crossroads with the Street of the Soma, opposite the Soma itself, the vast Temple of Demeter was set amid palms, olive trees and assorted fruit trees. As Demeter was the Greek goddess of nature and the harvest, the profusion of fruit was quite deliberate and a testament to the skills of the temple gardeners.

The pylon or *hecata* dedicated to Hecate was a huge dark red granite gate consisting of two pyramidal towers, each tapered and surmounted by a cornice. Atop this was a black basalt statue of the goddess Hecate. The overseer stood for a moment and took out the ring that Admiral Patroclus had given him early that morning. He held it up to compare the depiction on it with the statue above.

The basic image was the same, showing a seated woman astride a large dog. She had a snake wrapped round her neck, and in each hand she held a torch. The finely sculpted body and head showed a beautiful and seemingly untouchable goddess.

Scattered upon the ground all around the pyramidal columns of the pylon were fruits, flowers and numerous amphorae. The heavy smell of wine and olive oil made it clear that the pylon had already been dedicated by the pharaoh and his queen.

The sound of trumpets from within made Hanufer quicken his pace and mount the steps to the temple. At the top of the steps he was greeted by temple maids, who led the way into the great *cella*, the gathering hall where a multitude of people were standing in lines before the colossal statue of Demeter. Forming a human corridor through them were the royal guards, each bearing a sword and spear. Showing his pectoral of office to a captain of the guard, Hanufer was led to a position in the front line of dignitaries.

Ahead of him, on a specially erected dais in front of the statue, were Pharaoh Ptolemy Philadelphus and his sister-wife, Queen Arsinoe the Second. They were sitting side by side on thrones.

The pharaoh wore the royal *postiche*, a long false beard made of goat hair. He was wearing the *pschent*, the combination crown of Upper and Lower Egypt. Beside him, on a slightly smaller throne, Queen Arsinoe was crowned with a Greek crescent band with an ornamental Herakles knot at the front. Emerging from this knot was a silver uraeus, the stylised cobra of royalty.

A priest and priestess of Demeter were leading dignitaries, many of whom Hanufer recognised as scholars, officials and nobles, one by one up the steps to kiss the toes of first the pharaoh and then his queen. Among them were many emissaries of foreign countries.

Hanufer watched as the priests and priestesses of the temples of the other gods and goddesses throughout the city followed the most distinguished and eminent subjects. Among them was Nefrit. When he had seen her earlier, they had both agreed that they should not draw attention to themselves during the ceremony or the feast. Should they pass close to each other, they would give no sign of endearment other than a formal bow of recognition.

Soon Hanufer took his turn, received a nod of acknowledgement from the pharaoh and resumed his place in the line. Standing apart and opposite him was a small group of military and naval officers, and Admiral Patroclus himself.

As usual the vizier's expression gave nothing away, yet as their eyes met, Hanufer noted the slight raising of an eyebrow followed by a movement of his eyes along the line in which Hanufer stood. He leaned slightly forward to look down the line. At the end stood a woman dressed in a superb beadnet dress made of green and blue stones, which matched a pectoral of similar beading. She was holding a basket upon her beautifully coifed hair. He was taken aback for a moment, for she had the exact features that he had seen a few moments before on the statue of the goddess Hecate. This, undoubtedly, was Artemisia.

He looked back at Patroclus, who nodded subtly at the dais. Hanufer looked up at the pharaoh and his sister-wife Queen Arsinoe, and over the next few moments he registered three surprises. First, from time to time, the queen cast a cool look in the direction of Artemisia. Second, he noted an equal number of glances by the pharaoh, but his were accompanied by the suggestion of a smile.

The final surprise alarmed him the most. Upon the fifth finger of Pharaoh Ptolemy Philadelphus's hand was a ring, which looked to be a twin of the one he had in his possession — the one that Admiral Patroclus said had adorned the finger of the dead architect Usermontu.

Once all of the dignitaries had paid homage to the pharaoh and the queen, the next part of the ceremony began. Ptolemy stood up, took a couple of steps to the edge of the dais and raised his hands.

'Good subjects, we have already made the dedication to our goddess great Demeter in her temple. We have also dedicated the pylon you all walked through to her great helper who rescued her daughter Persephone, the goddess Hecate. Those of you who were present at the ceremony will have seen that the Lady Artemisia has been installed as a basket carrier to both Demeter and Hecate.'

He gestured for Artemisia to walk to the foot of the dais steps. When she did so, he raised his hands again. 'Welcome the Lady Artemisia, whom I now proclaim to be High Priestess of Hecate and basket carrier to Demeter.'

Artemisia stood and turned to face the assembly, still holding the basket on her head. Everyone present applauded, except for the guards. They remained motionless, ready to protect the royal couple if needed.

As he clapped, Hanufer stole another glance at Queen Arsinoe, who was making the motions of applauding without actually touching her hands together. He noticed that there was no warmth in her face as she looked at her brother-husband.

'The Lady Artemisia is a musician and dancer without comparison in Egypt. She will play the lyre for us so that we can send a musical message to the goddesses Demeter and Hecate.' He clapped his hands and two handmaids stepped forward — one to take the basket from Artemisia and one to hand her a lyre.

As the new High Priestess of Hecate began to skilfully play, Hanufer looked around at the faces in the assembly. It was clear that she had enchanted many of the men present, while an equal number of women gazed upon her disdainfully. Clearly she was a woman who stirred the emotions.

The feast followed soon after Artemisia's musical rendition. As usual, the pharaoh and his queen only partook of a little wine and a few mouthfuls of food which tasters had already sampled to ensure it was safe. The assembly then dissolved into standing groups and were served delicacies on platters and wine by numerous slaves who appeared from side doors to the gathering hall.

Hanufer began mingling, exchanging a word or two with people he passed as he headed towards Patroclus's small group. He immediately recognised the men surrounding the admiral. They were the general and army colonel, the naval captain and the two officials of the Nile Delta police whom he had passed as they had waited to enter the vizier's office that morning. The military and naval officers were Greek, and the police officers were Egyptian.

'Ah, Overseer Hanufer,' said Patroclus, waving a hand at the others, 'you may already have met General Argyros and Colonel Leonidas of His Majesty's Army, Captain Pakriatos of the Fleet, and *Archiphylakites* Heri-ib and *Hyparchiphylakites* Muthis of the Nile Delta police?'

They all bowed to each other.

'*Archiphylakites* Hanufer and I have met officially several times,' the Nile Delta overseer informed the vizier. He pointed to his deputy. 'And he has already met *Hyparchiphylakites* Muthis, who was in charge of the patrol boat that found the bodies of the murdered constable and the baboons on a shore of the Nile.'

Patroclus grunted assent. 'I remember the case well. I signed the death sentences to be carried out.'

Muthis was a well-built man with a shaven head, like Sabu. A short sword hung incongruously from the right side of his belt. Heri-ib wore an oiled wig and kohl around his eyes like Hanufer, and carried no weapon.

'I was pleased to hear that you found the criminals who killed your constable and the animals, sir,' Muthis said, addressing Hanufer. 'If I had my way, I would have dealt with them the same way they killed those great beasts.' Anger flickered in his eyes for a moment, then he bowed his head to Patroclus. 'My apologies for speaking thus, my lord.'

Patroclus waved a hand. 'I respect a man who cares for the animals. And baboons are, of course, associated with your god Thoth.'

Hanufer nodded and addressed Muthis. 'We had the baboons mummified and entombed with Constable Sinue. He too was fond of his baboons.' He looked around the group. 'Are you all here on official business? Is there some threat that I should be aware of?'

The officers all looked to Patroclus to reply.

'There is nothing that you need concern yourself with, Hanufer of Crocodilopolis. Suffice to say that we are all here for the Festival of Wepet Renpet.' He looked at the goblet of wine in his hand and then moved aside, gesturing for Hanufer to follow. 'What I do want you to be concerned about is the matter I told you about,' Patroclus said in a low voice. 'Now that you have seen the Lady Artemisia, what is your impression?'

Hanufer pursed his lips. 'She has presence, and I have noted how men and women look at her, my lord. She seems a most striking woman.'

'Then you saw how the pharaoh and the queen looked at her?'

'I did, my lord. A very noticeable difference in their regard.'

'Did you observe anything else?'

Hanufer nodded. 'I see that His Majesty is wearing a ring like the one that you gave me.'

Patroclus looked surprised. 'That I did not notice. It must be a recent gift from her. You have sharp eyes, Hanufer. Well, you can see that she has already attracted a large group of admirers around her. Go now and use your considerable skills to ascertain whether there is any danger posed to either the pharaoh or his queen.' With a grunt of dismissal, he returned to his group.

Hanufer had a bad feeling. For some reason, Admiral Patroclus was not telling him everything. Yet his own instincts, which he took to be a message from the gods, were telling him that there was danger nearby.

CHAPTER 8

Hanufer had not worked his way far through the assembly on his way to the cluster around Artemisia when he was stopped by a hand on his shoulder. He turned to see the long beard of Evenius the High Priest of the Temple of Proteus and Harpokrates, and beside him the priest Kephalos and the scribe Hatensor. Hanufer remembered that Hatensor had been reluctant to make eye contact with him that morning.

'What think you of the great pylon gate that Pharaoh Ptolemy has bestowed and dedicated to the goddess Hecate?' Evenius asked.

'It is magnificent. Quite beautiful,' Hanufer returned.

'Rather like the new High Priestess Artemisia herself,' said Kephalos. He bowed to Hanufer. 'We saw each other this morning at the vizier's office, but have not been formally introduced, my lord *Archiphylakites*. I am Kephalos, the High Priest of the Temple of Harpokrates in Canopus.'

'Indeed, I saw that you were waiting to see Admiral Patroclus along with General Argyros, Colonel Leonidas, Captain Pakriatos and two officers of the Nile Delta police. Did you all have an audience with Admiral Patroclus at the same time?'

The third member of the group, the scribe Hatensor interjected before Kephalos could reply. 'No, my lord. We were there to discuss the Wepet Renpet Festival, not talk of war. We had to wait until the officers finished their meeting with Admiral Patroclus.'

Hanufer noted the scribe's sulky tone. He was holding his empty goblet aloft to attract one of the serving slaves. His voice was slurred and his demeanour was less reserved than it had been that morning, when he would barely glance at Hanufer. He was uninhibited, if not a little drunk.

'There was talk of war?' Hanufer repeated.

'Hatensor, why don't you go and see if you can get us some more of those fishcakes they were serving?' Evenius suggested.

Kephalos quickly added, 'To answer you, my lord, Evenius and I serve the gods and were not included in whatever discussions the vizier had with the other military officials. And nor was Hatensor.'

The scribe scowled at Kephalos and then at Evenius. With an exaggerated bow, he said, 'Your wish is my command, sir. I'll have a look, but first I will pay homage to the Lady Artemisia.' He disappeared into the crowd.

'My apologies for our scribe's behaviour, my lord,' Evenius said. 'He sometimes likes his cups overmuch.'

'*Our* scribe?' Hanufer repeated.

Kephalos nodded. 'He is the scribe to both our temples here in Alexandria, and also to mine in Canopus. In addition, he is attached to the Ministry of Buildings and Monuments and seems to gain private commissions from individuals. As such, he travels a lot between here and Canopus and to other divine sites in the Nile Delta.'

'He is quite brilliant and as knowledgeable as any scholar in the Musaeum on matters of astrology and mathematics,' Evenius volunteered. 'For that, he is a most valuable scribe to our temples. How he fits in all his other commissions and appointments, I do not know.'

Another voice behind Hanufer spoke out sharply. 'Gracious words from you, Evenius, just because the book-keeper can add up numbers and has no fear of heights. He spends each day counting the steps at the Pharos lighthouse so he can spend the night counting the stars. He may spend a lifetime doing so but without really understanding the meaning of the simplest of numbers.'

Hanufer turned as two more men joined them. They were dressed in the Greek fashion and were clearly scholars. Both had goblets of wine, and it was clear that they had been eavesdropping on the conversation. He recognised the short, portly and middle-aged one as Lycophron of Chalcis, a poet and mathematics scholar of the Library, much given to making humorous remarks and playing with words. Pharaoh Ptolemy had ordered the librarian to put him in charge of the collection of books on the Comedies at the Library.

'And in the daytime he climbs the lighthouse to count the birds — a far more useful occupation, in my opinion,' said the second man. He was the tall and almost skeletally thin Posidippus of Pella, an epigrammatic poet and philosopher of the Musaeum.

Hanufer had met them both before at a social gathering at the Musaeum. Although they were separated in age by almost two decades, he knew them to be quite inseparable. It was widely speculated that they spent so much time together because they laughed at each other's witticisms when no one else did. He had also heard that Pharaoh Ptolemy and Queen Arsinoe retained them both as soothsayers.

They both roared with laughter at each other's interjections before greeting Hanufer and the two priests.

'You make fun of Hatensor,' Hanufer said challengingly. 'Perhaps it is a difference between Greek and Egyptian humour, but what was amusing in the things you said?'

Lycophron raised his hands in apology. 'Forgive us, Overseer Hanufer. The good scribe Sethnora is what you Egyptians call a rope-stretcher, and he is too arrogant for his own good.'

Hanufer looked puzzled. 'You called him Sethnora? Why so?'

Posidippus chuckled. 'Again, forgive my friend, Overseer Hanufer. Lycophron has a strange compulsion to jumble words and letters. He has done that with Hatensor's name and given him an alternative one.'

Evenius shook his head. 'It is the sort of frivolous pursuit that poets and philosophers get up to. But they should be careful of upsetting the gods.'

'It does seem a strange thing to do,' Hanufer remarked, sipping his wine. 'We Egyptians have more reverence for names.'

'As do I,' Lycophron returned. 'Often I give people names superior to those they were given at birth, just by a little reorganisation. So it is with Sethnora, or Hatensor if you prefer.'

'Both of you philosophers should perhaps pray more often to our god Harpokrates,' Kephalos said. 'You talk in riddles and think no one else understands you. Yet when your jests insult the gods and those that serve them, you risk their ire.'

Posidippus prodded Lycophron in the ribs. 'Mark that, my friend. The god of silence may silence you — or me.'

The two philosophers giggled and then bowed and took their leave.

'They go to seek mischief elsewhere,' said Evenius. 'You may not have realised it, but Posidippus was being sarcastic about Hatensor's counting birds. He himself boasts of his expert ability to make divinations by watching the habits of birds.'

Kephalos nodded. 'But speaking of mischief, it looks as if Hatensor has found some already.'

Hanufer turned and looked in the direction the priest was pointing. Hatensor the scribe was in a heated argument with two men. Hanufer could tell that they were either Egyptian businessmen, officials or scribes by their traditional wigs. One was quite stocky and was about forty. The other was younger, a well-built man of about Hanufer's age. They seemed to be remonstrating with Hatensor and trying to block his attempts to pass them and join the group of people surrounding Lady Artemisia.

'Artemisia!' Hatensor called out to her. 'It is I, your Hatensor. I need to have words with you.'

The commotion caught her attention, but Artemisia looked abruptly away and muttered something to someone behind her.

Evenius touched Hanufer's shoulder. 'Our scribe is drunker than I thought. He seems to be bothering people. Perhaps you, in your capacity as the Overseer of Police, should —'

Hanufer had already moved in the direction of the squabble, but before he could weave his way through the crowd he saw two more men from the group that surrounded Artemisia have words with Hatensor and the two other Egyptians. He presumed they were Artemisia's *somatophylakes*, her bodyguards. Then each took one of the scribe's arms and frog-marched him towards the exit.

Artemisia looked back at the Egyptians who had first been arguing with the scribe, but without glancing at Hanufer they both disappeared into the crowd. Yet as he advanced towards the group surrounding Artemisia, he became aware that the newly appointed High Priestess of Hecate was looking directly at him. Her smile was so beguiling that he stopped and returned it before bowing his head towards her.

She leaned backwards and said something to those around her. Then, with another smile at Hanufer, she turned and walked towards the exit. A group of people parted the crowd so that she passed unhindered.

Hanufer stood watching, then felt a hand on his arm. 'She is indeed beautiful, is she not, my lord, *Archiphylakites* Hanufer?'

He turned and saw Nefrit looking up at him. He had the distinct impression that there was a sharpness in her question and a hint of jealousy in her gaze.

Sleep did not come easily. Nefrit had told Hanufer that she would not visit his villa to sleep with him that night. She did so in a whisper, and then before he could engage her in further conversation, she had averted her eyes and gone to talk to another priestess.

So, his lover and wife-to-be was angry with him, yet he had done no more than smile at the *hetaera* who had just been proclaimed the High Priestess of Hecate. Perhaps her smile had seduced him into betraying thoughts he was unaware of. It seemed that Nefrit thought so.

Before lying down, he had laid some dried fruits before each of the figurines of Tutu and Bes and said prayers to banish the dreams that plagued him. But he found his mind straying to the two sudden deaths that required answers.

He recalled the look of contempt that Queen Arsinoe had darted at the Lady Artemisia. Then he thought of the scribe Hatensor, who had dared to attend the feast while obviously drunk. He went to the window and pushed open the shutters, staring out across the harbour to the Island of Pharos, where the powerful beams from the lighthouse shone out to sea.

In another part of the city, a group of four people were sitting on a rooftop terrace in the moonlight, watching the light from the Pharos lighthouse.

'He is becoming a danger,' said one.

'He has outlived his usefulness,' another agreed.

'What shall be done?' asked a third.

'The same as the others. Which means —' began the first.

'It is a job for me,' said the fourth. 'Fear not, none shall know. Not even him.'

All four laughed.

CHAPTER 9

Sabu had risen at dawn, as was his lifelong custom. Although Hanufer had offered him a room in the villa that Pharaoh Ptolemy had allocated to him, the big sergeant had opted to live in the barracks near the Gate of the Moon to the east of the Brucheum. He liked to be on hand to oversee the constables under his command. His first task of the day before he broke his fast was to take a report from the constables on guard at the barracks, and also from those of the night watch who had been abroad in the city.

It had been a quiet night with nothing of consequence for the guards to report, which pleased Sabu. He had other matters on his mind that he was anxious to report to Hanufer.

Taking a skin of water and some bread, he broke his fast as he walked to Hanufer's villa. There he met Timon, Hanufer's head servant, who was already up and at work, clucking around Delia the cook and Ophelia the housemaid to ensure that all was ready for when Hanufer appeared for his breakfast.

'I will wait for the *Archiphylakites* in the garden,' Sabu told him.

But Hanufer's voice called out to him from the rooftop. 'Come up the stairs, Sabu. I shall eat in the fresh air.'

Sabu grinned at Timon, who tutted at Hanufer's change to his arrangements, then mounted the stairs from the inner courtyard to the roof.

'I thought it best to talk up here, where we are most private,' Hanufer said when Sabu joined him. 'Will you eat with me?'

'I have supped, my lord,' he said.

'Then tell me the news that you are eager to share before we go to the headquarters.'

Sabu laughed. 'You know me so well, my lord. And you are correct. I did not think this should wait. It is about the death of Ahset. I talked with her friend Keket, as you told me to. She did not think that Ahset had any living relatives. As we already knew, both she and Keket were from Crocodilopolis, where they were house slaves to a scribe. They were sold to a rich man here in Alexandria, and were in turn sold by him to Gorgias's wife. I pressed Gorgias to show me the records of their sale to his wife. His wife seems to have been a very methodical woman with a good head for business. The man was an official, and one who built many of the villas in Alexandria.'

Hanufer sat forward. 'Did you get his name?'

'He was called Usermontu, my lord. I went back to headquarters and sure enough, Cario knew of him. He designed and constructed the new pylon gate outside the Temple of Demeter, where you said you were going last night. But more than that, my lord, Usermontu is —'

'Dead!' exclaimed Hanufer. 'That I already know.'

Sabu stared at his boss in surprise. 'You knew this, my lord?'

'I knew that this man Usermontu was dead, but I did not know that he had an association with Ahset or Keket.'

He told Sabu of the conversation he had had with Admiral Patroclus the day before. He also showed his deputy the ring that the vizier had given him. He explained that it was likely that Artemisia had given it to Usermontu.

'This design on the ring shows the goddess Hecate. It is the same image as that above the pylon gate outside the Temple of Demeter. Most worryingly, I saw a ring like it on the hand of the pharaoh.'

Sabu whistled softly. 'So, if Usermontu's death is suspicious, then Queen Arsinoe is worried that something could happen to His Majesty?'

'That is right. Yet because Ptolemy has made her a High Priestess of Hecate, I will have to be extremely careful in my investigation.'

He did not say anything about Nefrit's reaction to the smiles that were exchanged between himself and Artemisia, but he felt a spasm of guilt when he thought of it.

'The death of Ahset concerns me, too. As you reported to me, we know that both Gorgias and Keket had seen her last client many times before.'

'Yes, my lord. Gorgias said he was either a scribe or a scholar. Keket also said that he was a scribe or a priest. Both said that he had been drinking. Gorgias said that he was complaining about some difficulty at his work. Keket said that he was pompous and claimed to be cleverer than all of the scholars in the Musaeum and the Library, and that one day even the pharaoh would know his name.'

'A pompous, drunken scribe or priest,' Hanufer mused.

Sabu was reluctant to tell his boss that Keket had said she had slept with him a few times. However, he was on the verge of doing so when Hanufer sat forward and recounted the happenings at the feast.

'This scribe Hatensor fits that description, so I need to know more about him. Does he visit brothels? Could he have been Ahset's last client? When we get to the headquarters, we will send Pylyp and Filemon to seek him out. Come, Sabu, we have much to do. The Festival of Wepet Renpet and the divine Alexander's birthday celebration are but days away. We must be prepared for the procession to the Soma and for all the problems that can occur when the Nile rises and there is much drinking of wine and beer.'

Cario had Hanufer's desk prepared when they arrived at the headquarters.

'As you instructed before you left yesterday, my lord, I have put all of the papyri and ostraca that awaited your attention in your basket.'

Hanufer took his seat behind his desk and looked up as Cario hesitated. 'Anything else, Cario?'

The young man flashed an uncertain glance at Sabu, who had sat down and was starting to look in his basket. 'Sergeant Sabu asked me about a certain official, my lord. I ... I could not help but see that message that the vizier sent you yesterday. It is on the top of your pile in the basket, my lord.'

Hanufer respected Cario's intelligence, knowing that he could read and write well. He nodded for him to proceed.

'I saw that it was about the same person, my lord. Well, I know the house slave of a physician who was called to see the official when he died. He said his master was not happy about something and that he was visited by some rough-looking men that day. His master has not been the same ever since. He said he looked frightened.'

Sabu and Hanufer looked at one another.

'That is good to know, Cario,' Hanufer said. 'Fetch us some bread and beer. When you come back, give Sergeant Sabu the address of this physician.'

'Do you want me to investigate this, my lord?' Sabu asked when Cario had gone.

'I do, but be subtle about it. And remember to send Corporal Pylyp or Filemon to order Hatensor to report to me here. I want to interrogate him either today or tomorrow morning at the latest.'

'Shall I send them both, sir? If he is like most of the scribes I know, he may have other duties and may be hard to track down.'

Hanufer nodded. 'I know that he has many appointments. Meanwhile, I will look into Usermontu's business affairs and perhaps make enquiries about the Lady Artemisia.'

Hanufer left the *Dikasterion* and entered the palm tree-lined Emporium, which was the main square in Alexandria where all the bankers, moneylenders and merchants owned buildings. On the side of the square opposite the *Dikasterion*, many of the buildings housed the various ministries.

Though it was still early, the square was already packed with all sorts of people. Nobles and officials were being carried in litters or palanquins, and priests, servants and slaves bustled about on foot as street traders tried to attract their attention. In addition, there were work gangs of *demosios* slaves with their minders, clearing the streets of rubbish and horse and donkey dung and tending the palms and sycamore trees.

Admiral Patroclus had sent him the late Usermontu's address — a villa in the Brucheum. The vizier had also let Hanufer know that as an official in the Ministry of Buildings and Monuments, Usermontu had had offices in the Emporium. Hanufer was now paying these a visit.

A clerk working at a table in the entrance immediately recognised Hanufer's pectoral with his insignia of office and despatched a slave to fetch an official. Moments later, a young man dressed in a chiton, but with the traditional Egyptian wig, came into the hall to greet him with a bow.

He was one of the two Egyptians that Hanufer had seen the evening before, remonstrating with Hatensor. Hanufer was surprised but had long since trained himself never to show such a reaction.

However, it was clear from the Egyptian's expression that he recognised Hanufer, though the overseer could not be sure whether it was because he had seen him at some official occasion or at the feast the evening before.

'*Archiphylakites* Hanufer, you honour us by visiting our humble offices. I am Hak-mau, the acting *Architekton* of the Ministry of Buildings and Monuments. May I be of service?'

'I come for information, Hak-mau — about Usermontu. I believe he was a high official and also operated his business from here.'

Hak-mau's mouth became a thin line, and he looked downwards with a pained expression. '*Architekton* Usermontu was the chief builder of Alexandria, my lord. A good and kind official, and perhaps the most skilled builder in Alexandria after the great Dinocrates of Rhodes, who planned this city for divine Alexander. He was my boss.'

Hanufer clicked his tongue. 'Praise indeed. Then you will be able to show me all of his designs?'

Hak-mau looked surprised but nodded. 'All building designs in the city are kept here in the Ministry, and *Architekton* Usermontu had either drawn them or placed his seal of approval on the plans of other builders, including my humble self under his authority.'

He led Hanufer along a corridor, passing numerous doors where scribes and clerks were busy drawing or writing on large papyrus rolls.

In an office only slightly less sumptuous than that of the vizier himself, he offered Hanufer a seat behind a desk that was covered in papyrus plans. About the walls were racks from floor to ceiling containing large scrolls and piles of papyrus.

'Are there any particular plans you would like to see, *Archiphylakites* Hanufer?'

'The pylon gate to Hecate at the Temple of Demeter,' Hanufer replied, watching the scribe's reaction.

But Hak-mau immediately turned and went to the nearest rack to take out a large scroll. He returned and placed it on the desk, unrolling it on top of all the other documents and plans.

'A magnificent piece of work, in my humble opinion, my lord. It was *Architekton* Usermontu's greatest work.'

'Commissioned by Pharaoh Ptolemy, I understand. The columns and the gate itself are all red granite. From where did that come?'

Hak-mau smiled. 'From distant Assuan in Upper Egypt. If His Majesty wants it, it must be done, so no expense was spared.'

'And the statue upon it is basalt?'

'From the Fayum south of Memphis. Usermontu designed every detail, and we had ten sculptors work on it.'

'How are these materials brought to Alexandria? Is that organised through the Ministry of Buildings and Monuments?'

'We have contact with a stone merchant who is based in Canopus in the Nile Delta, my lord. He owns various quarries in the Delta, the Fayum and even Assuan in Upper Egypt.'

'He must be wealthy.'

Hak-mau shrugged. 'I do not know how much wealth he has, but he is certainly comfortable. In fact, he is here in Alexandria on business and for the Wepet Renpet Festival, and also because Pharaoh Ptolemy and Queen Arsinoe made an offering at the Temple of Demeter last evening.'

'I was at the feast, and I saw you and another man,' said Hanufer.

'Ah, then you possibly saw me with him. His name is Rekhmire.'

'An older man than yourself, quite well fleshed?'

'That was he, my lord.'

'And you seemed to be arguing with a scribe called Hatensor.'

Hak-mau sucked air through his teeth. 'Then I apologise that you saw that, my lord. Hatensor is a man who seems to drink too much. He has been doing that more so recently.'

'You know him well?'

'Quite well, my lord. He is a scribe to temples here and in Canopus. He is also employed by the Ministry of Buildings and Monuments as a surveyor. The man is a wonder with mathematics and numbers. But he is unpredictable in his moods. He can be rude and offensive. Indeed, because of that he had some sort of falling-out with Usermontu, who himself could be brusque. They clashed, and I do not think it was resolved before my boss's death.'

Hanufer made a mental note of that piece of information. 'I heard from some scholars at the Musaeum that he also has some expertise in the stars and watches them from the lighthouse on Pharos every night.'

'Indeed, that is true, sir. But it is because of his mathematical and rope-stretching skills that Usermontu employed him privately to survey and arrange quantities of various kinds of stone. As a result, he also gained commissions from Rekhmire.'

'So stone would come up the Nile and then reach Alexandria? How?'

'By barges on the Nile, then through the Delta along one of the tributaries, usually the Canopic River, and then along the

Canopic canal to Alexandria. Or sometimes it was moved directly across the desert, if it was smaller and more transportable, and then on boat across Lake Mareotis.'

'I saw that Hatensor was trying to talk to the Lady Artemisia, the new High Priestess of Hecate, but he was escorted out of the hall.'

Hak-mau winced. 'It was embarrassing, sir. Her bodyguards removed him and left him outside. What happened then, I do not know.'

'But before that, you and the businessman Rekhmire were arguing with him. Why was that?'

Hak-mau shook his head. 'That is even more embarrassing. It was about money. He said Rekhmire and Usermontu both owed him money and he wanted paying. We both said it was not the time or the place. Then he started shouting and trying to attract the attention of the Lady Artemisia.'

'I think I should talk to him. Do you know where he lives?'

Hak-mau looked blank. 'I have no idea, my lord.'

Hanufer nodded. 'So let us talk of Usermontu's sudden death. Do you know how he died?'

'I understand from his physician that he died in his sleep, sir.'

'He died over two weeks ago, I was told. So, as an Egyptian, his body will be undergoing mummification?'

'His body is in the House of Anubis at the Necropolis, my lord.'

Hanufer nodded. 'And who is going to inherit his wealth?'

'I am not sure, sir. His death was registered, as it is demanded by law in the *Dikasterion*, but his family is distant. I believe he has a nephew in Caria.'

Hanufer nodded. He recalled that Artemisia was also from Caria. 'Did he have friends, a lover, or a mistress in Alexandria?'

'I know little of his private life, my lord. Perhaps if you talk to his servants at his villa?' Hak-mau suggested. 'They will have been instructed by the court at the *Dikasterion* to maintain the usual running of the house until his nephew makes it known what he wishes to be done with his villas and his slaves.'

'He had more than one villa?'

Hak-mau nodded. 'He was the master builder of the city, my lord. He had several villas.'

'And which one did he die in? His main home?'

'No, my lord. It was in one of his other ones, which he used when he wanted to be alone to think or to design plans.'

'So, who found him?'

'One of his servants, when he did not return home.' Then, with slightly narrowed eyes, Hak-mau asked, 'Is there some reason you need to investigate this, my lord?'

Hanufer smiled humourlessly. 'Expensive stone transported from Assuan and from Memphis. And the Alexandrian chief *Architekton* has died fairly recently. We need to make sure that all measurements and transactions have been accounted for, since it is Pharaoh Ptolemy himself who has paid for the pylon gate.'

Hanufer noted the sudden glint of fear in Hak-mau's eyes.

CHAPTER 10

Sabu found the physician Galenos busily seeing patients at his practice off a fashionable boulevard south of the Canopus Way. He waited until the old physician showed a patient out and then introduced himself and showed his badge of office.

Galenos was a short man with a slight paunch and a curly, grey beard. To Sabu he seemed unduly nervous.

'Has there been some emergency that I must attend, sir?'

'No, I just need some information about one of your patients.'

Glancing at three waiting patients, one of whom seemed to be in considerable pain, he nodded. 'Then you had better come into my *iatreion*, Sergeant Sabu.'

After giving the patient a kindly reassurance that he would see him next, the physician led the way into his consulting room. Sabu saw that he walked with a limp and sat on an unusually high stool, either so that he would be above his patients or so that he did not have to bend the leg that troubled him.

The consulting room was elegantly furnished with a couch, a tall desk that matched the doctor's stool, and cabinets containing pestles and mortars and a range of surgical instruments. On a pedestal under a high window was a bust of Hippocrates of Cos, whom the Greeks revered as much as the Egyptians did the god Imhotep.

'Which of my patients do you want to know about, Sergeant?' Galenos asked, twirling his beard.

'A wealthy man called Usermontu. I understand he died about two weeks ago.'

Galenos continued to twirl his beard. He chewed his lower lip. 'Yes, he was a patient of mine. He died in his sleep. I was called by his servants, but could do nothing. He had been dead most of the night, I would say.'

'Had he been ill?'

'Yes. It was a blessing that the gods took him. His health was frail, and he drank excessive amounts of wine and took too much of everything. He had an imbalance of humours.'

Sabu nodded. 'I have heard the physicians Erasistratus and Herophilus talk of these humours. They are fluids inside the body?'

Galenos nodded. 'They are the vital fluids that give us life. We have four of them: blood, black bile, yellow bile and phlegm. Usermontu had too much blood, which made him sanguine. I wanted to bleed him, but he was squeamish and would not listen to advice.'

'What does sanguine mean?'

'He liked too much revelry. As I said, he drank too much and ate too much of everything.'

'What about the pleasures of the flesh? Did he enjoy that too much?'

Galenos started tugging at his beard. He shook his head. 'I think that was one thing he did not indulge in.'

'Not at all? Not with house slaves or with *pornae* or *hetaerae*? He had no attachments?'

Galenos shook his head.

Sabu sat upright in his low chair. In doing so, with his great stature he was level with the physician. 'Did anyone talk to you about his death?'

The physician's Adam's apple visibly rose and fell as he swallowed hard. 'No one, Sergeant Sabu.'

Sabu stared at Galenos for a few moments, noting that once again he was tugging at his beard. Then he nodded and rose. 'Thank you, Doctor, I will take up no more of your time. By the sound of that patient outside, your skills are needed.'

My boss will be interested to know that he's lied to me, he thought as he left the *iatreion*.

Hanufer visited Usermontu's villa in the Brucheum, where he talked with his servants, who were still grieving after their master's sudden passing. He then went to find Artemisia at the address that Admiral Patroclus had provided. It was an almost palatial villa set behind walls and with two tall columns by its gate, on top of which were small statues of Hecate. Hanufer saw that the columns were made of red granite and the statues of black basalt.

Two guards armed with spears stood to attention by the door. They immediately recognised and responded to Hanufer's pectoral of office by opening the doors and ushering him in. One of the guards struck a small gong inside the entrance vestibule. As its echoes disappeared, sandalled feet were heard coming down a corridor. An Egyptian whom Hanufer recognised as one of the two bodyguards greeted him with a smile.

'*Archiphylakites* Hanufer, welcome. The Lady Artemisia told us to expect you. Will you follow me?'

Surprised to hear that he had been expected, a few moments later Hanufer found himself standing in front of the newly appointed High Priestess of Hecate. Again, she was smiling at him. Seeing her close-up, he thought her even more beautiful. Her eyes were green and framed by kohl.

'Your bodyguard said you were expecting me, Lady Artemisia,' said Hanufer. 'I am intrigued as to why.'

'Because of the dreams,' she replied.

Hanufer stared at Artemisia in disbelief. How could she know about the dreams?

'And I would also like to have my property returned to me,' she said, still smiling at him, 'if you don't mind?' Seeing his look of confusion, she gestured for him to sit on one of the luxuriant chairs. 'Some wine, or beer?'

'Wine, please.' He watched as she poured two goblets from an amphora and handed him one. In the back of his mind, he heard Patroclus telling him that he and Queen Arsinoe suspected that Usermontu may have been poisoned. And then he thought of the conversation about Hecate being the goddess of witchcraft, poisons and shadows. He hesitated to put the goblet to his lips.

As if divining his thoughts, Artemisia smiled and took a sip herself. 'It really is very good wine from Upper Egypt. His Majesty has it sent to me. So, there is no fear of poison.'

Hanufer smiled and then tasted his wine. 'I would never have thought such a thing, my lady,' he lied politely. 'You are right about the wine; it is exceptional. But what exactly do you mean by your property?'

She gave a short, musical laugh. 'Why, the ring that I gave to Usermontu before he died.'

'And how did you know —?'

'One of my bodyguards saw you look at it and compare it to the statue on the wonderful pylon gate that Usermontu designed and built for His Majesty.' She held up her hand and showed him a ring on her middle finger. 'There are only three such rings. Since I am wearing one and another adorns the finger of the pharaoh, that one must be Usermontu's.'

Hanufer nodded, then saw an opportunity to ask about Hatensor. 'I think your bodyguards were busy last night. They rather forcefully escorted a scribe from the hall. Why was that?'

She shrugged. 'A nuisance of a man.'

'He was a scribe, I understand. Did you know him?'

She stared at him for a moment, then shook her head. 'I am often bothered by men who want me to give them my time. I think he was no one of consequence.'

'And what of Usermontu? He was a man of considerable consequence. Did you know him well, Lady Artemisia?'

'We were lovers, of course. I was a *hetaera*, so he was one of several wealthy lovers I entertained here in Alexandria. As he was so kind in building the gate to my goddess Hecate, I gave the ring to him as a gift.'

Taken aback by her candour, Hanufer sipped more wine and then lay the goblet down on a side table. 'And His Majesty? Why did you give him such a gift?'

'You know the answer to that question, Hanufer of Crocodilopolis. I have told you what I am. His Majesty wanted to meet me because of my skill in contacting the goddess Hecate. I showed him that I am an oracle and know many charms.' She sipped more wine, then added without a trace of embarrassment, 'And I charmed him into my bed.' She swept a hand around the great room. 'Now, I am a *hetaera* no more. He has made me the High Priestess of Hecate and given me this villa. Usermontu was in the process of building a separate temple for me, but now we will have to find another *Architekton*.'

'By "we" you mean His Majesty and yourself?'

Again she laughed. 'Of course! I hardly think Queen Arsinoe would gift a temple to me, do you?' She held out her hand. 'So, may I have my ring back? I presume that Admiral Patroclus gave it to you after his men searched Usermontu's villa when he died.'

Hanufer considered telling her that he needed it for his investigations, but now that he knew there were only three such rings and Artemisia was so candid, keeping it would serve no purpose. He was also keenly aware that she had the pharaoh's ear, so it would be risky for him to antagonise her.

'You are quite right. That is why I came, to return it to you.'

He took it from inside his chiton and handed it to her. She immediately slipped it onto the middle finger of her right hand and then beamed at him.

'It has been a pleasure meeting you, *Archiphylakites* Hanufer.'

Hanufer quickly finished his wine and then stood. It was clear that as far as Artemisia was concerned, the meeting was at an end. 'Just one other thing. What dreams did you refer to when I came in?'

Artemisia flashed another seductive smile at him. 'As I said, I am an oracle. I have dreams that men would pay much to have me recount.' She pursed her lips. 'And men tell me of their dreams so I can interpret them. So, tell me, Hanufer of Crocodilopolis, what do you dream of? Could it be crocodiles?'

Does she know that I dream of shadowy crocodile monsters, or is it just a guess? Hanufer thought. *Is it a trick? I must not rise to her bait.*

'I sleep well and rarely dream,' he lied.

'Really?' she replied. 'I also sleep well. It is one of the many things I do well in bed. I am accomplished at pillow talk.'

Hanufer felt his face grow hot. Had he not been in love with Nefrit, he could easily have fallen under her spell.

Once more, Artemisia seemed to divine his thoughts. She gave him a knowing smile as she picked up a small bell by her side and shook it. Almost instantly, the bodyguard who had shown him to the room came in and held the door open.

As Hanufer walked through the outer gates of Artemisia's villa, he wondered what her ambitions were and whether Queen Arsinoe had cause to be alarmed.

One thing was clear. Lady Artemisia had just given him a warning to leave her alone.

CHAPTER 11

Hanufer started to make his way back towards the police headquarters but decided instead to go to the Great Harbour and pay a visit to Nefrit first. To his immense disappointment, she was not there. One of the temple handmaids told him that she had gone to visit a friend who was sick. Hanufer did not know who this could be, for he was unaware of any mutual friend that was ill. But then, he thought grudgingly, she had lived in Alexandria longer than he and had had a wide circle of friends.

Puzzled and troubled that she might think him bewitched by the Lady Artemisia, he walked along the harbour on his way to the police headquarters, having decided to take a detour via the Musaeum.

The *peripatos*, one of the covered walkways that linked the Musaeum and the Great Library, provided some pleasing shade from the sun. There he saw Callimachus of Cyrene, the head librarian, sitting on one of the many benches. He was deep in conversation with three men. One looked like the affluent Egyptian he had seen the night before. The other two were foreigners, judging by their dress.

Hanufer stopped and greeted them. They all stood and Callimachus made the introductions.

'My friends, this is Hanufer of Crocodilopolis, our esteemed *Archiphylakites* of Police.' He turned to Hanufer. 'These gentlemen are three of the most valued benefactors to the Library. First, your countryman Rekhmire of Canopus.'

Rekhmire was a well-built man of around forty years with a slight paunch. Like Hanufer, he wore a wig and kohl around his eyes. They bowed to each other.

'I have heard of you, Hanufer of Crocodilopolis,' Rekhmire said with an affable smile. 'You made all of us Egyptians proud when we heard that you had been made *Archiphylakites* of Police by Ptolemy Philadelphus himself.'

Hanufer bowed. 'Actually, I saw you at the Temple of Demeter last night, when Lady Artemisia was made the High Priestess of Hecate.'

'Indeed,' Rekhmire replied. 'I am sorry, I don't recollect —'

'We didn't actually talk,' Hanufer returned. 'I saw you from a distance.'

Callimachus held out his hand towards a cheerful-looking fellow dressed in a long travelling robe and a head wrap tied with a silk cord. 'And this is my countryman Cecibus of Cyrene.'

'My pleasure, Hanufer of Crocodilopolis,' Cecibus said with a bow. 'You will perceive by my clothing that I have come fresh from the harbour, where my boats have docked and are being unloaded. I follow the teachings of the great Aristippus of Cyrene and find pleasure in everything and everyone. Any service I can do for you will make me even more joyful.'

Callimachus put a hand on his shoulder to silence him and then indicated the third man, a tall, sunbeaten man with a beard that would have been as bushy as the anatomist Erasistratus's had it not been heavily braided. His long black hair was neatly groomed and cut to shoulder length. He was dressed in a robe that crossed his right shoulder and came down to the middle of his calf. It appeared to be made of dyed antelope hide.

'And finally, Nasamon of Phthia in Marmarica.'

He and Hanufer bowed to each other.

'All three of these generous friends have made substantial contributions to the Library,' Callimachus said. 'As you know, it is Pharaoh Ptolemy's law that if any boat coming into Alexandria has books on board, they must either donate them or leave them for us to have copies made.'

Cecibus beamed. 'And as I just told good Callimachus, I have brought a complete set of the works of Aristippus of Cyrene on this very journey.'

Callimachus clapped him on the shoulder. 'Aristippus is our great philosopher, who studied with Socrates of Athens some hundred years ago. He founded a school in Cyrene, which I attended myself. I learned my love of words and writing there, which set me on the path that I followed to become the Head Librarian of the Great Library here in Alexandria, with the blessing of the gods and His Majesty.'

Hanufer looked impressed. 'I know of Socrates, for you showed me the great mural of him surrounded by weeping men and women as he drinks a cup of hemlock. And also your Plato, staring into the sea at some mysterious island. So stimulated was I that I have read some of the works of Plato that you hold in the Library.'

He did not mention that it was his recollection of the mural of Socrates that had helped him to solve a case some months before.

Callimachus laughed softly. 'While you, my friends, are donors to our Library, Hanufer is one of our frequent readers.'

Nasamon clapped his hands. As he did so, Hanufer noted the network of finely drawn tattoos upon the backs of them, which extended to every finger.

'I applaud all who read and have a thirst for knowledge. You may tell that I am a Marmarican. My culture is tribal, as you may know, and my country has had many conquerors. The Egyptians, Greeks, Phoenicians and Persians have all ruled us and established our towns and cities, each power leaving its influence on our religion, education and writing. For that reason, our library in Phthia is like this wonderful Library; it is the centre of a school where the wisdom of our greatest philosopher Augilos, an elder from the Augilae tribe, has been written down in our own language. I have brought five scrolls for Callimachus, all of which I have read and marvelled at.'

Callimachus laughed again. 'And which we will not be able to translate.'

Nasamon grinned, displaying ivory-white teeth. 'And therefore, even more reason for this humble man to visit more often.'

Rekhmire, seemingly determined not to be left out, clapped his hands. 'And I applaud you, my friend Nasamon. Both you and Cecibus have dutifully donated books every time you have sailed into Alexandria and we three have done business. Yet it is not just travellers who sail into the harbours that have to present books, but those like myself who enter by the Canal of Canopus. On this occasion, it was my privilege to donate a copy of our ancient *The Story of Sinuhe* to Callimachus when I arrived a few days ago.'

Hanufer looked quickly at him at the mention of the name, for it was the same as that of the constable who had been murdered in Crocodilopolis along with the two police baboons. But then he dismissed it as a mere coincidence, since it was one of the oldest pieces of Egyptian literature which virtually every educated Egyptian had read.

'A good choice, Rekhmire,' he said. 'I have read it several times and seem to get a different feeling about Sinuhe each time.'

Callimachus nodded. 'I understand that. I have read the copy and I agree: there are times when you feel sympathetic to the young official, especially when he succumbs to the charms of a woman. On the other hand, he can be cowardly and duplicitous. It is like this in life; people do not always act the way they should.'

Hanufer nodded. 'So, what business do you gentlemen do in Alexandria?'

All three looked at each other with a mixture of reticence and amusement.

'We do deals with our different commodities,' said Rekhmire, candidly. 'I bring stone of various types from my quarries.'

'Which we need for building our monuments and libraries,' said Nasamon with a broad smile. 'I bring animal hides, leather and dyed finery.'

Cecibus gave a hearty chuckle. 'And I bring all the cereals that you could want from our fertile northern region. But especially silphium, which only grows in a small area in the north of Cyrene.'

Hanufer nodded. 'A most valuable commodity, Cecibus. Our physicians in Egypt use it in several medicines.'

Cecibus retrieved a leather purse from beneath his robe and took out a silver tetradrachm coin. 'Look, it is so valuable to us that our royal mint prints a picture of a silphium plant on one side and the portrait of King Magas on the other.'

Hanufer took the coin and examined both faces. He noted that silphium was a bushy plant with a thick stalk; it looked like some of the vegetable crops that farmers grew in the fertile mud that was washed down the Nile during the inundation, but he knew that it was not grown in Egypt.

'And your King Magas is half-brother to both Pharaoh Ptolemy and his sister-wife Queen Arsinoe. Yet I do not see a resemblance to them in his likeness on this coin.'

Cecibus chuckled. 'To be honest, Overseer Hanufer, I don't care a fig what plant or which king is upon the coin as long as it is silver and feels heavy in my coffers.'

'We are businessmen, after all,' said Nasamon. 'We all have mouths to feed, and families and friends to look after.'

'Honest businessmen,' added Rekhmire. 'We have to look after the interests of those upon whose behalf we buy and sell.'

Callimachus smiled. 'And the better your deals and the more you trade, the more you have to visit Alexandria, which means — more books for the Library!'

Everyone dutifully laughed.

Hanufer saw an opportunity to probe a little further. 'I understand that you, Rekhmire, have supplied much of the stonework for many buildings and monuments in Alexandria.'

The businessman smiled deprecatingly. 'That has been my privilege. Limestone, granite, marble and basalt.'

'The pylon gate at the Temple of Demeter was done by you?'

'I supplied the materials from my quarries. The Ministry of Buildings and Monuments allow me to work with their sculptors and craftsmen. I also take private commissions.'

'I suppose you work with many surveyors and scribes? The reason I ask is that I saw a scribe arguing with you last night. I believe he is also a surveyor for the Ministry and works on other commissions.'

Rekhmire grimaced. 'Ah, you mean Hatensor. I am sorry that you saw that. Yes, the man is remarkably talented and I give him many commissions, but he is difficult to work with and he drinks too much.'

'I saw that he was also arguing with Hak-mau, who is now looking after the Ministry of Buildings and Monuments after *Architekton* Usermontu's sudden death.'

Rekhmire stared at Hanufer for a moment, then raised his hands in a gesture of despair. 'Hatensor was just being annoying. First he claimed that I, Usermontu and the Ministry owed him money for his work on the pylon gate. Then he said he was going to see what the Lady Artemisia would say about it.'

'I know that scribe,' said Callimachus. 'He frequently works at the Library — a man of many interests. He uses papyri from several of our departments. I have not noticed that he drinks. Perhaps he has a deference for the Library.'

'Personally, I do not begrudge a man a drink as long as he fulfils the work I expect of him,' said Cecibus with a laugh.

Nasamon scowled. 'But if he is employed in a dangerous activity or puts others at risk through his drinking, that is a matter I would be concerned about.'

'I would like to talk with him,' said Hanufer. 'He may be able to help me with some inquiries I am making. Do you happen to know where I could find him?'

'Perhaps you should ask one of the priests at the temples he is attached to,' Rekhmire suggested. 'I believe there is more than one devoted to Harpokrates in Alexandria. But really, I hope last night's little argument won't be the cause of trouble for him.'

Hanufer shook his head. 'I didn't say he was in trouble, merely that I would like to talk to him.' He bowed to all of them. 'I must not keep you any longer.'

It was very late in the afternoon and Hatensor was dimly aware of someone hammering on his door.

'Scribe Hatensor! If you are in there, open this door!'

His eyes snapped open and he felt an excruciating pain as bright sunlight shone in them. He shut them again, now aware of a thundering headache.

'Open this door, Scribe Hatensor!' a voice cried again. There was more thumping on the door.

Fear had become his shadow. He had been burdened with a huge responsibility, but things had taken an unexpected turn, and he had been browbeaten and disparaged by those who thought themselves to be his superiors.

He now tried to numb his fear with wine and women, but they made him more vulnerable. He therefore kept himself out of sight as much as possible. He knew that when he got to the lighthouse after dark, he would be safe. His friends would see to that.

When the star Sothis eventually appeared, the Nile would rise and with the Festival of Wepet Renpet, his work would finally be done. He would rise above them all, like the star Sothis itself. The thought pleased him.

It took him a few moments to realise where he was. He was lying on a bed in a barely furnished room. On a table he saw the remains of some food and an overturned amphora of wine.

'Open the door!'

His mind was still in a drunken daze, but he recognised that he was in a brothel. It was not the one he liked best, but it was the closest one to the *Heptastadion*. But where was the woman he'd paid?

He had been drunk at the feast last night, and those two fools had marched him out of the temple hall before he could talk to Artemisia. That was before they had beaten him in the guts and warned him off.

Somehow, he had made it to the lighthouse. He recalled making his observations of the stars and had duly recorded everything.

Yes, his scrolls and charts were here. He swung his legs over the side of the bed and shook his head to try to clear it.

More thumping on the door. 'We will break this door down if you don't unbolt it!'

He glanced at the heavy wooden bolt that prevented anyone interrupting when one of the women was entertaining a customer. It amused him to think that he must have bolted it himself after the woman had left him to sleep it off.

I wish you luck breaking that down, he thought. *You'll break your shoulders. But if you idiots are here to finish what you started last night, you'll be disappointed.*

The door shuddered as two heavy blows landed. Only then did Hatensor start to worry.

He rose, collected his bag with his scrolls and charts and crept to the window. It opened easily and noiselessly. His muscles ached from the punches he had received, but he managed to drop down into the alley below.

I'll go and lay low under Harpokrates' care until darkness comes, he thought. *Then I will watch and make the observations for the rise of the god Sothis. I will be safe then.*

Some minutes later, Pylyp and Filemon burst into the room as the wooden bolt finally snapped. Behind them was a worried-looking brothel mistress and several of her working women.

'He is like a ghost,' said Pylyp. 'We seem to have missed him yet again.'

'And we do not know where to look for him now,' agreed Filemon. 'Overseer Hanufer will not be pleased.'

CHAPTER 12

For a second night Nefrit did not visit Hanufer. He bitterly regretted having upset her, because he valued her counsel.

When he did manage to sleep, he found himself dreaming again. The shadow monsters returned, and he felt the usual fear.

And then a priestess emerged from the shadows. Raising her arms, she used powerful magic to make the monsters retreat. He felt relief and love flood through him, until she stepped forward into the light.

It was not Nefrit, but Artemisia — the beautiful, seductive green-eyed High Priestess of Hecate. She advanced towards him with her arms outstretched.

The fear returned and he tried to walk backwards, but he found himself sinking into quicksand. It did not seem to affect Artemisia as she walked over it, smiling at him.

Hanufer awoke in a cold sweat.

It was still the middle of the night. He went to stand by the window, where he took in the city, the Pharos lighthouse, the shimmering water of the harbours and the many torchlights within the Royal Palaces. He wondered if others were having a better night than he.

Queen Arsinoe had not slept after making love to her brother-husband, the pharaoh.

As usual, they had coupled vigorously by the light of countless oil lamps. He normally liked to look at her during the throes of passion, but this time, like the other times during these last few weeks, he had kissed her with his eyes tightly closed.

She had watched him and realised that the way he touched her and used her body was different. There was vigour, passion and urgency, but it was as if he was imagining that she was another woman.

That in itself was not unusual, for she knew very well that he often shared a bed with the Lady Bilistiche or the Lady Didyme. It was his right as the pharaoh to take mistresses as he wished. What was not right in her mind was that afterwards, rather than staying to talk about their children or her interests, he had been intent on leaving.

She had lain naked on the bed as he had tied the belt on his kilt.

'I will see you tomorrow,' he said, walking towards the door.

She felt emotions bubbling within her and decided to press him. 'That is an unusual ring you wear, husband.'

He looked at it, then shrugged dismissively. 'It is just a token of thanks from the Lady Artemisia for making an offering at the Temple of Demeter.'

'And for building her a pylon gate?'

'That too.'

'But she is a *hetaera*.'

He shrugged again. 'No longer so.'

Arsinoe gave a humourless laugh. 'Well then, she must be grateful to you for making her a high priestess of this new cult.'

'It is an old religion, not a new cult. She is a Carian, and it is fitting that she should want to worship her goddess here in Alexandria.'

'Fitting enough for you to build a new temple for her?'

He turned, fury in his eyes, although his expression was otherwise controlled. 'Who has told you this?'

'I am not a fool, Ptolemy.'

He looked at her for a few moments. 'No one would ever accuse you of that, Arsinoe. But I am Pharaoh, and I decide what buildings and temples are needed in Alexandria.'

He returned to the bed and kissed her on the forehead, then left.

And you are no fool either, Ptolemy, she thought when she was alone. *You never were when we were children, and you are not now. At least not in matters of state. In matters of love, I am not so sure.*

But then she began to wonder if she was the fool for speaking up. After all, her husband had repudiated their cousin, his first wife, who was also named Arsinoe. She had been exiled to Coptos in Upper Egypt.

Could it happen again? Was this latest mistress a greater threat than Bilistiche and Didyme?

Evenius was woken by a furious hammering on the door of his chamber. Dawn was only just breaking.

'Come in!' the high priest called as he swung his legs over the bed and rubbed sleep from his eyes.

The door opened. It was one of the temple boys whose task it was to bring fresh water to the priests so that they could wash away their sins before they went to pray to the gods Proteus and Harpokrates. 'Master, you must come quickly. It … it is horrible.'

Evenius stood and put his hands on the boy's shaking shoulders. 'What is wrong? What have you seen?'

'The scribe Hatensor. At the foot of the lighthouse.'

The great lighthouse was near the tip of the Island of Pharos. It stood some two hundred and twenty cubits high and consisted of three tapering tiers. Built on a foundation of great ashlar granite stones, its base tower was square, the middle octagonal and the topmost cylindrical. The whole was cased in limestone, so it shone brilliantly in the sunlight. It was also surrounded by a wall that was about the height of a man's shoulder. Opposite it, a hundred or so cubits away and overlooking the sea, stood the temple of Proteus and Harpokrates.

Evenius followed the youth through the temple pylon gate, which was topped with statues of the two gods.

Before they had gone fifty paces, Evenius saw a body lying sprawled on the marble ramp at the foot of the lighthouse, surrounded by a pool of blood.

'Wait, boy!' he called. 'I will go and see myself. Go and rouse our guest, High Priest Kephalos, and tell him to come hither. And then run across the *Heptastadion* and find the police night guards. Tell them there has been a dreadful accident.'

The boy ran off to complete his tasks.

Evenius watched him disappear and looked up at the statues of the two gods upon the pylon gate. Proteus, who knew everything but had to be tricked to make him tell his secrets, and Harpokrates the god of silence. Their stone eyes must have witnessed how the scribe's body came to be there and why the lighthouse guards were nowhere to be seen.

He said a silent prayer to them, then turned to go and see the body.

The sun had risen by the time the duty guards had investigated. Messengers and horses were sent to alert Sabu and Hanufer so that they could get to the scene as swiftly as possible.

When they arrived, Evenius and Kephalos told them how they had first seen the body, which was indeed that of Hatensor.

Hanufer and his deputy looked down at the mangled body that lay in a huge pool of blood. It looked as if Hatensor had been flailing about as he had fallen. His arms and legs were outstretched, and only half his face was visible. His right fist gripped a scribe's knife, its blade coated in blood.

'He is barely recognisable, but it is undoubtedly him, for I saw him only the night before last,' said Hanufer, kneeling down. 'It looks as if he fell from a great height and his body landed on the steps here.' He rose to his feet. 'I understand he went up the lighthouse every night and observed the stars. Do you know from where, exactly?'

Evenius nodded. His face was pale and his voice quaked. 'He did, my lord. He has been charting the sky every night for some years, and at this time of the year he was awaiting the rise of Sothis, when the Wepet Renpet Festival will begin.'

'And did Sothis rise this morning?'

The two head priests looked at each other and shook their heads.

'Hatensor would have been the first to tell us — but he did not,' Evenius said.

'And what of the watchmen?' asked Sabu. 'There should be two of them, I think. Are they still inside?'

Evenius shrugged. 'They have not come out.'

Hanufer bit his lower lip and stroked his two rings with his thumbs. 'And there should be *demosios* slaves up there as well. Have they not come down?'

The two priests shook their heads.

'We did not dare go inside,' said Evenius. 'We thought it should be up to you. In case anything dangerous —'

Hanufer nodded. 'We will look now.'

He turned to the four constables who were waiting for instructions. Two had been there since they were first alerted and the other two were the ones who had taken horses to Hanufer and Sabu.

'Cover the body now, and then two of you go to the hospital and deliver the message I am about to write to either Erasistratus or Herophilus. I want them to look at the body before it is removed to the hospital, where I would then like them to make a full examination. Fetch a wagon to take the body — the other two will stay and guard it.'

Once he had written his message and the constables had been dispatched on their duties, Hanufer again turned to Evenius and Kephalos. 'Where exactly did Hatensor make his observations?'

'Near the top, my lord,' Evenius replied. 'There is a room almost at the top of the uppermost tower, so it is beneath the fire room and the mirror room above that. It is ideal for his observations, as it has large open windows facing in the four main directions, so he could look out at the whole sky.'

'As I understand, the watchmen's duty was to keep the lighthouse safe. How many slaves keep the fire burning through the night?'

'Two *demosios* slaves tend the fires all night, my lord. The watchmen make sure no-one enters the lighthouse during the hours of darkness.'

'Except for Hatensor, I presume.'

'Apart from him.'

'Then we shall go and see what has become of the watchmen,' said Hanufer. 'You may both go, but I may need to talk to you later.'

'If you do not mind, Overseer Hanufer,' said Evenius, 'we would like to await the physicians. We have both agreed that it is only right that we should watch over our friend Scribe Hatensor's body.'

Hanufer and Sabu climbed the ramp leading up to the entrance and entered the atrium of the lighthouse. The oil lamps were still burning. The room containing a table and chairs where the watchmen usually ate or played knucklebones was unoccupied, and the remains of food and beakers of water looked as if they had recently been used.

Sabu led the way, with his short sword unsheathed as they mounted the first of many flights of stairs that spiralled up inside the lighthouse. The oil lamps and the numerous slit windows in the walls provided light.

Hanufer and Sabu had been up to the top of the lighthouse when they had first come to Alexandria and had had the working of the structure explained to them. All the way up they passed rooms containing the various types of fuel for the fire that had to be kept burning day and night. During the day, ships approaching the reefs in the bay were guided by the fire and the smoke that went up in a continuous plume. At night, great beams of light were reflected from the fire by the mighty polished mirrors in the dome at the top, beneath the statue of divine Alexander.

The rooms were full of wood, dried animal dung and large pithos jars full of oil. Three types of fuel had to be used, because in Egypt timber was in short supply. All of these stores had to be replenished every day by a whole team of slaves, and the ones nearer the top were taken up by the slaves to keep the fire stoked. It was a continuous process of moving stores up the lighthouse during the day; the slaves either carried them up the stairs or used the complex pulley systems that occupied the central core of the structure to raise loads up several levels at a time. At night, as the priests had confirmed, only two slaves were needed to keep the fires burning and they would carry replenishments from the topmost storerooms as they needed them.

Turning a corner, Hanufer and Sabu found the first watchman's body in one of the storerooms. He was lying face down in a pool of blood, which had soaked his tunic and part of his headcloth.

At a nod from Hanufer, Sabu turned him over, and they saw that his throat had been slit from ear to ear. His eyes were open wide, as if his life had been snuffed out in a moment of shock.

Without a word, Hanufer mounted the next set of stairs and Sabu followed. In another storeroom three further levels up, they found the second watchman. Once more Sabu turned him, and they saw that he too had had his throat cut. Close beside him was a half empty skin of wine. Unlike the first body, this watchman was only wearing a kilt. Blood had pooled around his shaven head.

Continuing up the staircase, they passed a discarded headcloth and a tunic that seemed to have been cast aside before they came to the room that Evenius had told them Hatensor had used for his observations. As they were in the topmost cylindrical tier of the lighthouse, the room was circular with large windows looking out in the four directions of the compass. On the floor there were various instruments, a water clock that had been kicked over, and a number of papyri and charts, some with footprints on them.

'There may have been a scuffle here, Sabu,' Hanufer said.

Sabu crossed to the open window and looked down. 'And this is where he fell from, my lord. It does not look as if the physicians have arrived yet.'

Hanufer gestured for the sergeant to follow as he mounted the stairs again. The air became very hot as they approached the fire room. A great door barred their way.

'You can come out,' Hanufer called. 'I am *Archiphylakites* Hanufer, the Overseer of the Alexandrian police. You are safe now.'

There was silence.

Hanufer pushed the door open and stepped into the smoke-filled fireroom. There were three great brass fire-bowls for the different fuels. Two curly-headed youths wearing leather aprons and mitts, both public slaves with the delta brand on their shoulders, lay on the floor. One lay on his back, his face fixed in a permanent scream. Several stab wounds in his chest had caused a pool of blood to collect around him.

Further on, the other slave lay face down, a stab wound in his back. It looked as if he had tried to run from his attacker. At a sign from Hanufer, Sabu gingerly turned him over to reveal that he had also had his throat cut.

By the time they had descended the stairs, Erasistratus had arrived from the hospital and was kneeling beside the body of the scribe.

The two high priests were standing a little distance away, watching.

'I don't quite know what you want me to do, Hanufer of Crocodilopolis,' the anatomist said. 'This man has probably broken every bone in his body and ruptured every organ within.'

'There are two watchmen and a *demosios* slave inside with their throats cut. Another slave is dead from stab wounds to his chest,' Hanufer replied. 'I would like you to examine all of their bodies in your dissection room at the hospital.'

'For what purpose? I don't think I'll be able to tell you more than I've just said.'

Hanufer pointed to the blood-covered knife in the scribe's hand. 'It appears that this man went on a killing spree in the lighthouse and then threw himself from the top.' He called the constables over. 'When Erasistratus has finished his examination, I want you to take the body to the hospital in the wagon.'

Sabu nodded 'Yes, and there are four more bodies within the lighthouse. They need to be taken, too.'

The two priests had come closer, their faces ashen. 'Hatensor must have gone mad,' said Evenius.

Hanufer nodded. 'That is certainly how it looks.' He turned to Erasistratus. 'I would like you to look at all of the bodies where they lie in the lighthouse before they are taken to the dissection room.'

Evenius shook his head in disbelief. 'The watchmen? But why?'

'This is the work of the evil demi-god, Cronos,' Kephalos added. 'All these deaths are without sense.'

'We Egyptians would say it was the work of the god Seth,' said Sabu.

Evenius stared in horror at Kephalos. 'Or of Hecate!'

Hanufer and Sabu looked at one another, both noting the priest's words.

Erasistratus stood up and brushed his knees with his hands. He snorted derisively. 'This was no god's work. A human hand was responsible.'

Hanufer nodded. 'It is evil work indeed, and you are right, a human hand did the deeds. But was it under the influence of a god — or goddess?'

Erasistratus looked scornfully at him and opened his mouth to reply, but he was silenced as Hanufer raised his hand.

'I suggest that you priests tend to your duties, and I shall begin my investigation.'

The priests agreed with alacrity and departed for the temple.

'Shall I come up with you, my lord?' Sabu asked.

'Yes, but first I need you to write and despatch a message to Admiral Patroclus and inform him of this horrific happening. Say that I shall call on him later this morning, after I have made further enquiries.'

Sabu pointed to the body. 'Well, you heard Overseer Hanufer,' he said to the constables. 'Let's at least load the scribe's body onto the wagon.'

While they began their grisly task, he sat down to write his message to the vizier, then joined Hanufer and the physician in the lighthouse.

CHAPTER 13

Erasistratus looked down at the body of the first watchman in the storeroom. The corpse was just as Hanufer and Sabu had left it after turning it over to find the slit throat.

'No other wounds, so his death is quite apparent. He had his throat slit from behind, and then he either fell or was dumped forward on the floor.'

Hanufer nodded. 'That is indeed how it looks. Let's see the second unfortunate fellow.'

Moving up the stairs, they entered the other storeroom where the second watchman's body lay on the floor.

'Note that his tunic and headcloth are missing,' said Hanufer.

'I see that,' replied the physician. 'Again, a mortal wound to his throat. And I note the wine skin. Perhaps he was taking that up to the scribe?' His eyes narrowed as he looked at Hanufer. 'You are not saying much, Hanufer of Crocodilopolis.'

'Let's go all the way up,' said Hanufer.

They mounted the spiral staircase, taking care not to disturb the inner pulleys and rope system used to hoist fuels up from the lower storerooms.

'There is the second watchman's uniform and headcloth,' Sabu said, pointing.

'And this is where the scribe Hatensor did all of his nightly observations,' Hanufer added, indicating the charts and papyri strewn about the floor, along with some writing reeds and a scribal set, a staff, a plumb-bob and the crushed remains of what looked like a water spirit level. 'See, it looks as if either he or his assailant trod on that, and a foot also smudged the writing on that papyrus.'

'It is an open window with a fairly low ledge,' Sabu said, looking down. 'Look, the constables have taken his body away, but you can see where he landed on the ground. The other two constables are there standing guard, as I ordered them to. And see, there is blood on the top of the next tier, and again on the lowermost.'

Hanufer joined him by the window. 'Indeed, it seems that his body struck and bounced off first the octagonal tier and then the lower square one before finally hitting the ground.' He pointed to the stairs. 'But there is more unpleasantness for you to see, Erasistratus.'

Sabu led the way up the stairs to the fire room. The heat from the fires and the sun made it incredibly hot. Already, blowflies had started to swarm, attracted as always to fresh blood.

Erasistratus examined the bodies of the two slaves. 'These poor young men,' he said, standing after a few moments. 'The one by the door was stabbed in the chest three times, and this other one must have tried to run but was stabbed in the back. Then for good measure, the killer slit his throat.'

'So, what do we think happened?' Hanufer asked.

'It looks as if the scribe Hatensor was either drunk and angered or affected by something he saw in the sky,' said Sabu. 'He was mad. Perhaps he went down first and induced the watchmen to go upstairs with a wine skin. Somehow, they went up separately.'

Erasistratus nodded. 'He followed the last one and slit his throat from behind. Then he sneaked up and did the same to the other one.'

'And what about the two unfortunate slaves?' said Hanufer.

Sabu grunted. 'He took the second watchman's tunic and headcloth and went up in disguise. He stabbed the first slave in the chest, then stabbed the other in the back before slitting his throat.'

Hanufer nodded. 'It fits the picture that we have seen, but what happened then? Do you really think he went back downstairs, tossed the tunic and headcloth aside and then — either still in his madness or overcome by guilt — took a running jump out of the window, bounced off the two lower tiers and smashed his body on the ground?'

The anatomist shook his head doubtfully. 'I cannot believe that.'

'Nor can I, my lord,' Sabu agreed.

Hanufer was rubbing his rings. 'I hoped you would agree with me. I think there was another person here. He killed the two watchmen and then disguised himself as one of them as he went up to murder Hatensor. That is why I want you to examine all four of these bodies as closely as you are able, as well as Hatensor the scribe.'

'But we know that the two watchmen were killed by having their throats cut,' said Erasistratus.

'But do we?' Hanufer persisted. 'Ahset had her neck broken and then her throat cut to make it look as if she died from the slit throat. I think that happened with the two guards.'

Sabu snapped his fingers. 'That would explain why the watchman's uniform and headcloth had no blood on them. After he had killed Hatensor and thrown his body from the window, the killer went up the stairs and murdered the two slaves. It would be after all that he tossed the tunic and headcloth aside.'

Hanufer nodded. 'And I think he had killed the two guards in the same way: from behind, breaking their necks one at a time to silence them. He only slit their throats afterwards as he made his escape.'

'But why?' asked Erasistratus, his clinical interest piqued. 'They were dead already, if you are correct.'

'If I am correct,' Hanufer returned, 'I think he sent one watchman up ahead to the scribe, taking the wine. He killed the one that went up with him, then did the same to the other. That left him free to kill Hatensor and toss his body out, to make sure he was dead.'

'So, he must have been known to the watchmen?' Sabu asked.

'Very possibly, which I think would have been the reason why they both had to die. And he killed the two slaves because there could be no witnesses.'

'But why kill the scribe in the first place?' Erasistratus asked.

'I think it was something that had to be done in a hurry,' Hanufer replied. 'Something so important that it couldn't be done without committing these other murders. He cut their throats to try to disguise how they died.'

'Again, why, my lord?' Sabu asked.

Hanufer led the way down the stairs to the room where the scribe had been making his observations. He pointed at the papyri, the charts and the other paraphernalia. 'Perhaps it is something to do with the observations he was making. This is the measuring equipment that astronomers and surveyors use.' He stroked his chin. 'It has something to do with the Wepet Renpet Festival.'

'And he was watching for the appearance of Sothis?' Sabu asked. 'But we don't know if he saw it or not.'

'I doubt if he did, but someone will have to continue his vigil until we know for sure.' Hanufer bent to start gathering the scattered charts, writing equipment and papyri. 'Note that his knife is not here, which indicates that it either was the weapon used to slit the throats and stab the slaves, or it was put in his dead hand later.'

'That seems to make sense, my lord,' said Sabu.

'It is the best I can make of it at present,' Hanufer said. 'In the meantime, I shall have to try to understand what all of these notes and charts are about. I shall have to consult High Priest Evenius and possibly also some scholars at the Musaeum.'

Sabu turned to the window. 'Shall I summon the constables to bring the bodies down, my lord?'

When Hanufer nodded, the big sergeant leaned out of the window. Putting his fingers to his mouth, he let out a loud whistle and gestured for the two constables below to come up.

'Do not tell anyone what we have just considered,' Hanufer said to Sabu and Erasistratus. 'For now, it is important that the killer thinks he has fooled us. The version of events that you both first described — that Hatensor went mad and killed the watchmen and the slaves, before taking his own life — must be the story we shall give.' He turned to Sabu. 'Sergeant, you must find out if these men and the two young slaves had families and friends. They must be notified at once, but for now we must say no more than we have agreed on.'

The Temple of Proteus and Harpokrates was typically Greek, with its entrance at the east. Hanufer passed through the pylon gate with the figures of Proteus on one side of the portico and Harpokrates on the other. He went through the colonnade that surrounded the main cella, where he found the two high priests overseeing the other priests as they made the first offerings of the day to both Proteus and Harpokrates. Catching Evenius's eye, he gestured for him to follow him outside, where he had laid down the pieces of equipment and the charts and papyri that he had removed from the lighthouse.

The priest listened in horror as Hanufer told him of the murders of the watchmen and the two slaves.

Hanufer pointed to the objects on the ground. 'These charts and papyri have been mixed up, but it is clear to me that Hatensor was working on something. I can see he has been making drawings and entering observations. Can you make any comment about any of this?'

Evenius knelt down and looked at the various instruments. 'He used these to observe the sky, I think. The staff and the plumb-bob he used in his calculations. But I see that there is no knife in his writing set.'

Hanufer nodded. 'He had the knife in his hand.'

Evenius shivered. He pointed to a sheet of papyrus on which the scribe had made various drawings and annotated them with hieroglyphic numbers. 'I think these would have been to do with measuring the horizon so that he could chart exactly when the stars appeared. And look, here he has made drawings of the sky and has written names beside some stars. But there is no mention of Sothis.'

'That is what I thought,' Hanufer agreed. 'Yet some of these drawings are of pyramids and mastabas, are they not?'

Evenius shrugged. 'Perhaps he was passing the time and they are to do with some other interest.'

'Do you think these pyramid and triangle drawings are to do with his work here, or could they be to do with other tasks?'

The high priest shook his head. 'I am a mere novice in the art of arithmetic and numbers, my lord. I am a humble priest of Proteus and Harpokrates. I regret that I cannot say.'

'Proteus is your god of prophecy, is he not?'

'He is, my lord. If you know the works of our great poet Homer, you will know that —'

'That Proteus had lived on Pharos since time was young and that he knew all things past, present and future, but would tell no one of them. To get him to give a prophecy, he had to be captured and bound tightly during his midday sleep. If one was not fast enough, he could turn into any creature and slither, run or fly to make his escape.'

Evenius nodded. 'Hence he was called the god of silence. Just like Harpokrates. Our function as priests of these gods is to venerate them so that evil does not occur and there will be no bad prophesies for the gods to make.'

'And do you have other shrines and temples to them in Alexandria? Are they under your care?'

Evenius nodded. 'We have a small temple to Harpokrates in Rhakotis near the Necropolis. I or one of my priests visit there every day to make offerings and to deal with any matters of administration. One of the junior priests stays there for five days at a time.'

'And would Hatensor visit this other temple, too?'

'He did so regularly, every other day.'

'And I understand that the Necropolis guards report to that temple?'

The high priest looked startled by the question. 'Yes, that is correct, my lord. The Necropolis is under the care of the gods Proteus and Harpokrates.'

'So, you will be aware of the recent tragedy, when one of the Necropolis guards was killed by another.'

Evenius looked pained. 'A horrible accident, I hear.'

'And you heard about the ghost? The guard who threw the fatal spear said the spirit appeared and attacked him. The spear apparently passed through him.'

'That part I did not know about, my lord.'

'Do you think it possible that the guard who threw the spear saw a ghost?'

'I think it highly likely, my lord. If one is going to see a ghost, then where would be more likely than the Necropolis?'

'Yet if you heard of the tragedy, why had you not been told of the ghost by the Necropolis guards? Surely that would have been a major thing to have been informed about, as they report to the Temple of Harpokrates.'

Evenius merely shrugged. 'It is a mystery, my lord.'

'A mystery,' said Hanufer. 'It seems that is something else that the two gods wish to remain silent about.' He started to pick up the papyri and instruments. 'One other thing: where did Hatensor live?'

Evenius hesitated. 'Yet another mystery, my lord. Neither I nor any of my fellow priests know that. I am not even sure if he had a regular dwelling. He spent several hours of every night in the lighthouse, and he often travelled to Canopus in the Delta, where he had other appointments. He also went to the Temple of Harpokrates in the city there, where my colleague Kephalos is the head priest.'

CHAPTER 14

An hour later, Herophilus joined his colleague Erasistratus in the dissecting rooms. He listened with much tugging of his beard to Hanufer's interpretation of the events that had taken place.

'You bring us many an intellectual challenge, *Archiphylakites* Hanufer,' he mused as he pulled on a leather apron that was stained with old blood. Together, the anatomists began their gory examinations while Hanufer and Sabu looked on.

At last, they rinsed their instruments and hands in some large ceramic bowls and conferred for some moments, before putting forward their conclusions.

'You were right, Hanufer,' said Erasistratus. 'At least with the watchmen and the scribe. They had broken neck vertebrae. The two young slaves were killed by being stabbed.'

'The necks of the scribe and watchmen were expertly broken, we would say, if there can be expertise in such a thing,' said Herophilus.

'How deep were the stab wounds?'

Erasistratus clicked his tongue. 'I thought you would ask that. They were deep enough to penetrate the slaves' hearts.'

'And the throat wounds on the two watchmen?'

'They were vicious injuries,' Erasistratus replied.

Hanufer pointed to the reed-cutting knife that had been laid aside while the anatomists had examined the body. 'Could he have committed these murders with that knife?'

Herophilus picked it up and shook his head. 'Not with this tiny thing. Which means —'

'It means that the killer was someone else who had a larger blade,' Hanufer replied. 'This killer is extremely dangerous, and to catch him I must allow him to think his ploy to put the blame on Hatensor has worked. Not a word about these findings must leave this room.'

The two anatomists nodded.

'And therefore, I must also ask you to write your findings down as precisely as you can. I think this could be of the greatest importance.'

'We will bring our findings along with anatomical drawings, as you have requested in the past,' agreed Erasistratus. He sighed. 'And we will try to make some time to teach some of our student physicians and surgeons so that they can learn how to treat bodies that are still alive.'

When Hanufer returned to the police headquarters, he listened as Corporals Pylyp and Filemon reported with much embarrassment that the day before, Hatensor had evaded them at a brothel by climbing out of the window. The two corporals expected a reprimand from the overseer, but it did not come.

'Did you identify yourselves to him?' Hanufer asked calmly.

'No, sir,' Pylyp replied. 'He had proved to be a difficult man to track down, but at last we found him in a brothel near the *Heptastadion.*'

'The keeper knew him and said that he had been drunk when he arrived the previous evening and had paid for the woman and the room,' Filemon went on. 'But since the woman said he was hardly capable of lovemaking, the keeper just allowed him to stay undisturbed in the room until he sobered up. We hammered on the door and shouted for him to open it, but when we got in he had escaped. Unfortunately, we couldn't tell which direction he went in, and despite trying all the other brothels and drinking houses around, we could not find him.'

Hanufer scratched his chin. 'He may have thought you were others coming to beat him again.'

'Again, my lord?' Pylyp asked.

'Yes, he was thrown out of the Temple of Demeter the night before by bodyguards of the Lady Artemisia, the new High Priestess of Hecate. Clearly, though, he was a man who was adept at evading pursuers, which is not a talent one would associate with an honest and industrious scribe.'

He dismissed the corporals, and once they were alone he turned to Sabu. 'Tell me, did you learn anything about the case of Usermontu?'

'Yes and no, my lord,' said Sabu. 'When I saw his physician Galenos, I could tell that he was lying to me. He denied that Usermontu had any dealings with women, and he was nervous when I asked if anyone had talked to him about the death afterwards. I did not press him on it then, for you had told me to be subtle.'

'Then we will investigate Galenos later. For now, the case of the lighthouse and the five murders that have been committed there must take priority.' Hanufer tapped the pile of charts and papyri in front of him. 'All this may yet be of great importance, for there is a link between Usermontu and Hatensor. The scribe worked for Usermontu. I need to know more about this. Among these charts, I can see that there are many drawings of the sky and many calculations. Without knowing exactly where some of the figures came from, it is a mystery.'

'But not all of these are drawings of the sky, are they, my lord? It looks as if he has been drawing pyramids,' said Sabu.

'And triangles,' agreed Hanufer. 'Lots of triangles. I need to discuss them with one more versed in mathematics than I.' He thought of the two scholars Posidippus and Lycophron, whom he had met at the Temple of Demeter. They had been sarcastic about the scribe. 'I also need to find out more about Hatensor, because someone wanted him dead. If he and the two watchmen were killed in the same way as Ahset, then there is much to find out. Those two poor young slaves were also brutally slain to stop them from identifying the killer. Their deaths must not go unpunished.'

Sabu struck his palm with his fist. 'They must have been terrified. I would like to face the killer up there in the lighthouse. I would toss him out of that window.'

Hanufer frowned. 'I know that in a fair fight there would be few who could match you, Sabu, but whoever this killer is, he must be taken alive to face justice. Unfortunately, we have little to go on, which is why we must start with Hatensor and find out all we can about him. Could he have been the scribe that had visited Ahset? And if he was, then who killed them both and why?' He sighed. 'But before that, I must report to the vizier.'

'What would you have me do while you pay Admiral Patroclus a visit, my lord?' asked Sabu.

Hanufer stood up, collected the papyri and charts and put them in a reed bag. 'I would like to know if Hatensor was the scribe that visited Ahset. Go back to the brothel where she worked and tell Gorgias the brothel-keeper that he may open for business again. While you are there, find out anything you can about the scribe from her friend Keket.'

Sabu did his best not to smile.

Admiral Patroclus was in an ill humour when Hanufer entered his office an hour later. Standing behind his desk, he jabbed a finger at the papyrus scrap on the desk in front of him.

'What happened at the Pharos lighthouse, Hanufer? Your Sergeant Sabu said in this message that there have been several murders!'

Hanufer outlined what had happened. 'In his dead hand he clutched his reed knife, my lord,' he said, concluding his explanation.

'So, you say that two watchmen and two slaves were killed by Hatensor the scribe? Had he gone mad and then jumped out of the lighthouse to kill himself?' Patroclus continued to fire questions without pausing to let Hanufer answer. 'How do you think Pharaoh Ptolemy will feel about this? Or Queen Arsinoe? Why did he do it? Did he have some idea of ruining the Wepet Renpet Festival? Was he stupid enough to think that if he, the observer, took his own life, it would stop the rise of the gods?'

'The murders did take place at the lighthouse, my lord,' Hanufer began. 'It is my belief that Hatensor was the single target and that the two watchmen and the slaves were just collateral damage.'

Patroclus leaned forward, his eyes wide. 'He was killed? But why? By whom?'

'I have yet to discover this, my lord.'

'So, you believe an assassin threw him out of the lighthouse?'

'I do, my lord. And I think that by placing the reed knife in his dead hand, he meant to make us think that Hatensor killed the watchmen and the slaves and then took his own life.' Hanufer decided not to mention the examinations by the anatomists at this stage.

'Was it to do with the star Sirius?' asked Patroclus.

Hanufer shrugged his shoulders apologetically.

'So how are you going to discover this? By waiting until this murderer strikes again or by asking a fortune teller?'

'I hope that there will not be another murder, my lord,' Hanufer replied as he stroked the rings on his fingers. 'I have already started making enquiries, and I trust that logic and diligence will yield the truth for me.'

'Well, they had better do. Are you up to this, Hanufer of Crocodilopolis, or do you want me to bring in extra help?'

'Extra help, my lord? From whom?'

'From a colleague of yours. Heri-ib, the *Archiphylakites* of the Nile Delta police. You know that he is here in Alexandria, as you saw him with me at the Temple of Demeter.'

'Has he not pressing matters of his own in the Nile Delta?'

'He is here in Alexandria for the Wepet Renpet Festival, since it is to do with the rising of the Nile. He is also liaising with myself and my commanders.'

'Ah, I did ask you at our last meeting whether there was any danger of war, my lord.'

'And as I said, we are always on the edge of a war footing. We have King Magas and the Cyrenaics and the Marmaridae to our west and the Arab tribes to the east beyond the Red Sea, but more importantly the Seleucid empire beyond them. The first Pharaoh Ptolemy was one of the *Diadochi* — the rival generals who fought to control his empire after he died. Now, the descendants of the others with their own empires would like to see Egypt weakened or conquered. Alexandria is the capital of Egypt, yet it is distant from the main part of the country and from the Nile itself other than through the Canopic Canal. I have to maintain a close eye on all that happens in Egypt, and Heri-ib, a most efficient police overseer, is my eye on the Delta.'

Hanufer nodded. 'I am grateful for the offer of his help, my lord. If necessary, I shall seek his counsel, but at this time I am content to follow my own investigations.'

'Then do so, but be prepared to answer questions from the pharaoh and his queen. I will have to inform them of these events, and they will want to know of your progress.'

'I must ask that you do not mention my theory of a killer to anyone.'

Patroclus gave him a hard look and then nodded. 'No one except His Majesty and Queen Arsinoe.'

As Hanufer left the Royal Palace and made his way through the Brucheum towards the Musaeum, he wondered if he would have to seek help. He had been stung by Patroclus' remarks about getting Heri-ib or a fortune-teller to help him.

Yet he did indeed intend to consult a self-proclaimed expert in bird divination.

He found Posidippus of Pella in a small, secluded square in the Musaeum. It was one of several spaces within the great building complex specially designed for the scholars and librarians to go to think. It had two date palms and a surrounding fringe of fragrant bushes, all of which were occupied by a variety of birds.

The tall, thin scholar was sitting on a bench, scattering seeds before a flock of eager pigeons, some of which were almost turquoise in colour. There were several perched on the bench beside him, while in the bushes there were some birds that Hanufer did not recognise.

Posidippus was whispering away to the pigeons on the ground, and it seemed that the birds were responding.

Hanufer took a step into the square, and many of the birds took flight. Suddenly, a hawk swooped into view and knocked one of the doves from the palm tree it had been perching in. It fell and the hawk caught the bird mid-flight, but immediately let it go and flew off. The dove plummeted to the ground and fell dead in front of the scholar.

'Oh dear! Oh dear! That is most ominous!' Posidippus exclaimed, gazing at the bird at his feet without looking around to see who had disturbed his peace. 'Whoever you are, I see that you are a messenger of ill tidings — of violent death.'

Hanufer gazed down at the body of the dead bird. *Is this a message from the gods after all?* he wondered.

'We met fleetingly on the evening of the feast, Master Posidippus,' he said, taking a seat on the bench beside the scholar.

'Indeed, *Archiphylakites* Hanufer,' Posidippus replied, tossing the remaining seeds in his hands onto the ground. 'You just saw the message the gods have allowed us to see. We have witnessed death first-hand, and you will now note that although I have scattered more food for my feathered friends, none will come to take it. Violent death has made them wary, and it will be a while before they venture here again.'

'Have you heard of what occurred this morning, or during the night? At the lighthouse?'

'I sleep late and have seen no living souls except those with wings. But I take it that there has been a sudden death.'

Hanufer knew that Ptolemy used the philosopher as a soothsayer, and he wondered if this was an example of his ability to receive messages from the Greek gods. He nodded. 'The broken body of the scribe Hatensor was found at the foot of the Pharos lighthouse.'

Posidippus clicked his tongue. 'So, the scribe fell from his perch. It is no great surprise, considering how he had fallen from grace these past weeks.'

'I had not heard that, Posidippus. Please enlighten me.'

'He is — or was — a man who likes his cups overmuch. And he was a lecher.'

'Tell me more of his lechery.'

'He visited prostitutes in all of the seedier brothels in the city.'

'How do you know this?'

Posidippus chuckled. 'The librarians and scholars here like to give the impression that they are all sober and industrious individuals who dedicate their lives to learning. But there are many who visit the fleshpots of Alexandria. They saw him when they visited the same establishments.'

'Does this include yourself?'

Posidippus looked shocked. 'I? No, my lord, I have but one love, and that is this Musaeum.' He looked upwards and pointed to a dove in the palm tree — the mate of the one that had been killed by the hawk. It seemed transfixed. 'The wonders of life and the messages from the gods give me all of the sustenance I need.'

'Why had Hatensor fallen from grace?'

'He paid too much attention to those who had risen far above his station.'

'Like the Lady Artemisia?'

Posidippus laughed. 'Exactly! I heard a rumour that she had entertained him fleetingly when she was a *hetaera*, but now she is above a lowly scribe. You saw how after the ceremony he tried to accost her but was ejected from the temple. Well, the same thing happened several weeks ago. He was beaten and warned off by one of the Lady Artemisia's suitors.'

'Who was this?'

'An official called Usermontu, who was the *Architekton* in charge of the Ministry of Buildings and Monuments. Hatensor had an official post with the Ministry, but Usermontu discharged him. News of that destroyed Hatensor's already dubious reputation.' Posidippus shook his head. 'A pity, for he had great skills in mathematics and astronomy.'

'Was Hatensor well known in the Musaeum, then?'

'He had no official appointment here, for he is no —' The scholar stared at Hanufer and hesitated.

Hanufer knew that he meant that the scribe was an Egyptian and not a Greek, an impediment to becoming accepted in either the Musaeum or the Library. However, he chose to say nothing.

'He is no scholar,' Posidippus continued. 'Yet I believe that through Usermontu's influence, Hatensor had a cubicle that he used. As the official in charge of the Ministry of Buildings and Monuments, which includes both the Musaeum and the Library, Usermontu was of course an honorary scholar.'

'Where is this cubicle?'

'I think it is in the Natural Philosophy section of the Library.'

Hanufer nodded. 'Usermontu had not taken away the privilege of this cubicle?'

'Not that I am aware, my lord. But Usermontu himself was playing a dangerous game by courting the Lady Artemisia.' He looked at Hanufer with narrowed eyes. 'You do know that she and the pharaoh —?'

Hanufer nodded. 'I know of that. I also know that Usermontu is dead.'

Posidippus raised his hands. 'Such is the way of life. The gods give it, and they can snatch it away.'

Hanufer tapped his woven reed bag. 'I have some of the papyri and charts that Hatensor was looking at in the lighthouse. Are you knowledgeable in mathematics and astronomy?'

The scholar shook his head. 'I am a poet and philosopher and have no great interest in numbers. But my colleague Lycophron, whom you also met at the feast, may be able to help. He knows more than anyone about the deeper meaning of all things that have a name, including the mystery of numbers. He has written several books upon this subject.'

'I planned to talk to him next, actually,' Hanufer said, standing. 'But you should know that Hatensor did not just fall from the lighthouse. It seems he jumped.'

'Horrible!' exclaimed Posidippus.

'Two watchmen and two young slaves were murdered, and Hatensor was clutching his blood-covered reed knife in his hand.'

'So, it seems he murdered them all and jumped,' Posidippus said slowly. 'That does not sound like the Hatensor that I knew.'

Once again, Hanufer did not divulge his conclusion that Hatensor had been the targeted murder.

There was a sudden thumping noise in front of them. Hanufer stared in amazement as the second dove's body lay next to the one that had been killed by the hawk.

'The poor thing,' said Posidippus. 'It could not live without its mate.' He looked slowly up at Hanufer. 'It is an ill sign, Overseer of Police.'

Hanufer felt a shiver run through his body. 'I will visit your colleague Lycophron to see what he makes of the things Hatensor was working on.'

They bid each other farewell.

Hanufer made his way along the colonnaded walk between the Musaeum and the Library. Once again, he had the unpleasant feeling that he was being watched.

CHAPTER 15

Hanufer entered the Library through a *peripatos*, a broad corridor with high slit windows. Off this were numerous tall alcoves, wherein scholars were working at desks, or standing to study books on high pedestals. It led into the main reading hall with its huge Doric columns suspending a magnificent dome. Huge racks from floor to ceiling were filled with scrolls and papyri, each shelf labelled in Greek. Ladders leaned against walls for the scholars and library clerks to reach the higher shelves.

The walls that were not covered in racks either bore murals depicting scenes of the great intellectuals of the past imparting their knowledge, or they had shrines carved into them containing both Greek and Egyptian gods. On a previous visit, Callimachus the head librarian had explained the murals to Hanufer. Hippocrates of Cos was shown under a plane tree teaching his students the art of medicine, Plato of Athens was staring at a far-off island, and incongruously, the great Socrates was depicted surrounded by weeping men and women as he drank a cup of hemlock. Hanufer's attention was caught by the mural of Pythagoras of Samos, showing him sitting at a table covered with geometric patterns, including pyramids and triangles.

Hanufer found Lycophron of Chalcis in the section of the Library devoted to all the books, texts and plays considered to be the Comedies. Pharaoh Ptolemy himself had ordered Callimachus to put Lycophron in charge of these works.

Hanufer found the little, portly scholar sitting on a high stool in an alcove, surrounded by books. He heard him chortling away before he entered.

'Ha, that's good! Oh, very witty!' Lycophron exclaimed. 'Oh, venerable, clever old Aristophanes, how I love your ingenuity and mirth!'

Hanufer coughed. 'Good day, Master Lycophron. Something greatly amuses you, I presume?'

The scholar looked up and wiped away the tears that had been rolling down his cheeks. 'Ah, *Archiphylakites* Hanufer, welcome. Pray take a seat.' He held up the book he had been reading. 'I am cataloguing the plays of the great Aristophanes, of whom you may have heard?'

'I know the name, but not the plays.'

'Then you have missed nuggets of pure gold and yet have much to look forward to. Listen to this from his play *The Frogs*. It is about the god Dionysus, the great strongman hero Hercules, the dramatists Euripides and Aeschylus and an assortment of common people and slaves. Dionysus dresses up as Hercules and talks to the Frogs, who are the chorus of the play.' He began to read aloud:

'What a sweat! I'm all wet! What a bore!
I'm so raw! I'm so sore! And what's more,
The blisters have come
On my delicate bum,
Where I've never had blisters before.'

Lycophron chuckled, then continued, '*Any minute now and it'll join in the chorus.*' He made a noise as if passing wind, then screwed up his face and made the noise of a frog. '*Brekeke-kex, ko-ax, ko-ax.*'

Hanufer smiled politely and waited for Lycophron to regain control of his mirth.

'Overseer Hanufer, you simply must see his plays whenever they are performed. He was one of our greatest poets and playwrights who wrote during the Peloponnesian Wars between Athens and Sparta.'

'I know of the Trojan Horse from the works of your great Greek poet Homer,' said Hanufer.

'Ha! The Peloponnesian War is recorded history, while the Trojan War is poetry and legend. Both feature Sparta, but do not confuse them. We do not know if there was such a place as Troy.'

'So Troy is not just another name for Athens?' Hanufer asked.

'No, no! It is but a legend. The two names have nothing in common, so we cannot even imagine that Troy was Athens.'

'I take it that you have not heard the ill news today?' Hanufer said abruptly.

To his surprise, Lycophron nodded. 'About Sethnora — I mean, Hatensor? Yes, a shame, but not a surprise.'

'That is actually why I asked about Troy being another name for Athens,' Hanufer said, laying his bag of scrolls and charts on the table. 'I am aware that you called the scribe Hatensor by this other name, Sethnora. It seemed to cause you and Posidippus much amusement. When I asked why, Posidippus merely said that you have a strange compulsion to jumble words and change names.'

'He is right, I do. I call this re-assemblage of names, parts of words and sounds an *anagrammatismos*, but I have shortened it to *anagram*. It reveals the inner secrets about a person. But I do it with a purpose rather than to be comedic. I explore and juggle with the components and sounds to uncover other meanings in names. Hatensor's secret meaning, his actual nature, can be discerned by rearranging his name. Hence Sethnora.'

Hanufer was perplexed. 'Which means what?'

Lycophron gave a thin smile. 'Say it slowly. Seth-no-ra. You and he are both Egyptian, so you can see that his nature is to follow Seth, not Ra. He is aligned with Seth the destroyer, not with Ra the sun god.' He sighed. 'So, I am not surprised that he fell from the lighthouse. He had evil intent, and Ra took his life.'

'Why do you think he had evil intent? What evidence have you?'

'I need none. I am not pleading a case, merely uncovering the mysteries hidden within a name.'

'As an Egyptian, I do not like this idea of yours,' Hanufer said with a frown. 'For us, the name is a part of the person's soul. We call it the *ren*, and without it the soul will never enter the afterlife. It is as important as the *ib*, which you call the heart, the *ka*, the *ba* and the *shuyet*, the shadow.' As he said the latter, he shuddered.

Lycophron gave a wan smile. 'Perhaps his two names mean that he goes to a different part of your afterlife.'

Hanufer shrugged, realising that the scholar was being flippant. 'Had you heard that there have been four murders? The victims were the two watchmen and the two slaves who tended the fires in the lighthouse. Hatensor's broken body was found at the foot of the lighthouse, and in his dead hand he was grasping his reed knife. It was covered in blood that did not seem to be his own.'

Lycophron nodded. 'I had heard, but I know nothing more.'

'Your colleague Posidippus said that Hatensor was a lecher.'

'I am aware of that, too. Again, it is implied in the name I reassembled. He followed the ways of Seth, the destroyer and seducer.'

'Posidippus also said that you understood the mysteries of numbers.'

Lycophron's face lit up. 'That too is correct. I can give you a personal meaning for any individual — I just need to know the exact moment they were born, the day, the season and the year. I have written a book on this aspect of soothsaying. Take the Wepet Renpet Festival. You know how important that is to everyone in Egypt, from the pharaoh and his queen all the way down to the lowliest slave working in the fields or the goldmines.'

'Or tending the flames in the lighthouse,' Hanufer interjected.

'Indeed! Well, when the star Sirius, which you Egyptians call Sothis, rises after having disappeared for seventy days, the Nile will flood and will inundate the fields. I am also aware how important the number seventy is to Egyptians. You mummify your dead for seventy days.'

'And although you are Greeks, you now live in Egypt and enjoy the rule of a pharaoh who was born here in Alexandria.'

'Indeed, and though we are Greeks living in Egypt, we all celebrate the Wepet Renpet Festival, since it falls so close to the birthday of divine Alexander. As you may have guessed, I have already calculated that this year something momentous will happen.' Lycophron gave a short laugh. 'But what exactly that is, I cannot say.'

'You know that Hatensor has been observing the sky every night for many weeks and months. All through that time, surely he was not just waiting for Sothis to appear? After all, we always hope that it will appear after those seventy days.'

'Indeed he was not. He told me that he looked to see each new star that rose and tried to identify them with the various pharaohs, nobles and people of importance who had passed into the afterlife. That, after all, is what you Egyptians believe, is it not?'

'It is. And even I, though not well versed in the sky and astronomy, know that there are five doorways in the eastern sky that open at dawn and allow the souls of those recently dead and entombed to enter the afterlife. One of the main ones, the one that is used by pharaohs and queens, is found where Sothis rises. Where the other four are, I have no idea.'

'Then you still have more idea about it than I do,' Lycophron replied with a chuckle. 'He made observations most nights from the lighthouse on Pharos. Perhaps he was recording things of real importance, or maybe he was just hope-stretching.'

'You like to make jokes, don't you, Master Lycophron?'

The philosopher beamed. 'Yes, jokes make people smile. That can only be good.'

'So, are you joking when you say he may have been hope-stretching? Indeed, you called him a rope-stretcher, if I recall correctly. You also said that he was too arrogant for his own good.'

Lycophron smiled innocently. 'Did I really? Perhaps it was too much wine, my lord. But as for being a rope-stretcher, he is indeed. I believe he held an appointment with the Ministry of Buildings and Monuments and was employed by various businessmen to measure and record and survey. That term rope-stretcher is an Egyptian one, is it not?'

Hanufer nodded. 'Let me show you some of the charts and papyri I found up in the lighthouse. Give me your opinion, if you will.'

As Hanufer unrolled the charts and papyri on the table, the philosopher looked them over. 'Well, he was certainly an adept scribe in both Greek and Egyptian demotic, I will give him that. And also clearly adept at using both Greek and Egyptian numbers, for he uses them interchangeably, it seems.'

'You can see he has made observations by each date, but Sothis has not yet been recorded.'

'No, but other stars have. Lots of them, actually. Yet I think there is more here. It seems as if he was trying to make things look too complicated for anyone to decipher but himself.'

'I agree, which is why I am seeking your opinion. As with your names and anagrams, can you see a secret meaning in these charts?'

Lycophron gazed for some moments, running a stubby finger along columns and strings of numbers. 'These are not all to do with the skies, I think.'

'You mean the drawings of pyramids and triangles?' Hanufer asked. 'I thought that I was fairly adept in arithmetic, but I am puzzled by many of these drawings.'

Lycophron nodded. 'Certainly he has drawn lots more triangles than pyramids. But of course, triangles make up pyramids. Reading through quickly, I would say that some do not make sense. He draws pyramids amid triangles, and some of these figures are calculations for the *seked*.'

'*Seked*?' Hanufer repeated. 'I am not familiar with that.'

The philosopher smiled. 'It is actually one area where your Egyptian mathematicians have been superior to ours. It is effectively the means by which your pyramid builders of the past constructed these wonders so perfectly. The *seked* is the slope of a pyramid, and it is the relationship between the height of the triangle and the length of a triangle that is formed when you cut a pyramid in half. Look.' Lycophron pointed to several of the triangles and figures with their Greek or Egyptian numbers and calculations alongside. 'Some of these look to be rope-stretching matters and others are to do with the skies. That is why some are the right way up and others upside down. But many of them relate to this upright line, which is the Pharos lighthouse.'

Hanufer nodded. 'That makes some sense, I suppose.'

Lycophron scratched his nose. 'Yet it is almost as if he is disguising his work, putting some figures and some drawings where they do not belong to make it look complicated. The other thing that occurs to me is that these papyri are probably not continuous. There may be some that are missing, which may make this seem more logical. All in all, I think he must only have had some of his work with him.'

'He had surveying and astronomy equipment with him,' Hanufer explained, describing them.

Lycophron shook his head. 'I do not have enough information here to make total sense of the numbers he has used, beyond saying that some of it is astronomical and some is rope-stretching.'

'You mean surveying work? Calculations of quantities and measurements of land and buildings?'

'Exactly. It probably has to do with his work for the Ministry of Buildings and Monuments, or private commissions, nothing more. He must have been carrying all of his work together. Or at least some of it. Perhaps his mind was not as organised as we all thought. Or perhaps his drinking has been making his thoughts and mathematical calculations jumbled?'

Hanufer started to put the work back in his bag. 'Again, that is what I thought. Posidippus said that Hatensor also had the use of a cubicle in the Natural Philosophy section of the Library. Do you know exactly where I can find it?'

Sabu told Gorgias that he could re-open his doors for business, much to the brothel-keeper's obvious pleasure. However, he was less pleased when Sabu told him that he needed to talk to Keket again.

'But she will have to —'

'It is the order of the *Archiphylakites* Hanufer. She may have important information about a case we are investigating. Not necessarily that of Ahset.'

His stern look was enough to make the brothel-keeper scuttle off to fetch Keket.

It was the third time that Sabu had talked with Keket, and each time he was sure that her smile grew broader and more genuine upon seeing him.

Rather than talk to her in the brothel, where he knew that the walls might be thinner than needed, he invited her to walk out with him down through the grid system of streets towards Lake Mareotis.

They passed through the city walls and ambled along the shore with its huge reedbeds, where fishermen were able to propel their flat-bottomed boats with long poles. Sabu had visited the area with Corporals Pylyp and Filemon, and they had explained that the reeds were so thick that local lake dwellers actually cut water paths through them in winding networks that were easy for them to negotiate, but almost impossible for anyone unused to the lake. As such, it had become a natural home for bandits and smugglers as well as fishermen and their families.

Beyond the reedbeds, the lake was deep and extended for many leagues. On the calm waters larger craft including barges and cargo ships could be seen coming to and from the Lake Harbour to the east.

Keket stroked back a wisp of her hair and looked up at Sabu. 'So, have you brought me here as Sergeant Sabu the Deputy of Police, or as a client, or for —?'

He gave her what he hoped was a reassuring smile. 'I am here on police business, but I hope you will also regard it as a friendly visit.'

'Not as a client? Because if you want, I could —'

He held up his hands. 'Look, Keket, I have to be here as Sergeant Sabu in the first instance. Can we deal with that first?' She pouted at him, and despite himself he put a hand on hers. 'You are a beautiful young woman, and I would like to be a friend, not a client.'

Her smile appeared again. She held onto his hand and drew close to him. 'Then there is no problem. We could just not tell Gorgias.'

He gently held her back. 'Police business first, please. Have you heard about the scribe who fell from the Pharos lighthouse today?'

She shook her head.

'His name was Hatensor, and my boss is wondering if he could have been the last client that Ahset saw. You said that you had also slept with him before?'

She stood back, looking shocked. 'He is dead?'

'He was found at the bottom of the lighthouse with a knife in his hand. It looked as if he may have jumped, after he had cut the throats of the two watchmen and stabbed to death two slaves who tended the fires.'

Hanufer had been quite clear on what he could and could not reveal, so Sabu did not mention the broken necks or his boss's theory that Hatensor had also been murdered.

Keket could not talk for a few moments as tears welled in her eyes. 'My poor Ahset. I hate to think of what happened to her. Yes ... I did sleep with him, when Ahset was busy. He was ... an arrogant man. He liked you to know that he was important.'

'Did he say in what way he was important?'

'No, he just let us know that he had the ear of the pharaoh. Neither of us believed that, of course. Men who come to us always say that they are more important than they are. It's their way of feeling powerful. Our job is to stoke that feeling for them and let them think that we would do anything to service them.'

Sabu did not like having to question Keket about such things. She looked more vulnerable than he had seen her before and he wanted to put an arm around her, but he knew that would be the wrong thing to do while he was trying to get information.

'Was there anything frightening about him? Anything that made you think he could have been violent?'

'Do you mean, anything that made me think he could have killed Ahset? No, he wasn't that sort. In fact, he was always a bit nervous. He listened for sounds in the corridor, as if he was suspicious that he could have been followed.'

'Did Ahset ever notice anything? Was he ever abusive to her?'

'It was she who said that he was nervous, and I noticed it after that.'

'Did he ever stay the whole night with either of you?'

Keket shook her head. 'Never. He said he had important work to do before dawn.'

'Always the same? Every night?'

She nodded. 'He said the same every time.'

'Then it is certainly Hatensor.'

Keket sighed. 'I am sad to hear of his death. He was an irritable and pompous man, but he was never unpleasant or violent to us. If you are saying that he killed those people, I cannot believe it.'

'What about his drinking? Did he get drunk?'

She laughed. 'Most men need a drink, but few can manage lovemaking when they're drunk. No, he'd have a couple first, then afterwards he'd maybe have more.'

'Did he seem drunk when he saw Ahset?'

'I didn't see them, so I couldn't say.'

'There was an empty amphora of wine. Would Gorgias have checked the room before Hatensor left?'

'No, he would already have charged him for that. It would have been left to Ahset to bring the empty amphora out in the morning. Gorgias is tight with money, and if there was any wine left, he would have taken it to sell to another customer.'

Sabu smiled. 'I think that's all I need to know.'

'Then if we've taken care of that, what about the other matter? I won't tell Gorgias if you don't.'

Sabu liked Keket very much and wanted to feel her supple body against his. But it would not be right. He kissed her gently, lingeringly, but that was all. 'I like you, Keket. I like you a lot, but there are matters that I must clear up before I can tell you more.'

She smiled up at him. 'I liked kissing you. So, clear those matters up quickly, Sergeant Sabu. Then I look forward to just calling you Sabu.'

CHAPTER 16

Hanufer followed Lycophron's directions to the Natural Philosophy section of the Library and asked a clerk to show him the cubicle used by Hatensor. It was one of perhaps twenty or so small, curtained areas where scholars and scribes could store the work they had been doing in the many pigeonholes built above each desk. The lighting was good, since each cubicle was roofless, but if someone was working after sundown an oil lamp was supplied for each cubicle.

All papyri borrowed from any of the departments in the Library had to be documented with Callimachus or one of his assistant scribes, so that they could keep track of the five hundred thousand works under its care.

Hatensor had been busy, Hanufer mused as he looked at the rows of pigeonholes, each of which contained at least one scroll.

He stretched each one out on the desk in front of him. Once again, most of the notes seemed to have been written in a way that only Hatensor would understand. Some scrolls were full of numbers and days, while others were filled with observations about the skies and the appearance of various stars, some labelled as past pharaohs who had become gods. Other writings compared the similarities and differences between the gods Proteus and Harpokrates. Still others were about the care of the dead, and the different customs of the various cultures that used the Necropolis. This interested Hanufer because it seemed so incongruous, until he recalled that Evenius had said that he and his other priests visited their temple near the Necropolis every day to make sacrifices and deal with matters of administration. But why would Hatensor have written notes about the care of the dead?

He shuffled through more papyri and found sketched plans of the Necropolis. Again, with some of these there were lots of numbers, and on some of them there were also depictions of pyramids and triangles.

Hanufer rested his chin on his fist as he pondered whether there was some clue amidst all of this as to why someone would have wanted the scribe dead.

He suddenly had the feeling that he was being watched. He spun round and pulled the curtain of the cubicle aside, but there was no one there.

Corporals Pylyp and Filemon had reported to Sabu as soon as he had returned from the brothel.

'We are sorry that we did not apprehend the scribe Hatensor last night, Sergeant Sabu, sir,' said Pylyp. 'We had expected *Archiphylakites* Hanufer to at least reprimand us.'

Sabu was drinking beer that Cario had just poured from a pitcher. He wiped his mouth with the back of his hand and eyed them sourly. 'Our boss is a fair man, and he can be stern if he thinks it is needed. It is a pity that the fellow took off, but obviously he knew someone was after him. He must have thought you were that person. Overseer Hanufer knows that.'

'Perhaps we should have gone to the lighthouse in the night and taken him with us to see the boss in the morning,' said Pylyp. 'At least he would still be alive.'

'And so too would the two watchmen and the two young slaves, poor devils,' agreed Filemon bitterly.

Sabu drummed his fingers on the desk. 'It is a bad business. And it runs deeper than we thought.'

'Deeper, sir?' Filemon repeated.

'Much deeper,' came Hanufer's voice from the corridor.

The corporals stood swiftly to attention, as did Cario.

Hanufer came through the door and sat behind his desk. 'Sergeant Sabu is quite correct. There has been much evil done either last night or very early this morning. And now we are going to take all of you into our confidence. None of you will tell anyone else what I am about to recount to you.'

Cario shuffled towards the door.

'Stay Cario. This includes you, too,' Hanufer ordered. 'There may be a special police task that I need you to undertake.'

With a grateful smile Cario stood back against the wall, conscious of the special consideration that he was being given by Hanufer.

'We are certain that Hatensor was the target of an assassin and that the others were murdered to cover up this crime.'

'But why would anyone be interested in this scribe, my lord?' Filemon asked.

'That is what I have yet to work out,' Hanufer replied. He nodded as Cario raised the pitcher of beer and picked up a goblet with a questioning glance.

They all waited while Hanufer slaked his thirst.

'So, tell me, what do you know about these lighthouse deaths so far?' Hanufer asked the corporals.

They looked at each other, then Filemon replied, 'The scribe Hatensor was found smashed to a pulp at the foot of the Pharos lighthouse. The two watchmen had their throats cut and the two young slaves had been stabbed. The scribe had a knife in his hands, so it looks as if he killed them all and then ended his life by leaping from the top of the lighthouse.'

Sabu nodded. 'That is what people believe at this time, and that is what they should continue to be told.'

'The actual situation is far more complicated than that,' Hanufer said. 'We had the anatomists Erasistratus and Herophilus examine the bodies, and they confirmed that Hatensor and both watchmen had their necks broken and the two watchmen had their throats cut as well. As for the two slaves, they were stabbed to death, but they did not have their necks broken. One of them was stabbed in the back and then had his throat cut. That indicates that the murderer was trying to make it look as if the watchmen had been killed by the slitting of their throats. It was the same with the murder of Ahset: the anatomists confirmed that she died from a broken neck and then had her throat cut. Remember that we told you her last customer had been a scholar or scribe? That was why we needed to talk to the scribe Hatensor. I believe that he was the last person to see her alive.'

Pylyp grimaced. 'So, if it was the same method, you must think that it was the same killer, my lord?'

'Exactly. That is why this information does not leave this room. It must not be divulged to anyone else. The killer has to believe that we think Hatensor was the murderer. He will then think that is the end of the matter and that he has been successful in covering up his crimes.'

Both corporals tapped their chests in unison, the sign that the order had been received and understood.

'But do we have any idea who the killer is, my lord?' Filemon asked.

Hanufer shook his head. 'We have many questions, but few answers.' He took out the scrolls from his bag and unfurled one. 'Hatensor wrote all of these notes and drew pyramids and triangles. But why he did so is not clear to me or any of those who knew him.'

Hanufer was not surprised when Tabid the vizier's messenger arrived and handed him Patroclus's summons to the Royal Palace for the second time that day.

He used one of the police chariots to get there quickly. Upon his arrival, he was led not to the vizier's office, but to one of the lesser throne rooms. There a royal clerk informed him that he should stand in front of the dais and wait upon the trumpet call, and that he should fall to his knees and bow his head until bidden otherwise.

To his surprise, the doors opened without ceremony, and he was in the process of kneeling when he heard the clerk give the same instructions to several people. He turned and saw that the scholars Lycophron and Posidippus had entered, along with Nefrit.

As they joined him before the dais, trumpets were sounded and the great doors at the back of the throne room opened. Admiral Patroclus came in, tapping a long staff on the marble floor as he walked in backwards ahead of Ptolemy Philadelphus and Queen Arsinoe.

Kneeling, all four visitors bowed their heads and averted their eyes as the royal couple ascended to their thrones. They waited until Patroclus ordered them to rise and kiss the toes of first the pharaoh and then the queen.

'Their Majesties have been informed of the deaths of the scribe Hatensor and of the lighthouse keepers and the slaves this morning,' the vizier told them once they had taken their places again before the royal couple.

'I am outraged at this heinous crime,' Ptolemy said. 'My vizier has informed me that he believes that Hatensor the scribe was also murdered.'

The two philosophers and Nefrit stared in surprise, but made no noise.

'So, five murders were committed, and a killer is loose in the city. Why are you not letting people know what actually occurred, Hanufer of Crocodilopolis?'

'Your Majesty, I am certain that Hatensor was the intended victim. The others were silenced to prevent the killer being identified. The scribe's blood-stained reed knife was placed in his dead hand to throw suspicion onto him. If we allow this version to circulate around the city, then the killer will think his plan was successful.'

'And what will prevent him killing again?' Ptolemy demanded.

'If he thinks we have accepted the idea that Hatensor was the killer of the others, it is unlikely that he will strike again.'

'But he must have done this for a reason. What progress have you made in discovering this?'

'I have begun enquiries, Your Majesty, and I have answers to some preliminary questions. I hesitate to say more, as it is important that my findings do not become public knowledge.'

'It is simple enough,' replied Ptolemy. 'You are here before your pharaoh and his queen, and they order that what is said here shall be as confidential as if we were talking to the gods. Upon pain of death, nothing of importance shall be passed to anyone outside of this room.'

Patroclus rapped his staff on the floor. 'Is that understood by you all?'

Hanufer raised a hand. 'If I may, Your Majesties, I must ask that I be permitted to share this with the most trusted men directly under my command, so that they can assist my enquiries.'

Ptolemy nodded. 'It shall be so. Now, what have you discovered?'

Hanufer had not wanted to mention anything to anyone outside his own staff, but now he had no choice. He told them that the anatomists had confirmed that Hatensor and the two watchmen had broken necks.

'It is not enough!' Ptolemy snapped. 'I want this killer found and brought in chains to suffer a suitable death.'

'Brother,' Queen Arsinoe interjected, touching her husband's arm. 'Perhaps *Archiphylakites* Hanufer requires more time.'

Ptolemy gave her a sour look. 'There is little time to give. We are on the verge of the Wepet Renpet Festival, and the Nile will soon rise — or not!'

Patroclus coughed to gain attention. 'Had the scribe Hatensor observed the rise of Sothis? It may not yet have occurred, since it usually occurs around the birthday of divine Alexander.'

'I think not, my lord,' Hanufer replied. 'It does not seem to have been recorded in his papyri. I have been going through them. Indeed, I sought the opinion of the scholars Posidippus and Lycophron soon after the event. I apologise to them both that I could not tell them of the murder of Hatensor.'

The pharaoh waved his hand. 'And so, what is their opinion?'

Posidippus shook his head. 'I know something of numbers, but not the same meanings that my fellow scholar knows about. So, I deferred to my colleague Lycophron, Your Majesty.'

Lycophron also shook his head. 'I looked at Hatensor's papyri, Your Majesty. From what we could determine, Sethnora — I beg your pardon, Your Majesty, I meant the scribe Hatensor — had not recorded it.'

Ptolemy looked annoyed. 'So, what had he recorded in these papyri?'

'A lot of mathematical calculations and drawings of the stars in relation to the lighthouse, Your Majesty,' Hanufer replied. 'But not the specific rise of the star Sothis.'

'And who is going to continue the observations at night?'

Patroclus answered. 'I have sent orders to Evenius, the high priest, and he is going to arrange for one of his priests who has knowledge of the skies to take over. More guards and slaves will be stationed at the lighthouse.'

Ptolemy grunted and looked at Nefrit. 'What do you think of this, High Priestess of Isis? Sothis is the spirit of Osiris, the husband of your goddess Isis. Is it possible that by killing the scribe, the rise of Sothis may not have taken place?'

Hanufer admired the confidence with which Nefrit spoke.

'If Sothis has risen, then whether a man sees it or not will not matter, Your Majesty.'

Ptolemy considered for a moment, then turned to the two scholars. 'And what say you both about this as soothsayers?'

Posidippus spoke first. 'When Hanufer came to seek me out in the Musaeum, we both witnessed a sign from the gods. A hawk swooped down as I was watching the birds in my little square. It took a dove that was perched on a tree with its mate, but instead of carrying it off, it dropped it at our feet. Moments later its mate, untouched by the hawk, fell to its death beside it.'

Ptolemy and Arsinoe stared at each other.

'What does that mean?' Queen Arsinoe asked abruptly.

Posidippus bit his lip. 'It could have many meanings, Your Majesty. It could relate to the fall of the scribe Hatensor from the lighthouse. If so, it could indicate that he was indeed killed by another. Or it could mean that the star Sothis will not rise, as its journey through the underworld has been prevented. The

Egyptian underworld, that is. Or it could mean that a violent death is soon to happen, or has already happened.'

'But had this scribe a wife?' Ptolemy asked.

Hanufer stroked his two rings. He debated whether to say anything about the murder of Ahset, but decided not to, since she was not Hatensor's wife. 'We do not think he was married, Your Majesty,' he replied, truthfully.

Queen Arsinoe put a hand on her brother-husband's shoulder. 'Or perhaps it could mean that the birds who occupy the highest place, the top of the tree, are —'

Ptolemy patted her hand and shook his head with a cold smile. 'You are not a soothsayer, my queen. Leave this to me.' He turned to the philosophers again. 'And what of you, Lycophron? Have you anything to add?'

'Only this, Your Majesty. You may have noticed that I began by calling the scribe Sethnora. That is what I call an *anagrammatismos*, but I have shortened it to *anagram*. This is a reformulating of the elements of his name. It produces a new meaning. Seth-no-Ra means that he secretly follows Seth, the brother of Osiris, but not Ra the sun. I think Hatensor had a brooding and evil side to him. He has paid the price, and the hawk that killed the dove shows this.'

Hanufer had thought the scholar was talking nonsense when he first heard his theory, but now there seemed to be some merit in the idea.

Before he could interject, the doors were thrown open. The pharaoh smiled and the queen stared angrily.

'Ah, now we may get some real meaning from this outrage,' said Ptolemy. 'Here is the High Priestess Artemisia.'

'A thousand pardons, Your Majesties,' Artemisia said, striding in front of Hanufer and the others and prostrating herself at the foot of the dais before crawling up the steps to kiss the toes of the pharaoh and his queen. 'I have come from the Temple of Demeter, where I saw the dark clouds of evil swirling in the oracle I cast in the flames. I saw a god in chains, held by his brother in the underworld where Demeter's daughter Persephone was abducted and held by Hades.'

Ptolemy grasped the arms of his throne. 'What does this mean?'

'The evil god Seth is threatening to hold Osiris, which may mean that the star will not rise and therefore the Nile will not flood. The crops will fail this year, and there will be famine — and danger to your rule.'

Ptolemy and Arsinoe stared at one another, then Ptolemy turned to them all. 'It seems that the gods have sent us warnings. They confirm that there are evil forces at work. Hanufer of Crocodilopolis, you must do everything in your power to catch this murderer. And do so quickly.' He then turned back to Artemisia. 'So, tell me, what must be done?'

'My goddess Hecate released Persephone by going to the underworld to light the way with a torch. You must make an urgent sacrifice to her before Ra dips down tomorrow so that she can do the same for Osiris.'

Hanufer glanced at Nefrit and saw that she was looking at him with an expression of ire. But then she looked away and he focused on how Pharaoh Ptolemy Philadelphus reacted to the High Priestess of Hecate.

Like the others, he listened with surprise as she told him what sort of sacrifice was to be made.

CHAPTER 17

As was usual after an audience with the royal couple, those who had been called to see them were not permitted to leave together. Instead, each were escorted out through different corridors in the labyrinthine palace network.

Hanufer had desperately wanted to talk with Nefrit, but she barely looked at him as she followed a guard down one corridor while he was forced to wait until first the Lady Artemisia and then the philosophers were taken on different routes. When it was his turn, he was led by another guard, but not down any corridor he recognised. He was taken into an antechamber, where he was offered wine and figs by a palace servant.

After some time, the door opened, and Patroclus entered alone. He made signs to the guard and the servant, who both instantly left.

'I thought that you may not have finished with me, my lord,' Hanufer said when they were alone.

'It is not just I,' the vizier replied, going to the door he had come through and opening it. 'There is another who wished to speak with you.'

Hanufer's jaw dropped as Queen Arsinoe walked in and sat down upon a couch. Immediately, he dropped to his knees and tapped his head on the floor.

'Let us dispense with these formalities, Overseer Hanufer,' she said, pointing to two chairs. Hanufer waited until Patroclus sat down before he followed.

'My brother-husband does not know of this audience, and that is how it must stay. As you will doubtless have seen, he is bewitched by the Lady Artemisia.'

'I saw that His Majesty seems to lay great importance upon her opinion,' Hanufer replied.

Patroclus leaned forward in his chair. 'Queen Arsinoe has permitted us to speak freely, Hanufer, so you do not have to guard your words here. Do you agree that His Majesty seems bewitched?'

Hanufer turned to look directly at the queen. 'I have little knowledge of bewitchment, Your Majesty, but I would agree that the pharaoh looks upon her with excessive favour.'

'Favour! He wears her ring, builds her a special pylon gate and is planning a temple. Now, after these outrageous murders, what is he going to do? He is going to follow her advice and make a sacrifice at the *temenos* close to the Temple of Poseidon tomorrow evening. And what is this sacrifice to be?'

'She said a dog, Your Majesty, for that is apparently one of the animals sacred to Hecate. And also a polecat and a fish.'

Patroclus nodded. 'According to Artemisia, they all have special associations with the goddess Hecate.'

'But which fish?' Queen Arsinoe demanded.

'I believe it is the red mullet, Your Majesty,' Hanufer replied.

'It is an affront to the gods to sacrifice a fish that feeds on the corpses of men drowned in the sea, and also a polecat that is known for frequenting dark spaces and lives by deceit. By permitting this in a sacred place like the *temenos*, Ptolemy is playing into the hands of Seth the destroyer.'

Patroclus grunted. 'You also saw that she requested permission to approach His Majesty and whisper in his ear.'

'I did, my lord,' said Hanufer. 'And I saw that after that, His Majesty called you onto the dais and had words.'

'There is to be another sacrifice,' said Patroclus. 'A baboon.'

Hanufer looked shocked. 'I have heard of baboons being sacrificed upon the death of a noted scribe, but only if they were specially trained pets. We had two baboons mummified after they were killed along with one of my constables when I was in Crocodilopolis, but I have never heard of one being sacrificed like this. Not along with fish.'

Queen Arsinoe nodded. 'Exactly! The worst thing is that he will be doing the witch's bidding in sight of the people.'

Hanufer held his hands up. 'I am not sure what you wish me to do, Your Majesty. I cannot prevent this. It is His Majesty the pharaoh's will.'

'Tell him, Patroclus.'

The vizier took a deep breath. 'Her Majesty is aware that I already told you about the death of Usermontu and the ring that I gave you.'

'May I ask why you were concerned about Usermontu, Your Majesty?' Hanufer asked. 'I understand that he was an official and had been the *Architekton* of many buildings and villas in Alexandria.'

Arsinoe frowned. 'I introduced Artemisia to Usermontu myself. It was foolish of me, just as it was foolish of me to have introduced her to my brother-husband, Ptolemy.'

Hanufer darted a startled glance at Patroclus, who merely raised an eyebrow, as if indicating that the matter was of little importance. But Hanufer considered it potentially of great importance and needed to know more. 'I was not aware that you had known the Lady Artemisia previously, Your Majesty?'

The queen sighed. 'I visited her in Canopus, as I had heard of her skills in interpreting dreams.'

Hanufer felt a shiver run up his spine as he recalled his own meeting with Artemisia. 'Could you tell me what you dreamed of and what she told you, Your Majesty?'

Queen Arsinoe looked shocked for a moment, then blushed with embarrassment. 'I had been troubled by dreams of the murder of my two youngest children, by my half-brother Ptolemy Keraunos. They were killed in front of me, and I have dreamed of them often.'

Hanufer was aware that Queen Arsinoe was the pharaoh's actual elder sister, but that she had had three children with King Lysimachus when she was young. After his death in battle, she had fled to Cassandreia where she had married Ptolemy Keraunos, her half-brother. He had heard that she had conspired against him with her two sons, hence their summary execution and her subsequent escape to Egypt to marry Pharaoh Ptolemy, her younger brother. It was for this reason that he was known as Ptolemy Philadelphus, meaning Ptolemy, sibling-lover.

'But then I started dreaming of our young son Ptolemy being dragged into the Nile and eaten by a crocodile.'

Hanufer fingered his Sobek ring. 'A distressing dream, Your Majesty.'

'It was, but Artemisia went into a trance and held my hand. She said that her goddess Hecate had taken her into my dream and told her that the crocodile had not eaten my son, but that he would protect him, for it was Sobek who ruled the Nile. One day, my son will rule the Nile and Egypt.' She held Hanufer's gaze. 'I know that you are from Crocodilopolis and that you, like all Egyptians, venerate Sobek.'

'We do, Your Majesty. And we are honoured that Pharaoh Ptolemy has renamed our city Arsinoe in your honour.'

She waved aside his attempted compliment. 'My dreams stopped after that. I was so grateful to her that I arranged for her to come to Alexandria. I introduced her to Usermontu, who had designed the stadium in my name in the east of the city. He fell under her spell as a *hetaera* and I believe they became lovers.' She frowned. 'Not long after that, I introduced my brother-husband to her when he had a difficult problem of state to solve. He had told me that it had caused him to sleep and dream fitfully. So he consulted her, and that was when he fell under her spell.'

Patroclus harrumphed. 'And then Usermontu died suddenly.'

'Poisoned by her, I am sure!' Queen Arsinoe spat.

'Forgive me, but why would she have done so, Your Majesty?'

She shook a hand irritably. 'Because he would have been a hindrance to her when she had designs upon seducing the pharaoh, my brother-husband. Patroclus investigated for me, but we had no proof, so —' She sighed and shrugged her shoulders.

Again, Patroclus interceded. 'Which is all just as I told you, Hanufer of Crocodilopolis. And here we are now, with this situation.'

Conscious that they were both looking expectantly at him, Hanufer said, 'I have already begun my investigations and have actually visited the Lady Artemisia. She told me that she and Usermontu had been lovers and that he was the architect of the pylon gate and of the new planned Temple of Hecate. But there was nothing to hint that she could be responsible for his sudden death.'

'So, you have no idea whether Usermontu was poisoned?' Patroclus asked.

'I did not have sufficient opportunity to question her further. But the fact that she has come from Canopus intrigues me.'

'Why so?' Queen Arsinoe demanded.

'Because it is possibly a link with the fall of the scribe Hatensor. I shall make further investigation.'

Queen Arsinoe stood up. 'I do not like these murders, Overseer Hanufer, so solve them quickly. Find out if the Lady Artemisia is involved in them, because only then will I stop worrying that I am going to become a widowed queen.'

Patroclus opened the door and the queen strode out without a further glance at Hanufer. 'You heard Her Majesty, Hanufer. Solve this mess swiftly.'

Hanufer was going over all that had been said during the meeting as he left the palace. First of all, he was determined to find out more about Artemisia and her connection with the city of Canopus.

He made his way to the Royal Harbour, where the fleet was at anchor. Immediately recognised by his pectoral of office, he was admitted to the maze of offices and greeted by a naval clerk. Asking to be taken to *Archiphylakites* Heri-ib, he was led by a naval clerk to an outer office where two constables of the Nile Delta police stood guard by the door. Inside he found *Archiphylakites* Heri-ib and his deputy Muthis poring over a number of maps of the city and the surrounding area.

After the customary formal greetings, Hanufer explained the purpose of his visit.

'We have heard about the spate of murders in the city, Hanufer,' Heri-ib said. 'If we can assist you in your enquiries, we shall. I have half a dozen Nile police constables with me, as well as Sergeant Muthis.'

'I may yet take you up on this offer, Heri-ib, but for now it is information that I seek. About the Lady Artemisia and about the city of Canopus.'

The Nile police chief looked surprised. 'Is the Lady Artemisia relevant to these murders?'

'That I am unsure of, but I must follow all leads, as you well know. You were at the dedication to the pylon gate at the Temple of Demeter. Did you see the fracas that the scribe Hatensor caused?'

'Yes, I saw him trying to bother the new high priestess, and he was marched out of the hall.'

'The fellow was clearly drunk,' said Muthis.

Hanufer nodded. 'He called out to her. As I recall, he said, "It is I, your Hatensor." That indicates that he was known to her. But she ignored him, and it looked as if she had her bodyguards eject him.'

'It did,' Heri-ib agreed. 'I do not know much about this scribe, Hatensor. He seemed to be attached to the Temple of Harpokrates in Canopus.'

'I am told that he was also commissioned by the Ministry of Buildings and Monuments here in Alexandria to do surveying work and organise supplies of various building materials with businessmen in Canopus and the Delta.'

'Canopus is a busy port city on the Canopus River in the Delta; there are many businessmen. The scribe Hatensor had not come to our attention. I only know of him because of his association with the Temple of Harpokrates.'

'The vizier, Admiral Patroclus told me that the Lady Artemisia was the priestess of a small Temple of Hecate in Canopus. He said it was more a shrine than a temple.'

Heri-ib pursed his lips and shook his head. 'I do not know of it. But I did know of Artemisia, who was a well-known *hetaera* in the city.'

'I do know of the Temple of Hecate, my lord,' said Muthis. 'The Lady Artemisia had a small villa in Canopus next to the temple, and she had a reputation as a dream soothsayer.' He looked uncertainly at Heri-ib for a moment, then continued, 'I know this because I made a votive offering myself and consulted her about bad dreams I'd had for some weeks after I'd found the body of your constable and the murdered baboons. Almost every night, I dreamt of baboons being shot with arrows by an unknown criminal.'

'I did not know this, Muthis,' said Heri-ib. 'What did she tell you?'

'She told me that it was a sign from the god Thoth that I should try hard to look after those who follow and worship him. I did not understand what she meant, and she told me that I must be a protector of the things they write.' He took a deep breath. 'I still do not know what she meant, and I can only say that I am glad I was not attached to look after this scribe who fell from the lighthouse.'

Hanufer thought for a moment, then asked Muthis, 'Had you previous knowledge of the scribe Hatensor?'

'Not exactly knowledge of him, but I did see him at her villa, rope-measuring in the grounds.'

'You saw him rope-measuring? Could he have been surveying a new building?'

'It is possible, my lord. I know little of the intricacies of rope-measuring.'

Hanufer nodded and addressed Heri-ib. 'Were you aware that Queen Arsinoe herself consulted the Lady Artemisia in Canopus, and it was she who brought her to Alexandria?'

Heri-ib nodded. 'I had heard this, of course.'

'Did you know of the *Architekton* Usermontu?'

'I knew of his reputation as a great builder, but I never met him.'

'The Temple of Hecate in Canopus had been built by local businessmen, I understand.'

Heri-ib shrugged. 'I don't know of that. It was not something that came to the attention of the Nile police.'

'Do you know of local businessmen who could have financed it?'

Again, Heri-ib shook his head.

'Usermontu was said to be a lover of Artemisia.'

Heri-ib shrugged. 'She was a *hetaera*.'

Hanufer pointed to all the maps on the table. 'Well, I thank you for all that, but one more question.'

'Please ask whatever you will.'

'Admiral Patroclus said that you are both here for the Wepet Renpet Festival.'

'We are, at his instruction.'

'Along with colonels, generals and captains? Tell me, why are you really here in Alexandria?'

Heri-ib smiled. 'I wondered when you would ask that, Hanufer of Crocodilopolis.'

After leaving the naval headquarters, Hanufer made his way to the nearby Temple of Isis to see Nefrit. He was greeted by one of the handmaidens, who informed him that Nefrit had not yet returned, for she had an important ritual to carry out somewhere else. Where that place was, she was unable to tell him.

Hanufer's strove not to show his profound disappointment. He hoped above all that she would come to his villa that night.

CHAPTER 18

Cario had spent the afternoon talking to his friend Paiania, the house slave of the physician Galenos, as Hanufer had instructed him to do. He reported on it to Hanufer and Sabu when they had returned to the headquarters.

'So, I helped him to clean the *iatreion* where his master sees patients, and then we ground up various herbs and filled jars ready for Galenos to make up his potions.'

'And where was Galenos, if he was not seeing patients in his consulting room?' Hanufer asked.

'He was visiting a patient in their home, my lord. That was fortuitous, because normally my friend Paiania has to go with Galenos when he makes a house call. It is not usually done in Alexandria for a physician to carry his own medicine chest, and Galenos is not a patient master. He can get angry with Paiania and … and often he will beat him if he does something wrong or is not fast enough in carrying out his work.'

Hanufer had been looking at some of the ostraca messages in his basket and looked up quickly, his interest piqued. 'Why did the physician not take your friend Paiania?'

'He did not know, except that he had visited the patient twice before and he had gone carrying his medicine chest himself.'

'Did he say what sort of case it was?' Sabu asked.

'No, sir. Galenos never discusses his cases with Paiania, even though he permits him to make up certain types of medicine. But Paiania said he can usually work out what sort of patient he has been to see when he cleans out his medicine chest. For example, he knows when he has been to see a woman patient or to one of the brothels, as he has to clean his speculums, the instruments he uses for looking —'

'Yes, I understand,' said Hanufer swiftly. 'Go on, what else can he tell?'

'If it is a surgical case, my lord, then he may take his various surgical knives and *macairia*. For this particular patient, he had taken bandages, sheep intestine sutures, needles and his cautery irons. More than that, when he returned he ordered Paiania to prepare more sheep intestine sutures, which I helped him to do. We had to go to the butchery market for fresh sheep innards to make them.' He wrinkled his nose. 'We had to stretch pieces of the gut on a special frame. It was smelly work.'

'So, it was some sort of injury that this patient had,' Hanufer said, scratching his chin.

'Who asked him to call?' Sabu queried.

'It was the same messenger who came each time — a burly Egyptian fellow was all he could say. The first visit was before dawn a few days ago. Paiania answered the door and roused Galenos. He said his master seemed worried when he talked with the man. Then Galenos visited again yesterday and today. He had also visited the patient late yesterday evening without being called upon. He said he must have arranged to visit again himself.'

'Did Paiania know where in the city the patient was?' asked Hanufer.

'No, my lord, but Galenos was gone a long time on each occasion, so it was either quite far or he had much to do.'

Sabu pursed his lips and looked at Hanufer. 'Would you like me to interview Galenos again, my lord? I could make him tell me about this case, or even make him show me where the patient lives.'

Hanufer thought for a moment, then slowly shook his head. 'No. It may or may not be important, but we must discover this subtly.' He looked at Cario and gave him an encouraging smile. 'You have done well, Cario. Another time, do you think that you can be subtle and perhaps follow the physician Galenos to find out where he visits?'

Cario grinned. 'I can be as subtle as a shadow, my lord.'

Hanufer suppressed a shudder.

Having sent Cario off to get some food for them, Hanufer listened to Sabu's modified account of his meeting with Keket at Lake Mareotis. The big sergeant omitted any mention of kissing.

'She did not know about the murders at the lighthouse, but from what she told me it was almost certainly Hatensor who had last visited Ahset. Keket had also slept with him when Ahset had not been available.'

'Why are you so sure it was he?'

'She said he was always nervous and twitchy. It was as if he expected trouble. He was irritable and pompous and always had to leave before the night was over, as he had work to do before dawn.'

'How did she react to his death?'

'She seemed sad, but not overly so. He was a customer, that was all. She did say that he was never violent, as some of the men are.' He shook his head. 'It is a terrible life that they have, my lord.'

Hanufer nodded. 'Indeed, and a dangerous one, too. But it is useful information, Sabu. I also had a most interesting and illuminating time. Queen Arsinoe clearly hates the Lady Artemisia, and she suspects that she poisoned Usermontu. The queen is convinced that Artemisia wanted to seduce the pharaoh and thought that Usermontu would get in her way. And we know that Ptolemy repudiated his first wife, Arsinoe the First and married Queen Arsinoe the Second. If it happened once, perhaps it can happen again.'

He told him about the conversation and of the forthcoming sacrifice of the baboon, dog, polecat and fish that was to take place.

Sabu listened, aghast. 'I can see why she would be worried, sir. And I can also see why even she cannot broach such a delicate subject with the pharaoh.'

'After I saw Patroclus and the queen, I paid a visit to *Archiphylakites* Heri-ib of the Nile police. I thought that I would find him at the navy headquarters in the Royal Harbour. He denied any deep knowledge about Artemisia or the scribe Hatensor. I already knew that Artemisia had been made a priestess of the Temple of Hecate that had been built by local businessmen in Canopus, but he professed ignorance of that.'

'It seems he was evasive, if you don't mind me saying, my lord.'

'That is what I thought, but I know that he is an efficient police overseer. I think that he is one who keeps his thoughts to himself and does not give much away. On the other hand, his deputy Muthis seems much more open. He had knowledge of the Temple of Hecate and told me that he himself had consulted Artemisia about bad dreams.'

'Does that tell us anything, my lord?'

'No, except that Muthis — who was in charge of the Nile police patrol that found Constable Sinue and the baboons washed down the river — was upset that the baboons had been shot with arrows. He is clearly an animal lover. Artemisia's explanation of his bad dreams about baboons was that he was being sent a message to protect the followers of

Thoth, since the baboon is one of the forms that Thoth adopts. As you know, Thoth is the god of writing, mathematics and therefore of scribes. Artemisia told him that he must protect scribes and the things they write.'

Sabu whistled. 'And then we have a scribe that is brutally murdered along with the lighthouse watchmen and two slaves.'

'That is so. Muthis said he was glad that he was not attached to protect Hatensor.' Hanufer pointed to the woven reed bag containing all the papyri and charts that Hatensor had been using. 'When I entered the office that Heri-ib and Muthis had been given — which was guarded by their own Nile police officers, I should add — they were studying maps of the city and charts of the harbours, the Island of Pharos and of the Canopus Canal leading to the Canopus River and Canopus itself. As I told you before, they have been consulting with Admiral Patroclus on several occasions, along with senior navy and military officers. Patroclus has brushed aside my questions each time about whether there are preparations being made for war. So, I asked Heri-ib directly why they were really here in Alexandria.'

'Will there be war, my lord?'

'Admiral Patroclus said that we always live on the edge of war footing, being surrounded by hostile countries. Yet he does not seem overly concerned. After all, Egypt is the mightiest country with the best navy and army. Heri-ib admitted to me that the real reason the Nile police are here is to investigate the smuggling of goods and commodities going in and out of Alexandria. But more importantly, if there are smuggling routes, there is just as likely to be a spy network.'

'That makes sense, my lord. Have they found anything?'

'They have identified smugglers of oil, spices and other minor things, using the Canopus Canal, but only insignificant criminals. So far, they have not detected any spies.'

Sabu nodded. 'He should perhaps also investigate the Lake Mareotis Harbour and the great reedbeds that line the shore to the south of the city. As Pylyp and Filemon told us, there are brigands and all sorts of nefarious activities that go on there.'

'I shall perhaps do that when next I see him,' Hanufer said.

'So, what are your plans, my lord?'

Hanufer tapped the woven reed bag full of Hatensor's papyri. 'We have some urgent things to investigate further. First, I need to make sense of these charts and papyri that we found. There seem to be a mixture of things he was studying. The philosopher Lycophron, who is versed in mathematics, does not think they are complete. I want to find out if he had other papyri elsewhere. High Priest Evenius did not know where Hatensor lived, or indeed if he had somewhere he could call home. If that is the case, I need to find out if he had places where he kept other papyri. One place that we need to look at is the other Temple of Harpokrates near the Necropolis, which is also where the Necropolis guards have to report.'

'I could send either Corporal Pylyp or Filemon to look there, my lord. They should be back soon. I ordered them to go to the barracks to drill the constables and make sure they are all absolutely clear on what they must do for the procession to keep the dignitaries safe. The palace guards will of course be there to protect Pharaoh Ptolemy and Queen Arsinoe.'

Hanufer thought for a moment. 'No, I think it would be better if you went, as you have a clearer idea of what to look for. A better use of their time would be for one to go to the Necropolis prison to check on the guard Kallisto and then go and see Sergeant Linus. We want to know if there have been any other sightings of ghosts.'

'I will give them your orders as soon as they come back, my lord.'

Hanufer nodded. 'That is good. Tell them to report back to me tomorrow.'

'And I shall see if I can find out anything more about Hatensor, my lord.'

The overseer sat back. 'The next important matter for me is to investigate Usermontu's death. Queen Arsinoe is convinced that he was poisoned. Indeed, I think she would dearly love to find out that he was poisoned.'

'But surely that is impossible to determine, my lord.'

Hanufer was stroking his rings. 'His assistant Hak-mau told me that his body is already being prepared for mummification in the House of Anubis. While we eat, I shall send Cario on another errand. Then I shall go to the Necropolis myself.'

CHAPTER 19

Later that afternoon, Hanufer entered the City of the Dead. The unmistakable smell of woodsmoke and burning flesh and the distant sound of wailing women wafted over from the Greek area of the Necropolis, evidence of a cremation taking place.

He made his way to the House of Anubis near the entrance to the Egyptian part of the City of the Dead. As he approached the embalming house, he became aware of a strange mix of pleasant and unpleasant aromas. This typically Egyptian scent felt more comfortable to him. Whereas the Greek cremation resulted in the reduction of the body to ashes and smoke, the smells of embalmment were all associated with the preservation of the physical and spirit body.

Hanufer waited by the great door. After a few minutes, he saw the familiar figure of Erasistratus the anatomist coming along the path. He was accompanied by a young slave boy bearing a heavy wooden chest.

'I received the message your *demosios* slave Cario delivered to me, Hanufer,' said Erasistratus. 'As you can see, I came at once. I have to admit that my interest was aroused by your strangely cryptic request to bring my instruments.'

He wrinkled his nose and laughed at the young slave, who was screwing up his eyes and pinching his nostrils. 'All right, young Nikos, you can stay out here until I come out.'

The boy looked relieved and laid the wooden chest by the door. With a bow, he took off down the path, out of reach of the odours.

Hanufer smiled and bowed. 'I thank you for coming. Djehuty, the father of the Men of Anubis, is expecting us,' he told Erasistratus. 'I wanted to be here before you entered because it is important that you understand that this is not only a house where embalming takes place, but it is also a temple where religious rituals are still being performed at the various stages of the process.'

Erasistratus tugged his black beard and nodded. 'Sergeant Sabu told me before when he visited my dissecting rooms that his father and his before him were embalmers and that generally it is a respected tradition passed from father to son. As he is the youngest of eight brothers, there were enough to carry on his family concern, which allowed him to become a Medjay police officer. I know it is serious work.'

Hanufer nodded. 'Exactly, so we must be respectful of the dead who are being prepared for the afterlife.'

'Lead me into your Egyptian world of the dead. I look forward to seeing if there are techniques that may be of use to me in preserving organs for my students. Although, Hanufer, you still have not told me why I am here with my *macairions* at hand.'

Hanufer put a finger to his lips. 'You will see soon.' He pushed open the huge door and they entered.

They found themselves in a dimly-lit corridor with a very high ceiling and were immediately confronted by the towering figure of a man with the head and neck of a black jackal, dressed in a white kilt and a leopard-skin robe. Beyond him at the end of the corridor was a huge statue of the god Anubis, carved from black obsidian.

Erasistratus uttered an exclamation of alarm and took a step backwards.

'Have no fear, Erasistratus,' said Hanufer. 'This is Djehuty, the father of the Men of Anubis.'

As Erasistratus's vision adjusted, he saw that the man was wearing a cartonnage head mask that was painted black and shaped like a jackal head. The mask covered his shoulders, and it became clear to Erasistratus that it exaggerated his height. Looking closer, he saw two holes in the jackal's neck and through them the eyes of Djehuty.

'Welcome, Hanufer, and the esteemed physician Erasistratus,' he said. He held up his hands, to show an odd-looking tool in each one. 'I have just performed the opening of the mouth ritual on the mummified corpse of the Lady Taweret, the widow of Kenamon, one of the captains of His Majesty's fleet.'

'It is so that in the afterlife she will be able to breathe again,' Hanufer explained to the anatomist.

Djehuty nodded. 'In the older days, this ritual would be done by a Sem priest as the body was laid in the tomb. Nowadays I, as the father of the Men of Anubis, perform this before the body is placed in the sarcophagus that will hold her *akh* for eternity.'

He turned and pointed into an open doorway, where two young men dressed only in white kilts and wooden sandals were lifting a mummified body from an upright position against a wall to place it in a brightly painted sarcophagus.

Djehuty held the tools in his hands up for Erasistratus to see. 'This is an *adze* and this other a *peseshkaf.*' He tapped them together, and instantly a boy appeared, took the tools from him and waited while he removed the Anubis mask and the leopard-skin robe.

'That is my youngest son. He and his ten brothers all assist me in our sacred duties. My two eldest are seeing to the Lady

Taweret's sarcophagus and making it ready for her family to collect and take to the tomb where her husband lies waiting for her.' Djehuty was a wiry-looking man of about fifty years. He was shaven-headed like his sons, and his arms and hands bore the healed scars of old burns. 'Come then, Hanufer told me that you would like to see the processes that we use in preparing the body for the next life.'

'That is excellent,' Erasistratus replied. 'My reason for examining bodies is to learn the purpose of all the organs within it. I am particularly interested in how you preserve the flesh, so I can see if there are methods that I can use in the dissecting room.'

Djehuty eyed him unsmilingly. 'We already know all the parts of the body and of the person, since we Egyptians have been preparing bodies for the afterlife since time began.'

Hanufer touched the physician's arm and gave him the subtlest shake of the head. Erasistratus took the hint and nodded to the embalmer.

'Please, show me.'

Djehuty led them along the corridor and pushed open a stout door. They entered a room where a preserved body was balanced on a table on two blocks of wood, one under the ankles and one under the neck. A man and a woman stood comforting each other as they watched two more of Djehuty's sons, who were winding thin strips of linen bandage round the body.

'We will not disturb them, for this is a solemn process. This man's family will oversee the placing of all of the protective amulets and talismans that will be wrapped on his body. They will help his spirit as he passes through many gates to the Hall of Truth.'

'Protect him from what?' Erasistratus asked.

'From the *Ammut*, the eater of hearts.'

'A goddess with the hindquarters of a hippopotamus, the forequarters of a lioness and the head of a crocodile,' Hanufer explained.

Erasistratus grimaced. 'A formidable deity to avoid.'

The embalmer gestured for them to follow him to another great room on the other side of the corridor, where two more of his sons were working over the naked body of a young man. One was pushing a hook up the left nostril to pull pulverised brain tissue from it, while the other was pulling intestines from a large incision in the abdomen.

None of Djehuty's sons talked. They just worked quietly and efficiently on the tasks allotted to them.

'We have no use for the head jelly, but the bowels we preserve. After my son has squeezed all the contents out, they will go into a bath of natron, which makes them shrivel and become like a softened animal skin. The same will be done with the liver and the tiny sac of green juice that lives beneath it, and also the stomach and the lungs. All of them will be treated in natron baths and left until they are ready.'

He drew attention to the four walls and the statues in the recesses in each of them. 'These are the four sons of Horus. Each one looks after a particular organ, and when they are prepared they will be put in the appropriate jar and sealed. Imsety, who has the body of a man, will look after the liver. The baboon-headed Hapy will protect the lungs. Jackal-headed Duamutef will watch the stomach, and Qebehsenuef, who bears a hawk head, will protect the bowels.'

'And each of them in turn is protected by one of our gods,' added Hanufer. 'Isis protects Imsety, Nephthys does Hapy, Neith does Duamutef and Serqet looks after Qebehsenuef.'

'And what of the heart?' the anatomist asked.

The slightest hint of a smile crossed Djehuty's lips. 'We call it the *ib*. It is where we hold our thoughts and feelings. It must stay inside the chest but usually, if the person's family can afford it, we treat it with oils and then wrap it separately before replacing it. And the body cavities are washed out first with palm wine and then packed with honey, fat and perfumed herbs, so that they maintain the body build they had in life. Those that can afford it have frankincense, myrrh and other rich perfumes packed inside them, too. Then we sew up the body.' He shrugged apologetically. 'But those who cannot afford such expense do not have the bowls removed. Instead, we pour juniper oil up the back passage. This will, over time, dissolve everything inside, and we drain it after a full passage of the moon.'

In the next large room he took them into, the smell of brine was so strong that Hanufer and Erasistratus had to wipe tears from their eyes. Here three of Djehuty's sons were each covering bodies with dry natron powder.

'Here the bodies are covered with natron to draw out all the water from them. This will last for thirty-five days, and the natron will be changed three times. The whole process of preparing the body lasts seventy days.'

Erasistratus gave a short laugh. 'Ah, yes, the mystical seventy number that you Egyptians are so fond of.'

Hanufer scowled at him and Djehuty stared at him in disbelief.

'After the evil Seth murdered and mutilated the body of his brother Osiris and scattered the parts about the world, it took the goddesses Isis and Neith seventy days to collect the parts and resurrect him,' Djehuty told him.

Hanufer again touched Erasistratus's arm, signalling for him to be sensitive to the Egyptian beliefs.

'And this is also why we venerate the rising of Sothis — which you Greeks call Sirius — every seventy days,' Djehuty went on. 'The Wepet Renpet Festival begins when the star rises in the morning sky and the Nile will start to rise again.'

'Forgive me, I mean no disrespect,' the anatomist said.

'Respect for the dead is important,' Djehuty replied taciturnly. 'All that we do here in the House of Anubis is done with deference, dignity and respect for the dead person so that they will be able to pass into the afterlife. Every single part of it is a sacred matter. But Overseer Hanufer explained the importance of the matter you are here for, and I have seen that all has been made ready for you.'

Without another word, he gestured for them to follow him to the end of the corridor and then down another to a room at the end. Pushing open the door, he led them in. Upon a table the naked body of a slightly portly man was being washed by another of Djehuty's sons. The nose had been packed, and the large stitched incision on the left side of the abdomen was obvious.

At their entry Djehuty's son quickly finished, bowed to his father and stood waiting.

'We will leave you now,' Djehuty said. 'Neither I nor any of my sons will witness the desecration you intend and for which we have broken the forty days of drying the body in natron.'

Once they had gone, Hanufer pointed to the naked, partly dried-up body. 'So here, Erasistratus, is the reason I asked you to be present. This is the body of *Architekton* Usermontu, the chief builder of Alexandria.'

He quickly explained that the death of Usermontu had been sudden and that it was suspected that he had been poisoned.

Erasistratus gave a snort of derisive laughter. 'I think you have too much faith in what I can tell you, Hanufer of

Crocodilopolis. What do you expect me to do, go searching in jars to examine his stomach or his bowels? I don't know how you would tell if a man was poisoned, especially not when he has been eviscerated and dried out like a fig.'

'I am not interested in his stomach,' Hanufer replied. 'I want you to examine his neck.'

Erasistratus smiled. 'Hence you wanted me to bring my instruments. Very well, if you will turn the good Usermontu over, I will get my *macairions* and fine dissecting tongs and we shall begin.'

Hanufer watched as the anatomist went about his work.

'It is like working with leather. There is no give in the muscles and tissues at all,' Erasistratus said as he inveigled his fingers into the hole he had made in the back of the corpse's neck.

After a few moments, he nodded. 'You obviously suspected this for some reason, Hanufer. And you were right. This man died from a broken neck.'

'Can you write a report with —'

'With drawings, like the others? Yes, I will do that as soon as I return to the hospital. Herophilus will also be most intrigued about all of this.'

'But do not mention it to anyone else, Erasistratus. That is vitally important.'

'I will be as silent as a mummy, Hanufer. You would have to get old Djehuty to use that *adze* and his *peseshkaf*, or whatever he called it, to open my mouth.'

The group of four met after dark in the usual place. They drank wine on the terrace under the moon. From the other side of the harbour, the lighthouse beams shone over the city.

'Are the men under control?' asked the first.

'Don't worry, they are under my command,' replied the second.

'The injured one wasn't.'

'He's been taken care of.'

'Permanently?'

'No! We look after brothers.'

'Can you trust the one you brought in?' asked the third.

'We will for as long as we need. Then I'll see.'

The first swirled his wine, watching the reflection of the moon in his goblet. He looked at the fourth. 'You said that interfering dog was sniffing too close. I think it's time we took care of him.'

'The usual way will be risky.'

'A subtler way, then?'

'That's just what I was thinking. Now is the right time.'

Once more, all four laughed.

CHAPTER 20

Nefrit did not come to Hanufer's villa that night. He was bitterly disappointed, as he had wanted to ask her so many things.

Did she really think that he was under the Lady Artemisia's spell? What did she think about the way Queen Arsinoe had looked at the new High Priestess of Hecate when she had entered the throne room? And when he told her, what would she make of the news that a baboon was to be sacrificed along with the fish, polecat and dog?

But more importantly, he wondered if she thought there could be any serious connection between Hatensor's murder and his observations of the sky. Could disposing of the scribe possibly prevent Sothis from rising? Or rather, could his killer believe that to be the case?

Before he retired to bed, he drank a cup of wine and made his small offerings to Tutu and Bes. When darkness came, he slept fitfully and had dreams of monsters chasing him from the shadows.

Hanufer awoke in a cold sweat while it was still dark and made his way up to the flat roof of his villa. Sitting on a stool, he looked up at the sky, focusing on the stars he recognised and then on the myriads that he did not. He looked towards the Pharos lighthouse, imagining himself in the room where Hatensor made his observations beneath the great fire and the bronze mirrors that sent out great beams of light. He felt sympathy for the slaves who were tending the fires and undoubtedly thinking of their fellow slaves who had been so brutally murdered.

He looked towards the west and the City of the Dead and wondered whether any ghosts would be visible this night. And then he settled down and looked towards the east, where he knew that Sothis should appear, hoping that he might catch a glimpse of the star as it rose.

But he fell asleep and did not wake until the great disc of Ra had risen. Even if Sothis had flown above the horizon, it could not be seen now.

He wondered if others had been watching — both living and dead. Immediately he thought of those who had so recently suffered violent deaths.

An image of Ammut, the eater of hearts, suddenly entered his mind: the goddess with the hindquarters of a hippopotamus, the forequarters of a lioness and the head of a crocodile.

Are you the monster of the shadows that plagues my dreams? he mused as his thumbs stroked his two rings with their images of Maat and Sobek. He closed his eyes.

I pray to you both to help me find the truth of these deaths and bring the killer to justice. It would be justice if Ammut devoured his heart — whoever he is.

When Hanufer arrived at police headquarters, Sabu and the two corporals were waiting for him. As usual, Cario had been up since dawn and had arranged both Hanufer and Sabu's desks.

Hanufer took his seat and gestured for Sabu to take his while the two corporals stood to attention, ready to give their reports.

'I think you will be interested to hear news of our investigations, my lord,' said Sabu.

'You may sit on the stools, Pylyp and Filemon,' Hanufer instructed. 'Let me hear your news first, Sabu.'

'As you know, sir, yesterday afternoon I went to the Temple of Harpokrates in Rhakotis. It is not far from the Necropolis, but is on this side of the canal that runs from the Eunostos Harbour to Lake Mareotis. It is a much smaller temple than the one on the Island of Pharos, but it is only dedicated to Harpokrates, not to Proteus, who is only worshipped on the island. Leonidas was the young priest whose turn it was to stay there for the next five days. He showed me around.

'Like the Pharos temple, it has a *pronaos*, which is a porch at the front. Then there is the *naos*, where the statue of Harpokrates stands and they do their priestly worshipping, then an *adyton*, which the priests use to prepare offerings. At the back, there is a room for the priest to sleep overnight, and behind that an office. That is where the records are all kept. There are racks of scrolls on three walls, all neatly arranged and labelled.'

'And was there anything that we would find useful among all those racks?'

'Nothing there, my lord. I went through everything, but I did not find anything that resembled any of those papyri that we found with his things in the lighthouse.'

'Did Leonidas know Hatensor well?'

'Fairly well, my lord. He was reticent when I asked what he was like, because he obviously did not wish to speak ill of the dead. When I told him the importance of knowing all about him, he was more cooperative.'

'So did he think that Hatensor was a likeable man?'

'Not exactly, because he could be irritable when he was disturbed. He would go there at noon every other day to write up whatever the priests told him to do. Also, the Necropolis guards would report to the priest on those days and he would document everything they told him.'

'Was Leonidas surprised about the murders?'

'He could not believe that Hatensor would do such a thing. He thought him tetchy at times, but he mainly thought that he was an anxious man. He said he bragged a lot, often about women he had slept with. Leonidas and his fellow priests all thought he exaggerated his tales about his amorous conquests.'

'Did he know that he visited brothels?'

'No, he said that Hatensor implied that he was a great lover and that women fell for his intellect and his charms.'

'Was he ever seen to be violent?'

'I asked him that, and he said he had never witnessed anything to suggest it was in his nature. He did say that he drank a lot and often had a skin of wine or a jug of beer with him when he was working. His drinking had increased a lot over these last few weeks. He thought that as his drinking increased, he had become more nervous and he seemed to work harder and harder. He knew that he had many appointments elsewhere and somehow managed to keep up with them all.'

'Did Leonidas know where he lived?'

Sabu grinned. 'He said that Hatensor was always cagey about that, my lord. Leonidas and some of the other priests had asked him that before, because all of them also knew him from his regular visits to the other temple on the Island of Pharos and his nightly vigils in the lighthouse. He told all of them that he kept his home a secret in case the husband or brother of any of his lovers tried to find him. When Leonidas probed him about his nightly visits to the lighthouse, he just laughed and said he felt safe there, because the watchmen looked after him. Again, that is why he felt so surprised about the murders.'

'Perhaps it was a husband or a relative of a lover that did it, my lord,' Pylyp suggested.

'Indeed, it is a possibility,' Hanufer agreed. He signalled for Sabu to continue.

'Leonidas said he thought Hatensor inadvertently gave him a clue one day when he'd drunk too much. He'd made a joke about being unsteady on his feet when he got up to relieve himself, and he said that it was a good thing he was used to his boat wobbling in the night when he stood and passed water over the side into the reeds.'

'A houseboat?'

'Yes, my lord. I told you that bandits, smugglers and folk who want to lead a discreet life frequent the reedbeds on the shores of Lake Mareotis, where they have cut all sorts of channels so that they can disappear. So, I went there and found some fishermen who recognised my description of Hatensor. They took me to his boat.'

With a triumphant smile, Sabu stood up and retrieved a large basket from under his desk. Taking off the lid, he lifted out a pile of papyrus scrolls and laid them on Hanufer's desk.

'He did not have many possessions on the houseboat. Mainly clothes, rope-stretching equipment, some dried food and a lot of empty wineskins. But then I found this cache under a little table with writing sets, reeds and ink blocks. He had several oil lamps, and it looked as if he did much work there.' Then, as an afterthought, Sabu added, 'Ah yes, and he had two small figurines of bearded gods.'

Hanufer gave a rueful smile. 'Those would be Sia and Hu, two of the gods who protect scribes. They ride in the celestial boat that carries Ra as he sails through the underworld each night. Part of their duty was to prevent Ra from falling into the underworld sea and disappearing forever.' Hanufer carefully unrolled one scroll after the other until the surface of his desk was covered. Like the other papyri they had found, there were several with demotic and Greek writing and numerous drawings of triangles and pyramids. 'Let us hope that with a little study, we can see if the missing parts of this great puzzle are here.'

Sabu turned back to the basket and drew out yet more scrolls. He handed these to his superior. 'I thought these ones were particularly interesting. They are not in the same hand, that much I can tell.'

Hanufer let out an exclamation of surprise. 'These are documents bearing the seals of the Ministry of Buildings and Monuments, while these have been taken from the Library. Look, there is Callimachus's seal.' Placing them in a neat pile, he nodded approvingly. 'That is excellent work, Sabu. I will study these later. So now, Corporals, let me have your report.'

'Very good, my lord,' said Pylyp, straightening himself on the stool. 'Following Sergeant Sabu's orders, we went first of all to the Necropolis guardhouse. Sergeant Linus was there, taking the reports from the guards under his command. The first thing he told us was that he was worried for his friend Kallisto, as he was refusing food and water.'

'He said it wasn't just that he is feeling guilt,' said Filemon. 'He said he's stricken with grief for having sent his comrade to the next world.'

Pylyp nodded. 'All the other guards were quick to agree with him and told us in no uncertain terms that he's innocent. They think it could only have been an accident.'

'Then Sergeant Linus informed us that they all told him they have had a bad feeling about the site of Dion's death for some time.'

Hanufer sat forward. 'Bad in what way?'

'Some of the men are sure that that part of the Necropolis has been haunted for a while,' said Pylyp. 'They say there are few birds around there, despite the bushes being full of berries.'

'And others said they have heard ghost noises at night,' Filemon added. 'But what can you expect, when there are dead bodies buried all about? And they said it's not just there, but at three or four other places around the Necropolis.'

'And they kept coming back to their comrade Kallisto's claim that his spear passed straight through the ghost before it struck his fellow.'

'Had any of them seen a ghost?'

Both corporals shook their heads.

'They only heard noises,' Filemon said.

Pylyp pursed his lips. 'A couple of them did say they had noticed strange smells.'

'What kind of smells?' Sabu asked. 'There will always be smells in the Necropolis. Burning flesh lingers for hours after a cremation. So, there would be that, woodsmoke, the smell of ashes and the odours of mummification from the House of Anubis.'

'They just said it was strange, but couldn't be more specific,' replied Pylyp. 'They were all angry that we have not been back to investigate or to bring Kallisto to trial. All of them, Sergeant Linus included, want to speak up for Kallisto.'

'We, of course, emphasised that the other sudden deaths have had to take priority,' said Filemon. 'They weren't happy, my lord, but Sergeant Linus silenced their grumbling and we left.'

'You said the right things,' Sabu said approvingly.

'Then we went to the Necropolis prison and saw Kallisto,' Pylyp continued. 'I must say that I don't like that turnkey,

Nikias. He curses the prisoner whenever he passes his cell, and I'm not surprised Kallisto doesn't eat or drink. I wouldn't put it past Nikias to spit or —'

'Understood,' Hanufer said quickly. 'We will reprimand him when Kallisto is brought to trial. Did you learn anything further when you spoke to him?'

'We questioned him about the ghost, my lord,' Filemon replied. 'He said it was not so clear in his memory, despite the fact that he has thought of little else. He wept as he talked about hitting his comrade with a spear and trying to remove it from his head. I asked if he could absolutely remember seeing the spear pass through the ghost.'

'And did he?' Hanufer asked.

'Again, he seemed uncertain. He said it shimmered in the moonlight and in the half-light from the lighthouse. He said it was making noises, snorting noises like a beast, and it seemed to be coming for him.'

'Did it actually see him?' Hanufer queried.

'That's what he said,' Filemon continued. 'I asked him to show me. Well, my lord, there is not a lot of room in that cell, so we got Nikias to let him out into the corridor. He did his best to show us. If you will allow me, my lord, I could show you if we go into the corridor here.'

They all filed out. While Pylyp took up a position like the guard Kallisto, Filemon went to the other end, dropped into a hunched position and came forward, swinging his arms and moving in a zigzag down the corridor.

'It was making these snorting noises like a beast, my lord,' sad Filemon.

'Was that the pace it moved?' Hanufer asked.

'That's exactly how he described it, my lord,' Filemon returned.

'Not exactly coming at him,' Sabu remarked.

'He said it momentarily turned one way and then the other, its arms still swinging. Fearing for his life, he threw his spear.'

'And he thinks it went through it?' said Hanufer.

'He was absolutely sure when we first talked to him after it happened, my lord,' put in Pylyp.

'As he was when I interrogated him myself,' said Hanufer.

'Yet he seemed less certain this time,' said Filemon. 'It was as if, thinking of nothing else, he has a clearer picture in his mind. He thinks he struck it and it made another noise. He said it was shimmering and yet made of smoke. Then the spear went through, and all he could see then was his comrade, mortally wounded.'

'Then it just disappeared,' said Pylyp.

'Or he stopped looking and turned his attention to his fallen friend,' Hanufer said. 'Did he actually see it vanish?'

'We don't know, my lord,' said Filemon. 'That's where he can't be any more specific.'

Hanufer nodded and led the way back into the office. He gestured for them all to sit down again.

'After that, we thought we ought to revisit the place in the Necropolis, my lord,' said Pylyp. 'Sergeant Linus assured us that no one has actually been to the area. But when we got there and looked around the exact spot where we found the blood and the footprints, it had all been brushed.'

'Was there a stone there?' Sabu asked. 'I left it there and made a mark on a small rock to mark it.'

'We found the rock, sir,' Filemon said. 'It had been tossed into the bushes. But the ground had definitely been brushed with the branch of a shrub. We found that thrown away. There was no trace of blood-soaked dirt.'

'So, a ghost that bleeds, leaves footprints and then comes back to brush the whole area as if making sure it covered its tracks. It becomes more mysterious. And how you described this ghost is even more puzzling than it seemed at first.'

'Puzzling in what way, my lord?' Sabu asked.

'It sounds like a very strange ghost that moves like a crouching man!'

From the far end of the outer corridor, there came the sound of a raised female voice. They heard Cario trying to calm her, then the sound of hurried footsteps.

A moment later, Iput, one of the Temple of Isis handmaids, turned into the doorway and ran straight to Hanufer's desk.

'I'm sorry, my lord,' Cario blurted out. 'I tried to stop —'

But the young woman ignored him and stared beseechingly at Hanufer. Her eyes were red from crying.

'What is it, Iput?' asked Hanufer.

'It's my Lady Nefrit, sir. She … she has gone!'

CHAPTER 21

Hanufer was horrified to hear that his beloved Nefrit had not returned the day before and had not been seen by any of the temple handmaids since she had gone to the palace.

Iput was clearly distraught. 'When she did not come to the palace to supervise the dressing of divine Isis this morning, we were worried that she might be ill,' she said. 'But her bed had not been slept in. So, I … I went to see if she had stayed —' She hesitated, casting quick glances at the others in the office. 'I went to the villa, but was told by a servant that, that —'

Hanufer understood that she had gone to his home and had talked to his ever-discreet Timon. 'So, you were told to come here to see me. Did you go anywhere else?'

'To the palace, but the guards would not tell me anything and they sent me away.'

'They would do, of course,' Hanufer said. He turned to Sabu. 'I will go with Iput. The Lady Nefrit may have been taken ill at some friend's home, so I will go and see. Meanwhile, I'd like you to compare the papyri that are definitely Hatensor's with the ones we previously found.'

'Shall we get some of the constables to help you, my lord?' Filemon asked.

Hanufer shook his head. 'I will deal with this myself. I'd like you two to visit the senior scribe to the chief judge of the *Dikasterion* and give him the message I shall write in a moment. The Necropolis guards are right; it is time that we brought Kallisto to the court for a hearing. Then go to the Necropolis prison again, and on your way fetch a physician to see the prisoner. Get him to give a medicine to Kallisto to make him eat and drink. He may seem less confused then.'

'Remember what I said about Nikias the warder, my lord,' Pylyp reminded him. 'We thought he may have been tampering with his food and drink.'

'Then I also want you to make Nikias understand that Kallisto is a prisoner and is to be dealt with in a civilised manner. If I hear otherwise, tell him he will feel my wrath.'

'Which physician should we bring, my lord?' Filemon asked.

'Perhaps Galenos, my lord?' Sabu suggested. 'It might give us an idea of how good a physician he is.'

'No, get Hessi, the Egyptian physician who practices in Rhakotis. He is nearer, and I trust his practice. Besides, I have other thoughts about Galenos.' Hanufer took a fresh piece of papyrus and began to write a message to the chief judge's scribe. 'Cario, arrange the police chariot for me and then come back here. I have an important task for you.'

With Iput standing behind him, clutching onto the rail of the chariot, Hanufer drove quickly along the busy Canopic Way. He then turned left onto the Street of the Soma and on towards the Brucheum and the Temple of Isis.

Together they mounted the steps that led up to the white marble building with its vaulted roof. Twin statues of Isis stood on either side of the great door that opened into the *purgatorium*, the colonnaded court with the small stream that ran through it. This was a place that Nefrit loved, for it was actually water from the River Nile that was used in sacred ceremonies in temples throughout Egypt. This purifying water was diverted from the Canopic Canal that ran from the town of Canopus on the west of the Delta, some five leagues from Alexandria.

Then they entered the garden where he and Nefrit had first kissed, and then went into her private quarters. But there was no sign of her having been there recently, not even a whiff of her perfume.

'Do not worry, Iput,' Hanufer said as the young woman began to weep again. 'I will try the homes of some of her friends and will find her.'

As he left the temple and returned to the chariot, he yet again had the unsettling feeling that he was being watched. But though he saw many people going about their business, none seemed to be paying any attention to him.

After calling at the villas of several of their mutual friends in the Brucheum, Hanufer found himself driving the chariot towards the palatial villa of the Lady Artemisia. The large gates stood open, so he passed between the two large red granite columns topped by their black basalt statues of Hecate.

As before, two guards armed with spears stood to attention by the door of the villa.

They watched Hanufer dismount from the chariot and hand the reins to a servant who had suddenly appeared from the shadows at the side of the villa.

One of the guards struck the gong inside the vestibule, and moments later the bodyguard that had greeted him on his previous visit met him with a bow.

'Welcome again, *Archiphylakites* Hanufer,' he said with the hint of a smile. 'The Lady Artemisia said to expect you.'

What does that mean? Hanufer wondered. *Does she know something of Nefrit's disappearance?*

Acknowledging the man with a curt nod, he followed him through the same room where he had met the Lady Artemisia the last time, and then out through a large door into a garden heavy with the scent of lotuses that covered an ornamental pond. On the other side of it under a palm tree he saw her. She was sitting on an ornate wicker chair with a table in front of her, staring intently at a crystal which dangled from a chain held between her finger and thumb. The crystal was oscillating over a glass dish full of water.

The bodyguard coughed softly to attract her attention, but was silenced when she raised a hand. She continued to watch the crystal moving round and round. Hanufer took the opportunity to observe her keenly, for it seemed as if she was in a trance. Dressed in a pale blue peplos pinned at the shoulders and a belt of silver, she looked even more stunning than before.

After a few moments, she gave a little laugh and then slipped the chain over her head. Then she stood and turned with a smile. '*Archiphylakites* Hanufer, welcome again. Will you join me in drinking a little honeyed wine? Or perhaps some goat's milk?'

'Thank you, but I have recently quenched my thirst, my lady.'

She nodded to the bodyguard, who departed after bowing to her. 'Then sit with me under my favourite tree. I have been looking at the signs.' She touched the chain about her neck, drawing Hanufer's attention to the brilliant green crystal that now nestled in her cleavage. He looked up swiftly and saw how well it matched her beautiful green eyes.

'Beautiful, don't you think?' she said with a smile. 'My jewel, I mean. It was a gift from Ptoly.' Her smile was more conspiratorial this time. 'I mean, from His Majesty.'

Hanufer was in no doubt that her use of what was clearly a pet name for her lover, the pharaoh, was another subtle warning to him. He smiled and lowered himself onto the wicker chair opposite her. 'My reason for visiting you today is official, my lady.'

'Oh, how tedious. I thought you had come to see me as a friend.'

He ignored the seductive smile. 'You will doubtless have heard about the deaths at the Pharos lighthouse.'

'Ah, yes, a scribe killed two or three people and jumped to his death.'

'The scribe's name was Hatensor. He was the man that your bodyguards ejected from the Temple of Demeter when you were initiated as the High Priestess of Hecate here in Alexandria. If I recall correctly, you referred to him as a nuisance of a man and said that you thought he was of no consequence.'

'It sounds as if Alexandria is better off without him now,' she replied.

'There were four deaths, actually: two watchmen and two public slaves who tended the fires. At your initiation feast, he seemed to know you. I was there and saw him try to talk to you. Are you sure you don't know more about him?'

She sighed. 'Very well, I did know him when I was a *hetaera* back in Canopus. That was before I became a Priestess of Hecate. He was a client of mine when he visited the city. As you know, I have skills as a soothsayer, and he had many worries that he wanted me to ask the goddess Hecate about.' She shrugged. 'I may have slept with him once or twice.'

'Only once or twice?'

'Yes, it was not long after I came to Canopus from Caria. When you begin a business, you take all the clients that are willing to pay for your talents. As I became better known and the richest of my clients built a temple to Hecate, I only allowed those I really liked to share my bed.'

'Do you know why he came to Canopus?'

She shook her head. 'I have told you all I know. He was a scribe, he had money but he became a nuisance. When Queen Arsinoe brought me to Alexandria and Ptoly became my lover, I had no need of him or any others — unless I really like them.'

Her lips quivered into the most seductive of pouts, and Hanufer felt his cheeks burn.

Artemisia laughed. 'I make you uncomfortable, do I not, Hanufer?' she asked. 'Well, have no fear. I can tell that you are besotted with another, just as she is with you. Although she is not enamoured of me.'

'How do you know this, Artemisia?' Hanufer asked, following her lead and using her name.

'I was a *hetaera*, which means that I can read the feelings of others as surely as I can read the signs.' She raised her crystal and kissed it. 'She loves you, and she thinks that you are attracted to me. I have Ptoly, and though I find you attractive, to have another lover would be very risky.'

Hanufer was taken aback by how forthright she was. He cleared his throat to bring his mind back to his purpose. 'But you did have another lover, didn't you? The architect Usermontu.'

'I did, but he died. So now there is nothing to be concerned about.' She looked at him with narrowed eyes. 'But I see that you still have concerns, Hanufer. About your Lady Nefrit, I think.'

'What makes you think that, Artemisia?'

'I told you, as a *hetaera* I can sense feelings.' She raised her crystal. 'Would you like me to ask Hecate anything for you? Perhaps she could put your mind at rest.'

'Thank you, but I venerate my own gods, Sobek and Maat,' Hanufer said, raising his hands and showing her his rings. 'I shall seek their guidance if I need to.' He stood and bowed. 'I thank you, Artemisia. You have told me what I needed to know about Hatensor.'

She smiled at him. 'Remember, Hanufer: if you change your mind, I have the ear of Hecate.'

As instructed by Hanufer, Cario had gone to the physician Galenos's house. Going down an alley off the fashionable boulevard of sycamore trees, he entered the garden to the rear and waited until he saw his friend Paiania emerge.

'My master Galenos has had me grating *silphium* roots while he sees patients,' Paiania said, holding his hands up to show how stained they were.

'It must be a wonderful medicine.'

'It is. He uses all parts of that plant. From the hollow stems he can make a medicine that cures all coughs; from the leaves he makes remedies for the stomach and bowel. The perfumed flowers make people want to tumble in bed.' He grinned and made a lewd movement with his pelvis. 'And from the sap he makes a medicine that makes men hard, and yet can make women soft and yielding. Still more wondrous, the grated black root can stop a woman having babies. Galenos uses this a lot and sells his remedies to half the brothels in Alexandria.'

'Where does this wondrous herb come from, Paiania?'

'From Cyrene. He has a personal supplier who obtains it for him. He may not be a physician in the hospital, but he is one of the most sought-after physicians in Alexandria.'

'Are the medicines he makes from it expensive?'

'Assuredly. My master showed me a tetradrachm silver piece from Cyrene. It has a picture of a silphium plant on one side because it grows more there than anywhere else in the world. He said that the god Apollo has a fountain, and it falls as rain through a hole in the sky in that small place.'

'A tetradrachm would pay a skilled craftsman for more than a week,' said Cario with a whistle.

'Yes, a free craftsman,' returned Paiania bitterly. 'And a tetradrachm is nothing to Galenos. His purse clinks at the end of every day when he goes out visiting. He empties it every night and keeps his money locked away somewhere in his *iatreion*. I don't know where, and it would be more than my hide is worth to spy on him.'

Cario put a sympathetic hand on his friend's shoulder. 'No, you must do your work and do his bidding, my friend. That is what we *demosioi* must do. I only wish your master was as kind as mine.'

Paiania clicked his tongue. 'Perhaps he will be more relaxed soon. When he has difficult cases to deal with, his temper is hot, but when they get better he becomes mellower.'

'And will he be visiting today?'

'He will. After he has seen his patients in the *iatreion*, he said he is going out to see another, but again without me to carry his chest. It is the same one I told you about, for he ordered me to pack fresh dressings and also put in a jar of honey and some of his special willow concoction.'

'What is that for?'

'His patient must be making much pus and be in great pain.'

'Can I help you with this silphium or with any other tasks? I have some time before my master expects me back.'

'No, you had best go. If he comes out and finds me talking with you, I could expect to feel his rod.'

Cario left his friend and let himself out of the garden. He went back up the alley to the front of the house and hid in the shadows of some acacia trees, waiting for Galenos to come out.

Hanufer drove the chariot to several more of Nefrit's friends' houses, but without luck. No one had seen her in the last day. Having run out of ideas, he made his way to the little public square with the column of Sobek, where he felt the god's presence. There was rarely anyone there, and as it was surrounded by palm trees, it was a calming place for him to go and silently worship.

Oh, Nefrit, where are you? he thought as he approached the column. *Have you had an accident? After this, I shall visit the hospital to make sure you have not gone there.*

From his chiton he took out his little bag of figs and grains, as he had done some days before to make an offering to Sobek and his wife, the goddess Renenutet. He was about to place some figs on the pedestal between the feet of the statue when he saw a shiny white object.

Picking it up, he recognised it instantly. It was the broken end of an ivory cow horn. He was certain that it was part of Nefrit's headdress.

His heart thudded and he quickly looked around. He felt sure that someone was watching him. And whoever it was had his beloved Nefrit.

CHAPTER 22

After delivering Hanufer's message to the senior scribe to the chief judge of the *Dikasterion*, Pylyp and Filemon returned to Rhakotis and found Hessi, the old Egyptian physician. Their boss had told them that he was a pious man and had a reputation for being a caring doctor, provided the patient scrupulously followed his advice and treatment. If they did not, then he would castigate them with the imprecation that they should pray to their own feet, for they clearly thought themselves a better physician than he. He would then leave them to cure their own illness or die.

Hessi lived with his wife in some comfort in a typically Egyptian villa surrounded by sycamore trees in the most exclusive part of Rhakotis. His wife was a pretty woman who looked to be a third of his age. She greeted Pylyp and Filemon and introduced herself as Hemetre, before offering them beer while they waited for her husband to finish treating a patient. They accepted gratefully.

'Has your husband worked here for long?' Filemon asked.

'We heard that he is much in demand by Egyptians,' Pylyp added.

Hemetre smiled at them as she poured beer from a jug. 'Hessi is the oldest physician in Alexandria and has practised here in Rhakotis since the days of the first Pharaoh Ptolemy. He actually brought me into the world and treated all of my family. I am his third wife, and he has given me two sons already.'

It was not long before the elderly physician came out with his patient, a very grateful-looking young woman who was clutching an infant to her chest. Once she had gone, Hemetre informed her husband that the two corporals were waiting to see him on important business. Smiling at her and patting both her shoulders, he ushered them into his consulting room.

They found themselves in a large, square room with an open window that let in a welcome breeze. A large statue of a man with the head of a scarab beetle dominated one wall. In front of it was a table crammed with pots and jars, pestles and mortars, and yet more figurines of other animal-headed gods and goddesses.

Hessi sat behind his desk and gestured for them to sit.

As Hanufer had told them, he was an elderly physician of over eighty summers. His hair had long since left him, but he declined to cover his head with a wig. Instead, he wore a silver headband, on the front of which was a brightly coloured scarab beetle. Other than this, he wore a kilt and a loose bag tunic with a large apron pocket.

He scowled in response to their request that he come with them to treat a patient. 'I am a man of mature years, and my patients come to me,' he replied tartly. 'If they are so ill that they or their family think that they are at the great door of death, then they must be brought here on a stretcher.' He smiled sarcastically. 'Or they can always see a Greek doctor.'

'I am afraid it will not be possible to bring this patient,' said Pylyp, ignoring the old physician's jibe. 'He is a prisoner in the Necropolis prison. Our boss *Archiphylakites* Hanufer instructed us to get you to treat him.'

The old physician scowled again.

'He said he trusts your opinion, sir,' Filemon added quickly.

Hessi nodded at the compliment. 'Overseer Hanufer is a wise man, and I respect him, too. But as I said, I am a man of mature years, and I do not waste my time and my breath unnecessarily. What is the matter with this prisoner?'

'He will not eat or drink,' Pylyp returned.

'And why is he a prisoner?'

'He is accused of having killed someone. A fellow guard.'

'Were they enemies?'

'No, they were comrades,' Pylyp replied. 'It is thought to have been an accident.'

'How did the guard die?'

'Unpleasantly,' said Filemon. 'A spear through his head. Straight through his eye and into his brain.'

'That does not sound like an accident.'

'That is as much as we can tell you, sir,' Pylyp put in. 'The prisoner will have to be tried in the court as the law demands.'

Hessi shook his head. 'So many violent deaths lately. The whole city knows of the murders in the Pharos lighthouse and of my friend, poor Hatensor's end.'

Sitting at Hanufer's desk, because it was larger and had more room, Sabu went through all of the papyri that they had accumulated in connection with the case of Hatensor. He placed all of the ones that had been found in the Pharos lighthouse in one pile. Next to them, he placed the ones that Hanufer had brought back from the Library, and beside that the cache of papyri he had taken from the scribe's houseboat.

Then he went through the first pile, looking at each piece of papyrus. Although he could not read as well as Hanufer, he was adept enough in Egyptian demotic and had picked up enough Greek to be able to differentiate those documents that related to the skies from those ones that seemed to do with his rope-stretching work.

Reaching no firm conclusions, Sabu turned to the second pile from the Library. He separated the papyri that consisted mainly of numbers and dates from ones that related to the names of gods, especially Proteus and Harpokrates.

He noted that Hatensor had seemed interested in the deaths of pharaohs and the places in the sky where they now lived. The scribe had also written many notes about the disposal of the dead in the Necropolis.

Sabu smoothed down a piece of papyrus with a sketch of the Necropolis on it. Turning it over, he found more sketch maps of its different areas — possibly part of the work Hatensor had done as a scribe to the Temple of Harpokrates.

Turning to the cache of papyri from the houseboat, he put the documents written in Hatensor's hand in one pile and made a separate pile of the papyri that bore the seals of the Ministry of Buildings and Monuments and of the Library of Alexandria.

Unrolling them, he saw that they were all annotated maps of Alexandria. One of them showed the Island of Pharos with the lighthouse and the Temple of Proteus and Harpokrates, the two harbours separated by the *Heptastadion*. Another showed the positions of all the great cisterns, canals and underground channels that supplied the city with water. Some of the sketch maps Sabu had seen in the pile from the houseboat were rough copies of these, but on them the scribe had again been drawing pyramids and triangles, as well as lists of numbers and calculations.

Leafing through the piles, he found the sketch maps and then laid them on his own desk, for there was no room left on Hanufer's. Alongside them he placed the actual maps and plans from the Ministry and the Library.

Sabu wasn't sure what to make of it all, but he thought that Hanufer would be able to discern something.

The two corporals stared at Hessi.

'Hatensor the scribe was your friend?' Pylyp repeated.

'Certainly. I brought him into the world, and I treated him whenever he was ill. All of my patients are my friends.'

'Was he ill, Doctor? Did he ever show signs of madness?'

Hessi guffawed. 'You mean, was there anything to suggest that he would kill anyone? Not at all. As a child he was mischievous, but when he was at scribe school, that was more or less beaten out of him. Yet he liked women, work and wine, though in which order I cannot say. I have heard the stories that he went mad and killed the guards and the young slaves who kept the fires going, but I do not believe it.'

'Why not, Doctor?' Pylyp asked.

'Because he was a squeamish child who grew into the most squeamish man I ever knew. He fainted at the sight of blood.'

'When did you last treat him for anything?' Filemon asked.

'About a week ago. He wanted me to make up his usual supply of silphium sap. I make pills of it.'

'For what condition?'

Hessi cackled and pointed at Pylyp's groin. 'To make him as potent as the Serapis bull itself.'

The corporals exchanged a knowing look, each thinking the same thing: the aged physician clearly took his own medicine.

'But you didn't come to ask about poor Hatensor,' said Hessi. 'You told me that a prisoner will not eat or drink.'

'It seems he is grief-stricken because it was his friend that he killed. Can you help him?' Pylyp asked.

'I do not visit patients, but I see that this is an unusual situation. I will make up some pills and you can take them to him. If he takes them, then they may help him. If he doesn't take them, then they won't. It is as simple as that.'

They watched as he crossed to his table and started to place ingredients from various jars in a mortar. There were insects, seeds and worms. Filemon winced at the sight.

'A person is like the Nile,' Hessi explained as he began to pound them with a pestle. 'The body is full of channels that carry the life blood. If there is evil in the *ib* — which you Greeks call the heart — then channels get silted up. If there is great sorrow, the stomach shrivels, and if there is guilt, the liver swells and produces bile that makes one too sick to eat or drink.'

He added some oils and ground the mixture until it became a thick paste.

'I am making a medicine that will help his sorrow, if he is genuinely full of remorse. If his guilt is because his friend is dead, then it will help his liver. But if he has guilt because he meant to kill the victim, then it will not work. It will do nothing and he will die, as he would deserve to.'

The corporals were taken aback and Filemon was about to say something when Hessi abruptly raised his hand for silence.

'There must be quiet now, for I must ask the god Khepri to help.' He pointed to the statue. 'Each day, Khepri rolls the great disc of Ra across the sky, and each night he rolls it into the underworld, so that it will rise anew each day. To do this, Khepri takes the form of the scarab, the dung beetle that rolls its eggs in a dung ball.'

They watched as he poured the paste onto the table and then deftly started rolling tiny balls under his palm, all the while praying in Egyptian to Khepri. At last he had ten small pills, which he wrapped in a sycamore leaf and presented to Pylyp.

'Give them to him and get him to swallow one at a time, washing each one down with a mouthful of palm wine. If they stay down, he will begin to feel thirst and hunger. That will mean he is innocent. If he vomits them back, he will continue to shrivel inside and likely die. If he lives and thrives, let me know, then I will send Overseer Hanufer my fee. If he dies, I want nothing to do with his death or his guilt, so there will be no fee at all.'

Pharaoh Ptolemy Philadelphus made vigorous love to Artemisia in her bedchamber for two hours before they fell apart and lay beside one another, regaining their breath.

'You are like the Greek god Priapus, Ptoly,' Artemisia giggled. 'You carry me to heights of delight I never thought possible.'

'You inflame me, my love.'

'I like to hear you call me that — my love!'

'And I am moved when you call me Ptoly. No one has ever been permitted to use such a name since I was a boy. Even then, it was only my mother. My father always behaved like the pharaoh and was not affectionate.'

'Are you, Ptoly? To your own son, I mean.'

'I am, but I am also teaching him that he must be strong. One day, he will have the weight of Egypt upon his shoulders. His people will depend upon him.'

'I cannot imagine how hard that must be. It makes it so important that you have a strong support by your side.'

Ptolemy turned and stared at her for a moment, before smiling. 'You mean my queen.'

'And your vizier, Admiral Patroclus.'

'They help. You are also a great help, Artemisia.'

'Like the Ladies Bilistiche and Didyme?'

'They help, each in their different ways. But none of them have your great skills and powers.'

Artemisia smiled demurely. 'I am merely a channel, Ptoly. I am a mouthpiece to Hecate, that is all.'

He touched her lips. 'A mouthpiece. A beautiful mouth, and this evening you will intercede with her for Egypt when we make the sacrifices to ensure that Sothis rises.'

He kissed her tenderly, then they made love again before he left.

After bathing, she drank a cup of wine to wash down the strong brew of silphium she had taken.

A child would be an inconvenience, she mused as the wine took the bitter taste from her mouth. *One thing at a time.*

Cario wished he had taken some water with him as the sun continued to rise high in the sky. Although the acacia trees shaded him from the burning heat, the dryness of the air was making him feel thirsty. Yet he did not dare leave his post in the alleyway, lest Galenos should leave his villa while he was gone.

He felt guilty that he had not taken his friend Paiania into his confidence, especially when he had told him so much about Galenos's coming and goings. But Hanufer had emphasised that he had to be subtle.

He had watched for the better part of two hours, and his eyes were starting to flutter closed when the physician came out of his villa. He was on his own and was carrying his medical chest himself.

Cario waited until Galenos had walked some way from his home up the long sycamore boulevard before he left the alley and started to follow. Up ahead Galenos turned right onto one of the busy streets lined with market stalls. He was soon barely visible amid the crowds in the busy street. Cario noticed that he was darting glances sideways and backwards.

Keeping a good distance away and pretending to look at market stalls every now and then, Cario followed Galenos until he entered the gamma sector of the city, which consisted of the Soma and the surrounding villas and mansions of the wealthy citizens. And then he was approached by a large Egyptian, an artisan rather than a merchant or businessman. Even from a distance, Cario saw the physician's demeanour suddenly change. He stiffened, looked worried and seemed to clutch his medical chest tighter, but then they passed a few words and kept on moving.

Cario kept to the shadows and followed. Once more, he saw the physician darting glances in all directions. The large Egyptian walked beside him, directing the route they took, which again seemed haphazard, leading off the main streets and into the network of alleyways between the high-walled villas.

With fewer people around, Cario slowed down so that he could merge with the shadows, yet still kept them in sight.

Then the Egyptian suddenly stopped at the end of an alley and spun round, staring directly at Cario. Galenos also turned and saw him, his eyes opening wide. He tugged the other's elbow and muttered something.

By Apollo, he recognises me! thought Cario.

In a panic he started to turn on his heel to run, but he never completed the move. He felt a thunderous pain in the back of his head, before falling unconscious.

CHAPTER 23

Hanufer was in turmoil after finding the ivory cow's horn. He started to drive the chariot back towards the police headquarters when a mounted messenger intercepted him.

'Admiral Patroclus wishes to talk to you straight away, my lord,' the messenger called out as Hanufer drew to a halt before him.

It was the last thing Hanufer wanted at that moment, but he turned his chariot in the wide street and followed the messenger to the palace.

When he was shown into Patroclus's office, he was surprised to find Heri-ib and his deputy Muthis already in discussion across the desk from the vizier.

'Sit, Hanufer. You know Heri-ib from the Nile police. He and his sergeant have some disquieting news. They have uncovered a network of spies.'

Heri-ib nodded to his fellow overseer. 'I had already told my friend Hanufer that we were in Alexandria to investigate whether there could be spies,' he told Patroclus.

'Spying upon whom?' Hanufer queried.

'Upon Egypt,' Patroclus interjected. 'On the navy, the army, His Majesty Ptolemy Philadelphus, on myself and — on you!'

Hanufer stared disbelievingly. 'Did you say upon me?'

Heri-ib nodded. 'Indeed. As the Overseer of Police, you are an obvious person for a network of spies to want to know about. If they know what you are investigating without you being aware of them, then they can take precautions to keep their main activities a secret.'

Hanufer remembered all the recent occasions when he'd thought that he was being watched. Could it be true?

'I have actually seen at least three different people following you, my lord,' Muthis proffered.

'And how did you know this?' Hanufer asked indignantly.

'Because I arranged to have you followed,' Heri-ib declared. 'Sergeant Muthis and our constables are skilled in these matters, and —'

'And I ordered it,' said Patroclus. 'I don't care if your feelings are hurt, Hanufer. My concern is the safety of Egypt, of his Majesty and Queen Arsinoe. Anything that threatens such safety is a danger. I offered you the help of Heri-ib, but you refused. So, I asked him to make sure all was being done properly.'

Hanufer was seething but knew better than to allow his emotions to show.

'It would help if you told us what cases you have been investigating lately,' Heri-ib said. 'The vizier has told us of Queen Arsinoe's concerns, so we know about the death of *Architekton* Usermontu and the deaths in the Pharos lighthouse.'

Patroclus drummed his fingers on his desk. 'I have a bad feeling about all that is happening. We have this sacrifice that Pharaoh Ptolemy is going to make later today. I had the most horrific difficulty in ensuring that we have the sacrificial creatures ready, especially the baboon, but if this somehow does not work and Sirius does not appear —'

Sergeant Muthis gasped in horror. 'A baboon, my lord? Surely not? They are sacred animals and are like people.'

'That may be,' said Patroclus, 'but the sacrifice is to be of a fish, a dog, a polecat and a baboon. The Lady Artemisia says that is what is required for the goddess Hecate.'

Heri-ib nodded. 'It has happened before, of course. My predecessors kept records of many pharaoh's rules, and on the years when Sothis did not appear at the expected time, the Nile did not rise and there was famine.'

'And if there is famine, the rule of the pharaoh is under threat,' added Patroclus. 'And if we have internal unrest, then that can affect the army, navy and the security of the country.'

Hanufer wondered whether to talk about Nefrit's disappearance and his discovery of the ivory cow horn. He decided he needed help, so he described his morning's search.

'So, we come again to Artemisia, the High Priestess of Hecate!' exclaimed Patroclus. 'Queen Arsinoe considers her a threat to herself personally. What did you think when you saw her today, Hanufer?'

'I am unsure, my lord. She offered to seek the goddess Hecate's advice, but I declined.'

'Do you think she could help?' the vizier demanded. 'It would be difficult to coerce her, since she is His Majesty's mistress, but —'

'I would rather not risk His Majesty's ire,' Hanufer said quickly. 'But I have no idea where Nefrit is being held. And now I am seriously worried that she is in grave danger.' He reached into his chiton and placed the ivory cow horn on the desk. 'I found this on the pedestal of the statue of Sobek. It is Nefrit's, I am certain. And I have no doubt that this was meant for me. It is a warning to me to back down.'

'I agree,' Heri-ib said with a grim nod. 'The Lady Nefrit's life is in danger.'

Cario slowly came round, instantly aware of nausea. He tried to work his jaw, only then realising that he had a rag in his mouth. It was dark and he could see nothing.

He was seated on a cold floor, his back propped up against a pillar of stone to which his torso had been lashed. His legs were in front of him, and as he tried to move them he realised that they were also bound.

He listened hard, thinking he could hear movement nearby. Then he heard the sound of breathing.

Not daring to move in case the sound was coming from an animal, he tried to breathe as shallowly as possible.

Sabu was still working on the papyri when Hanufer returned. In addition to the two desks, he had spread them out on the chests by the wall and on the floor.

'My apologies for using your desk, my lord, but I needed to be able to see them all at once. I shall gather them up now.'

'No, leave them and I shall look. I need to occupy my mind with all that is happening. Especially with this sacrifice that is to be made when Ra goes down.'

Sitting behind his desk and gesturing for Sabu to do likewise, he told him of his unsuccessful search for Nefrit and his subsequent meeting with Patroclus and the Nile police officials.

Sabu listened with increasing horror, for he was well aware of his boss's relationship with the High Priestess of Isis. 'Should I call all the men and organise an extensive search, my lord?'

Hanufer lay the cow horn on the desk between two papyri. 'No, Sabu. This is obviously a warning to me, but I have not yet had the actual message. Under the circumstances, the best thing that I can do is to concentrate on the investigations we already have. It is because of one of these cases, that is clear, although the Lady Nefrit has no connection with any as far as I can see. That being the case, we must be close to discovering something.'

'You told me that the Nile police are here trying to uncover spies, my lord. Are they any closer?'

'Yes and no. They know who is being spied upon, and they have even seen several people who have been following and watching me, but they have not apprehended anyone yet. Now that the situation is becoming urgent, Overseer Heri-ib is going to make their presence in Alexandria obvious. They are going to have constables patrolling all of the harbours and the Canopus Canal. And if we need help, they will immediately come upon my request.' He pointed to the papyri. 'So, tell me, what progress have you made?'

Sabu recounted how he had divided the three lots of papyri and then subdivided them according to whether they were to do with administration, rope-stretching or sky-watching.

'It looked as if he had deliberately mixed them up. But I did not want to reassemble them into three types, in case the original three caches could be important. That is why I have scattered them all about the office. The ones on and about your desk are the first ones we found in the lighthouse. Those around my desk are from the library, while the ones on the chest and on the floor beside it are from his houseboat.'

'And what do you make of his drawings?'

Sabu rubbed his chin. 'I cannot understand any of the pyramids and triangles, my lord.'

Hanufer stood and went around the office, looking at the papyri with drawings. 'I don't think they make sense at all, Sabu. And I think that is precisely why Hatensor drew them.'

'I don't understand, my lord.'

'The notes he has made only really relate to some of the drawings. They make no sense because they were only drawn to disguise the relevant ones. So, let us focus on those.' Hanufer pointed to one on his desk. 'These figures here relate to rope-measuring. See, these are quantities of building materials. These drawings have no relevance here. But look at this one next to it. That long, thin triangle is related to the figures beside it, which are times of the night. Yet this third papyrus has pyramids and triangles, and these figures do relate to it. He has calculated the *seked*, the slope of the pyramid he has drawn.'

'But what does this tell us, my lord?'

'I am not sure, other than that this is clearly to do with his sky-watching and this other is to do with a building and calculations for it. All in all, Hatensor was successful in making his writings only discernible to himself.'

Sabu snapped his fingers. 'My lord, I am sorry, I put these ones under my desk.' He bent and produced the documents that Hatensor had taken from the Library and the Ministry of Buildings and Monuments. 'These are detailed maps of Alexandria. This one shows the Island of Pharos with the lighthouse and the Temple of Proteus and Harpokrates, and the two harbours separated by the *Heptastadion*. There is also a sketch of this map, and again he's drawn triangles, pyramids and lots of figures. But look, the pyramid is the wrong way up. At least, it's different from most of the ones he's done.'

Hanufer leaned down and examined the drawing.

'And look here, sir,' Sabu said, producing another sketched plan of the Necropolis. 'He's done a few of these with the outlines of various tombs, and again the upside-down pyramids.'

Hanufer studied it for a few moments. 'Most intriguing. And he has calculations of the *sekeds* on these.'

The sound of heavy *cothurnus* boots was followed by the appearance of Pylyp and Filemon. After informing them of Nefrit's disappearance and of the Nile police's confirmation that spies were active, Hanufer instructed them to report on their visit to the Necropolis prison.

'The physician Hessi is a most remarkable man,' said Pylyp. 'He refused to visit because of his age, but he made up some pills and prayed to the god Khepri. Well, they had a miraculous effect upon Kallisto. After taking them and washing them down with wine, he demanded food and he said his mind had cleared. We questioned him again about that ghost and the spear going through it. This time, he said it seemed to bounce off it.'

'He still thought it looked as if it was made of smoke, because it was steaming,' added Filemon. 'We asked if there was any smell, and he said there was. He had noticed it before the accident. He said it was like vinegar.'

'Vinegar!' exclaimed Sabu. 'There must be all sorts of bad smells in the Necropolis.'

'But when he said the spear may have bounced off the ghost, we thought we ought to go back to the place it happened,' Filemon continued. 'As we found before, it had been smoothed over, but we tried to work out exactly where the ghost was and where it might have disappeared if it was a man. We found it, sir. It was covered by a large flat stone, but as soon as we shoved it aside, we smelled the vinegar. It was a shaft, sir.'

'Did you go down?' Hanufer demanded.

'It looked deep and dark and we didn't have a rope. We think there may have been foot and handholds gouged in the rock, but we thought we should report it to you, sir, and then investigate further.'

There was a knock on the door and a constable announced the arrival of Erasistratus and Herophilus. He then stepped back to allow the two anatomists to enter.

'We have brought you the reports you wanted with our detailed drawings of the injuries,' Erasistratus said, handing Hanufer a roll of papyri.

'And a gift,' added Herophilus, turning and snapping his fingers.

Immediately the hospital's young slave Nikos came in, carrying two dead chickens. He hesitated until Herophilus pointed to a space on the floor, and he lay them down.

'You will understand when you read the reports and look at the drawings.'

Hanufer unrolled the papyri and quickly read the findings before turning to the next scroll and examining the drawings.

'Essentially, you can see how the middle neck bones, of which there are seven in total, have been broken on the left in each case,' Erasistratus pointed out.

'We looked at how one can wring a chicken's neck,' Herophilus went on. 'Erasistratus sent young Nikos to bring ten of them from the market, and one by one we experimented and opened their necks. These are two to explain. The chicken on the left had its neck wrung the usual way, which is basically done by pulling the head and twisting. That doesn't always break the bones, but it dislocates the bones, or pulls them apart. Death comes with the spinal cord from the brain being snapped. The one on the right had its neck twisted and pushed sidewards at the same time. Its neck bones are broken. You simply couldn't wring a person's neck. It would have to be twisted and pushed sideways at the same time. Why don't you show them, Erasistratus?'

The anatomist gave a short laugh and then beckoned Nikos to come forward and turn his back to him. 'Have no fear, young Nikos. I'm not going to break your neck, just turn your head.' He stood behind him and encircled his shoulders with his right arm. 'You have to do this from behind and ensnare the person's arms. Then you have to wrap your other arm around his face and grab the back of his head.'

Nikos tensed and made a whimpering noise.

'Then twist and pull to the side at the same time and — snap, instant death.'

He released Nikos and tousled his hair.

'Do you see our point?' Herophilus asked. 'The direction of the twist is all important.'

'Of course!' Hanufer suddenly exclaimed. 'The directions.'

'That's right,' Erasistratus began, 'you see —'

But Hanufer had started looking at the various maps of Alexandria and the corresponding sketch maps that Hatensor had made. 'It begins to make sense,' he said. 'Strange, almost unbelievable sense. And thanks to our two good anatomists, who have given me the key word — direction.' He drew their attention to the maps. 'Hatensor's sky-watching pyramids and triangles were all orientated east to west, but all of these are north to south. Look at the points of these triangles: they rest on definite places. And they are done in sequence. They are charting positions in the city.' He snatched the maps and sketches of the Necropolis. 'Look at these. Hatensor was charting specific tombs. As you said, Sabu, these triangles are upside-down and the calculations of the *sekeds* are written here.'

'I don't see, my lord,' said Sabu.

'Hatensor was calculating the slopes of shafts underground. That was an air shaft that you found, and that ghost was a living tomb-robber.'

CHAPTER 24

Cario heard footsteps from beyond a door. Someone seemed to be descending a staircase. Bolts were thrown back and a man with a torch entered the room.

In the light of the flame, Cario could see that he was a tall man with a braided beard and long black hair, dressed in a robe made of some sort of hide, and he had tattoos on the backs of his hands. He smiled, his white teeth gleaming in the light.

'So, have you two met?' he asked with an ugly laugh. Cario did not recognise the accent, but he knew that he was neither Greek nor Egyptian. 'Or did you both at least realise that you had a companion in the darkness? You were both unconscious when you were brought here. And one of you has gone without food and water for a considerable time!'

Cario felt his heart pounding. Tearing his eyes away from the man, he was shocked to see the Lady Nefrit, bound and gagged like him. She looked terrified.

'I am sorry for the gags, but although no one outside this building would hear you, the twenty men who live and work here would not appreciate cries for help. Especially not from a woman. Some of them are very rough indeed.' He laughed again. 'And now you should know why you find yourselves here as my guests. It is because of that interfering dog Hanufer. He needs to mind his own business and leave us to ours.' He turned and whistled up the stairs, then inserted the torch into a ring holder on the wall.

Moments later, footsteps on the stairs were followed by the entrance of Galenos the physician, carrying his medical chest.

'Since you were so interested in where my good doctor was going, my man thought he ought to bring you to join the Lady Nefrit. And now that Galenos has done such a good job on one of my other men, he is free to take a little something from each of you to send as a warning to our precious Hanufer.' He turned to the physician. 'Get out one of your knives. A little finger from each of them will do.'

Galenos stared in horror. 'No … no! I … I cannot.'

'Open the chest and take out a knife!' the man said menacingly.

Galenos clutched his chest and shook his head vigorously.

'In that case, I'll use mine,' the tall man said, pulling out a curved blade from the sheath on his belt. He spun Galenos around, grabbed his grey beard from behind and yanked it upwards before raking the knife across his throat. A fountain of blood spurted from an ugly wound and the physician fell to his knees, a horrible gurgling noise coming from his throat as he dropped the chest. His eyes rolled and his body started to convulse as he fell forwards. Moments later, the room was filled with the noise of his death rattle, before he was still forever.

Nefrit and Cario stared in horror, unable to move.

'He had to go, of course, since he had seen too much,' the man said nonchalantly, stepping over the pool of blood. 'The good thing is that no one knows where he was going to. Now, where was I? Ah yes, a little finger each.'

He waved the blade back and forth and approached Nefrit.

Hanufer explained his reasoning as they looked over the sketched plans of the cisterns and waterways, the Necropolis and the maps of the city.

'Look at this map of the Necropolis and where he has drawn the pyramid on it. The two angles cover two tombs. I think it looks as if one tomb was entered from the surface and they entered the other via an underground tunnel. It is something that has been going on since ancient days. But look at this upside-down triangle. He has calculated the *seked*, the slope. Some of these documents from the Ministry and from the Temple of Harpokrates show the positions of the tombs and how deep they are.'

Erasistratus tugged his beard. 'So the *seked* was his way of telling the direction they had to dig the shaft and how far.'

'And I believe they threw vinegar on the limestone, my lord,' said Sabu. 'It makes cracks in the rock. That explains the smell.'

'And the tomb-robbers would use those cracks to hack the rocks out of the tunnel,' Hanufer added. 'Sometimes, they probably used fire to heat the rocks before throwing the vinegar on it. That would also explain why they created air shafts. I suspect that one of the robbers was partially overcome and climbed out for air. He would probably have been covered in limestone dust, and as he coughed and spluttered, clouds of it would have come off him. It would have looked as if he was made of smoke or steam. If Kallisto the guard thought he was a ghost, I can see why he threw his spear. It must have struck the tomb robber, wounded him to cause the blood on the ground, and been deflected to strike the guard Dion.'

'So a horrid accident and nothing more, my lord!' said Pylyp. 'Shall we take some constables and investigate, sir?'

'We will do that later. I want you and Filemon to come with me. Bring five constables.'

'And what shall I do, my lord?' Sabu asked.

'I want you to go to the Royal Harbour, where you'll find *Archiphylakites* Heri-ib. Tell him that I think I will want his assistance after all, and the expertise of the Nile police.'

'We shall return to the hospital, unless you have further need of us,' said Herophilus.

'Your help has been of immense importance. Please look to your patients now.'

Once they had left and Sergeant Sabu had gone on his mission, Hanufer looked at the mass of papyri. 'We had better tell Cario not to disturb anything,' he said to the constables. 'But where is he? I would have expected him to be back by now.'

Cario was not sure whether the man who had murdered Galenos had left the torch in the wall to be cruel, for the sight of the physician's body in the pool of his own blood was horrible.

The man had laughed when instead of cutting off their fingers as he had threatened, he had merely cut some locks of hair from both the Lady Nefrit and himself.

But one thing was clear. If he had slain Galenos without a thought, there was little chance that they would leave alive. Especially not Cario, a lowly *demosios* slave. The Lady Nefrit, though, surely he would not kill her? But could he afford not to now? Whichever way he looked at it, there was no answer. They seemed doomed.

He looked across and saw Nefrit staring at him and nodding her head vigorously. She was trying to attract his attention. Then he saw that she had somehow managed to wriggle a hand downwards so that she could move her fingers.

He realised she was trying to indicate Galenos. But why?

Then he saw the physician's fallen medical chest, which lay just inches from his feet.

Looking up, he saw her nod. She was flicking her fingers at him. He understood. There was no way he could free a hand, but he could perhaps shove the chest across the floor to her.

Straining every muscle, he managed to push himself down so he could extend his legs a little more and get his feet against the side of the chest. Praying to every god he could think of, he managed to propel it towards Nefrit.

He watched hopefully as she moved her feet to manoeuvre it slowly towards her hand. Then she managed to lift the lid as she moved the chest closer. Moments later, she had one of the physician's *macairion* knives in her hand.

Turning it, she moved it by feel and managed to begin cutting through the rope. Cario prayed that she would not drop it and that the man would not return yet.

At last the ropes parted and she was able to release her hands. Soon after that, she had cut more ropes and freed herself.

'Cario!' she whispered after removing her gag. 'Now we must free you and arm ourselves. It is our only chance.'

Minutes went by as she cut his bonds. Then they rummaged through Galenos's medical chest so that each of them had a blade in each hand.

'We must wait on either side of the door,' Nefrit whispered. 'And as soon as that monster returns, we must both strike to kill. You go for his heart and I'll go for his eyes.'

Sabu took the second police chariot to the Royal Harbour along with one of his constables. He left it with him to look after while he went directly to the naval offices, where Hanufer had said he'd find Heri-ib.

Sergeant Muthis was just coming out of the office with two Nile police corporals. Recognising Sabu's insignia on his chiton, he hailed him.

They greeted one another as officers of the same rank, then Sabu said, 'My boss has sent me to speak with *Archiphylakites* Heri-ib. We have made progress in our investigations but seek the assistance of the Nile police.'

Sergeant Muthis beamed. 'Then my boss Heri-ib will be most pleased to help. Here, let me introduce you.'

He nodded at one of the corporals, who opened the door to the office and stood aside to let Sabu enter.

Heri-ib was sitting in a chair behind his desk, his face staring sightlessly at Sabu. There was a huge gash in his throat, and the front of his chest was covered in blood.

Sabu sensed what was about to happen and felt hands grab at him. Instantly he swung his arms upwards and backwards, his fists connecting with teeth and noses.

'Unfortunately, Heri-ib is indisposed,' came Muthis's voice behind him, immediately encircling his shoulders with one arm while his other hand covered his face. 'Just as you will be in —'

Sabu threw his head backwards, crunching Muthis's nose. Grasping his right arm with one hand and his left hand with the other, he bent forwards, pulling Muthis's arms to throw him over his shoulders.

The two corporals were staggering, with blood pouring from their faces. Sabu grabbed each by their necks and smashed their heads together. They slumped to the floor.

'So that's how you killed all those poor people — always the same way, you bloody coward!' he yelled, diving forward as Muthis scrambled to his feet, reaching for his short sword at his right hip.

But Sabu was faster. He grabbed the wrist before Muthis had cleared the sheath, and using both hands he snapped the wrist so that the bones broke and the sword fell to the ground.

Muthis howled in agony. Sabu's great right fist then ploughed into his lower jaw, breaking teeth and hurtling him back so that his head crashed into the wall. He slid down it, landing in an unconscious heap.

Going to the door, Sabu called his constable and ordered him to use his manacles to tie the two corporals together. As soon as he had done that, Sabu bundled Muthis into the chariot. They headed to the barracks to find a quiet cell, where the sergeant intended to persuade Muthis to cooperate.

The sun was setting. The appointed time for the sacrifice of the fish, the dog, the polecat and the baboon had arrived. Patroclus had ensured that the important event was well attended, especially as Pharaoh Ptolemy Philadelphus and Queen Arsinoe would be there.

Accordingly, a great crowd had assembled around the *temenos*, the circular sacrificial arena which was reached by passing through the grove close to the Temple of Poseidon. This area with its sacrificial altar was used by several of the temples dedicated to the different gods, both Greek and Egyptian, since no animals could be slaughtered within such sacred spaces.

As usual, the high priests would carry out the sacrifice, which would involve high priestesses of different religions parading as basket carriers. Inside the baskets there would be the axe or the ceremonial blades used to dispatch the sacrifice.

Cheers rose from the crowd when the great chariot driven by the pharaoh entered the arena. Queen Arsinoe stood behind her brother-husband in the chariot, and both acknowledged the crowd.

But when the sacrificial creatures were brought forward, the fish carried in a tank, the dog, polecat and baboon on leashes, the cheers turned to murmurs of discontent.

The dog and the baboon seemed to know what was about to happen as they were led towards the altar, where the Lady Artemisia had her hands raised to the sky. She was making a speech, asking the goddess Hecate to accept the offerings.

Suddenly the baboon swept his great arms out, knocking the priest holding its leash to the ground. The baboon grabbed it, hit out at the other priest holding the dog and polecat's leashes, and bounded off through the crowd. The people parted to let the dog, baboon and polecat escape.

Their cheers obviously angered Ptolemy, who glared at Artemisia before driving his chariot out of the arena.

Many were relieved that the animals had gone, for the dog and baboon were associated with the god Thoth. And many saw from the smile on Queen Arsinoe's face that the failed sacrifice had pleased her.

The Lady Artemisia looked less than happy.

Footsteps came down the stairs.

Cario and Nefrit were petrified yet determined. They stood on either side of the doorway, their weapons raised.

The bolts were drawn and the door was thrown open. Both of them took a step and swept their hands downwards.

Their wrists were caught in a strong grip.

'Enough!' called out Hanufer. 'You are safe.'

CHAPTER 25

'What of that monster?' Nefrit asked after she had buried herself in Hanufer's arms and wept for relief as he kissed her head. Cario had discreetly taken himself up the stairs, where Pylyp and Filemon met and greeted him effusively.

'We have found only one person in this villa, my beloved. He is a tomb robber and he is no threat, as he is wounded and we have tied him up for now. It was he that the physician Galenos was treating, for a wound that was festering.'

'But that ... that man said there were twenty or so rough men living and working here.'

'He said it to fill you with fear. This is one of two villas built together. Both belonged to the architect Usermontu. This one has been used as a base and a place to treat the wounded man. My men and I have been watching from the orchard and I think we saw Nasamon leave the villa. Does he have a braided beard and long hair? Is he dressed in a hide robe?'

Nefrit shuddered. 'He ... he threatened to cut our fingers off to send to you as a warning.' She pointed to the gruesome corpse of the physician. 'He ... he cut that man's throat in front of us.'

She buried her face in his chest again and he held her close.

'I am going to get Cario to take you back to police headquarters now. I must go to the villa next door and deal with the man, whose name is Nasamon. He claims to be a merchant from Phthia in Marmarica.'

'Take care, my love. He is a monster.'

After despatching Cario and Nefrit, Hanufer called out to his two corporals. He drew out one of Hatensor's sketch maps of the cisterns and underground water systems of Alexandria and spread it on a table in the villa.

'These are the points where the underground systems emerge,' he said, pointing to places on the canals. 'The Nile has not yet risen, so they are not full. One of these is where the men we pursue will come out. Get one of the constables to go back to the headquarters and despatch two constables each to these points.' Moistening his finger and dabbing it on his ink block, he marked the various points. 'And here, Pylyp, is where I want you to go — take one constable with you. Filemon, myself and the rest of the constables are going down there now.'

'But, my lord, that will leave only three constables and us. Will that be enough?' Filemon asked.

Hanufer nodded. 'We have the advantage of surprise and we are armed.'

The villa garden next door was a mass of rocks and rubble.

'They have been mining here for at least two weeks,' Hanufer explained as they cautiously let themselves into the villa. Like the one that Nefrit and Cario had been kept in, it had a cellar, the wall of which had been hacked open, and there was a mineshaft ahead of them. It led into a tunnel about five cubits high and the same amount wide. Oil lamps were burning in cavities that had been cut into the rock.

'It goes downhill,' Filemon whispered as they began their descent.

'It does, and it is exactly at the angle that the scribe Hatensor specified,' Hanufer replied. 'This tunnel is one of the upside-down triangles he had drawn.'

They carried on in silence until they reached the end of the tunnel, which flattened out for several more cubits.

Hanufer went first. He held up one of the oil lamps that he had taken from a cavity and entered a large hall with Grecian statues at the edges. In the centre was a huge pedestal with several marble steps.

'Where are we, my lord?' Filemon asked as he and the three constables joined him.

'We are in the tomb of the divine Alexander,' Hanufer replied. 'And the tomb-robbers have taken his body and the gold and glass sarcophagus in which he was brought here from Memphis.'

'But how? Where?' Filemon asked.

'There!' said Hanufer, raising his oil lamp and pointing to another tunnel entrance. Like the one that they had come through, this one also went slightly downhill. 'Can you hear water?'

'I can, my lord. It sounds like —'

'Like a barge being moved along a canal.'

They followed the tunnel and soon found themselves inside a vast hall with a wide waterway.

'This is one of the main cisterns of Alexandria,' said Hanufer.

As they advanced along the path beside the waterway into another tunnel, the sound of voices ahead was soon followed by the appearance of flickering shadows.

'Come now, Filemon, we must charge them. Have the men make as much noise as possible.'

And they did, rushing along the walkway, shouting and scraping their swords against the walls of the tunnel.

Ahead, a great sarcophagus was being dragged along on a barge by six men. Hearing the police officers, they dropped the ropes, cried out and fled in the opposite direction.

'Stop! Turn and fight these curs!' cried Nasamon. Seeing Hanufer, he drew his sword and rushed at him. 'You interfering dog. I was going to send you pieces of your slave and your woman, but —'

'But I am going to take pieces of you instead!' Hanufer cried angrily. He turned to Filemon. 'Go after the tomb-robbers. I shall deal with this mongrel.' He dropped into a fighting stance, with his sword at the ready.

Nasamon came at him, his sword in one hand and his knife in the other.

Hanufer waited until he was within contact distance and then threw a handful of rubble dust that he had kept in his chiton pocket. It struck Nasamon in the face, temporarily blinding him.

It was sufficient time for Hanufer to hack down on the wrist of his enemy, causing his sword to fall.

Nasamon screamed and lashed out sideways with his dagger, only to have his other wrist slashed.

'You should have cleaned up after your robbers a little better,' Hanufer said contemptuously. 'Tempted as I am to chop a few fingers off, the law will deal with you.' He punched the Marmarican in the face and he hurtled backwards onto the barge, where his head connected with the gold sarcophagus and he slumped downwards. 'Meanwhile, divine Alexander can have you.'

Sabu had returned to the headquarters after incarcerating his prisoner at the police barracks. There he had been told by Cario and Nefrit where Hanufer was. He had joined him, taking more constables to help the others round up the tomb-robbers. But first, they had to notify and bring the vizier and the royal guards to the scene.

Admiral Patroclus was horrified as he stood in the tomb now lit by many oil lamps and watched as a dozen of the royal guards brought the sarcophagus of divine Alexander back and raised it onto its marble plinth.

'So, this outrage is what all these deaths have been about, Hanufer of Crocodilopolis?' he demanded.

'It is, my lord,' Hanufer said. 'But thanks to the gods, we have prevented it. Hatensor the scribe had not merely been watching the sky for the reappearance of Sothis; he had also been charting the exact position of the shafts and the estimated time it would take for the robbers to dig their tunnel from the villa of Usermontu to the Soma.'

'The murders in the lighthouse?'

'Committed to silence Hatensor. The murderer was Muthis, the *Hyparchiphylakites* of the Nile police. His badge of office was sufficient to permit him entry to the lighthouse by the guards. He also murdered the *Architekton* Usermontu, whose villas they used to mine this tunnel.'

'You do realise how devastating this would have been had they succeeded and removed the body of divine Alexander?' Patroclus said, aghast.

'I do, my lord. And if they had managed to sell it to one of the powers that are not friendly with Egypt, I think it would have meant war.'

'A war that we may not have won, since divine Alexander's body could have united the *Diadochi* successors against Pharaoh Ptolemy. You will make a full report of all this to me and to His Majesty.'

'I will, as soon as I have completed my investigations, my lord. I will have to interrogate Muthis and Nasamon, the Marmarican.'

'Do whatever is needed to make them talk, but do not kill them. I believe the pharaoh will want to decide their fate.' Patroclus stared at the tunnels. 'We shall have these sealed up again, and these cisterns and canals will have to be rerouted.' He chewed his beard thoughtfully. 'But if tomb-robbers managed it once, they could again. I will consult His Majesty. We may even have to move the tomb of the divine Alexander to a secret place of greater security.'

The following morning, Hanufer took the maps and papyri which the scribe Hatensor had either borrowed or purloined from the Ministry of Buildings and Monuments and gave them back to Hak-mau.

'I am grateful, *Archiphylakites* Hanufer,' said the deputy architect as he unrolled them on Usermontu's desk, now his own. 'I wonder how Hatensor managed to get them? Perhaps Usermontu allowed him to take them before they had their great argument. They are important ones, and I am not sure if we have copies. I shall have to check.'

'He had made sketch maps of some of them, like this one,' Hanufer said, producing a scroll. 'As you will see, he drew pyramids and triangles on them.'

Hak-mau looked on as Hanufer unfurled it on the desk. 'Hmm, curious. All sorts of calculations on them, too.' He pointed to some jugs on the side table. 'Would you care for some palm wine, or perhaps a mug of beer? It is a hot morning.'

'Some beer would be welcome,' Hanufer replied.

The architect poured a mug of beer and then a goblet of wine for himself.

'Delicious,' said Hanufer after taking a sip. 'What do you think he was calculating?'

Hak-mau drank some wine. 'They look like *sekeds*. That is the incline of the pyramids. It is a bit of a mystery, since as far as I am aware he was not involved in any monumental work. At least not in Alexandria.'

Hanufer raised his mug to his lips. 'Perhaps it could have been elsewhere? Canopus, for example.'

'Possibly. He did work for Rekhmire and one or two wealthy citizens there.' He wiped his brow. 'Goodness, it is hot this morning.' He took more wine and smiled as Hanufer drank more beer.

'It ... it is, indeed,' Hanufer muttered. 'I suddenly feel very hot.'

'The heat can make one very tired, my lord. That beer will cool you down, though. Usermontu used to like it, and I have continued to have it stocked here.'

Hanufer raised his mug to his mouth and then tried to place it on the desk, but he missed and it went clattering to the floor.

'I ... am ... sorry,' he mumbled, taking a deep breath. 'I'm very ... clumsy his morning.'

Hak-mau smiled as he drained his goblet. 'Yes, clumsy indeed, Overseer Hanufer. Perhaps the beer was stronger than you thought?'

Hanufer stared at the mug on the floor. 'Or ... poisoned?'

The architect smiled. 'A proven combination of hemlock and some special concoctions that bring on swift clumsiness, numbness and paralysis. The heat you are feeling is a sign of its success.'

Hanufer grasped the edge of the desk and tried to pull himself forward, but instead lost his grip and slumped back again.

Hak-mau laughed. 'As you see, it is very fast. Soon you will not be able to reach out at all, and then your speech will go.'

'So ... what now...? You slit my throat?'

'Like Muthis did with the others after he broke their necks, you mean? No, your fate is not in my hands.'

He strode to an inner door and pulled it open. A moment later, Kephalos the High Priest of the Temple of Harpokrates walked in.

'We were in the process of making plans for your death when you so kindly came here this morning,' the priest sneered.

'We ... stopped ... you,' Hanufer rasped.

'You took our workers and you took back the corpse of the so-called Great Alexander. But we will cause war some other way.'

'You were ... taking it to Marmarica? Or to ... Cyrene?'

'That was the original plan — to take it to King Magas of Cyrene. But it could have gone to the highest bidder. The emissaries of all the empires are here to see the tomb of Alexander at the start of the Wepet Renpet Festival, and to celebrate his birthday. It would have been spectacular if Patroclus had opened the tomb and found it empty, and there would have been fortunes paid to become the possessor of the Great Alexander's body. Undoubtedly, there would have been war, but what would that have mattered? There are always fortunes to be made in war. And I and my friends would have been rich beyond our dreams. But you ruined that.'

'We have ... Muthis ... and Nasamon ... and the...'

'And the others?' said Kephalos. 'Not one of them will say a word, no matter what you threaten or how you beat them.'

Hak-mau laughed. 'They are all men of honour. Brothers.'

'You're ... just ... tomb-robbers ... and murderers.'

'Tomb-robbers!' exclaimed Kephalos. 'You dare to use that slur? My family have been experts at removing the chattels of your nobles and pharaohs for generations. We are kings of our craft.'

Hanufer's eyes opened wide and he struggled to utter words.

'You didn't know that, did you?' Kephalos taunted. 'Just as you did not know that I am Egyptian. Born in Thebes, I walk, talk and act like a Greek, and had little difficulty with entering the priesthood of Harpokrates and working my way up to Head Priest over the years. Harpokrates was one of our gods before the Greeks took him over, but as the god of silence he's always been the god of our family and brotherhood. But I am as Egyptian as you are. So now you must know that the men you impaled in Crocodilopolis were all members of our family. They were my nephews, Hak-mau and Muthis's cousins. Not Nasamon, though. He was a fanatic. He wanted war between Cyrene and Egypt, so that his country could crush Cyrene.'

'Usermontu ... Hatensor ... they —'

'They were our men, but both had tongues that waggled. We could not risk them bragging to prostitutes. They had to die — and with them any who might have listened to their pillow talk. That is why Muthis killed the two prostitutes and Usermontu.'

'So ... now...?'

'So now we will take you on a trip to Lake Mareotis. We have a stake already sharpened for you to be impaled upon. You will feel the agony that my nephews experienced and you will not be able to cry out when the crocodiles come for you, attracted by the blood that drips down the stake.'

Hanufer suddenly leaned forward and shook his head. 'I thank you for confirming your guilt. You will find your poison did not reach my lips but was tipped against this desk leg. It was the same that was given to Usermontu, I presume.'

As the two men stared in shock, Hanufer reached into his chiton and drew out a small trumpet. He raised it to his lips and blew three loud blasts.

Both of them made a move for Hanufer, daggers drawn. But he leaped up, drew his sword and with a couple of deft moves he sliced through muscles and tendons to instantly incapacitate them.

Moments later, the door burst open and Sabu and his two corporals rushed in to restrain the two cursing men.

The Lady Artemisia was sitting in her favourite place beneath the palm tree on the other side of her ornamental pond. She was dangling her crystal over a bowl of water when she was interrupted by her bodyguard, who coughed to attract her attention.

She held up a hand to silence him.

'I think it is you who needs to be silenced,' came a curt voice.

Artemisia spun round, aghast. Queen Arsinoe was standing in front of the pond.

'It is discourteous to sit in my presence, but I will allow you that — since you will be leaving Alexandria soon. And if I were you, I would not stop until I had left Egypt entirely. The sacrifice you advised was clearly not favoured by the gods. My brother-husband has admitted his shock and disappointment in you. He told me you had beguiled him and misled him about your skills, so now he wants no more to do with you.' She opened her hand to reveal the ring that Artemisia had given the pharaoh. 'He gave me this to return to you.'

She tossed it contemptuously across the pond. It landed in the bowl in front of the High Priestess of Hecate.

'In other words, you are banished — never to return, upon pain of death!'

Artemisia was lost for words and sat staring at the retreating figure of the queen.

Choking back tears, she rose and called on her maids to begin packing.

That night, Nefrit stayed with Hanufer.

After some hours, he woke and gazed admiringly at her. To his relief, he had not dreamed of shadows or monsters, and he thought that because of Nefrit's presence, the wings of Isis must have once again enfolded them.

Yet Nefrit suddenly seemed to shudder in distress and awoke. She told him that she had dreamed of being back in the cellar, where she was confronted by the monster Nasamon who threatened to cut off her fingers.

Hanufer took her in his arms, kissed her and comforted her before they made love until just before dawn.

Then, rising and drinking palm wine, they went to his flat roof terrace and watched as Sothis rose with the sun.

EPILOGUE

The next day, Hanufer reported everything to Pharaoh Ptolemy and Admiral Patroclus.

As Kephalos had said, neither Muthis nor Nasamon would cooperate at first, but at last they did admit that they had all been involved in the daring plan to rob the tomb of Alexander and take the body and sarcophagus to King Magas of Cyrene, or to the highest bidder among Egypt's neighbours. Ptolemy Philadelphus was furious that his elder half-brother should have been involved, and he ordered Patroclus to ensure that any attack from Cyrene could be instantly dealt with.

Hanufer told them that Sergeant Muthis, deputy architect Hak-mau and high priest Kephalos were all related to the tomb-robbing dynasty and that they had long thought it their right to plunder the tombs of the rich nobility and of the pharaohs and queens of Egypt.

He had told them of the architect Usermontu's part in their plan, and of his murder when they thought he might divulge it while in the throes of passion with his mistress. He was careful not to say who that mistress was, although it was clear to the pharaoh who he meant.

Ptolemy himself asked whether the Lady Artemisia was involved in any of the crimes.

'None, Your Majesty. The criminals merely feared that she might became aware of a plan.'

He told them of Hatensor's involvement: because of his rope-stretching and mathematical expertise, the scribe had been able to work out exactly how a tunnel could be sunk from one of Usermontu's villas to the tomb of Alexander. Then he had shown how the sarcophagus could be taken via a tunnel that breached one of the cisterns and thence via the underground water system to the canal. From there, the plan was to load it onto a boat, cross Lake Mareotis and sail down the Nile, then travel back up the Delta and onwards to whatever foreign port was chosen.

'Like Usermontu, they murdered Hatensor in case he divulged their plans to the prostitutes he slept with. They murdered two of the poor women, who were innocent victims of their scheme, as were the lighthouse watchmen and the public slaves who tended the fires.'

He recounted how they had used Hatensor's methods to practise robbing tombs in the Necropolis, and explained that the wounded robber — the 'ghost' — had been in the process of completing such a raid on a tomb when he must have had to come up for fresh air, probably because he was choking.

'That was when he was seen by the Necropolis guard Kallisto, who thought he was a ghost because of the limestone dust that he was covered in. As he coughed, he must have shaken the dust from him, giving the impression of smoke. Kallisto threw his spear, which wounded the fellow as it sliced through his back, but it did not stick in him and instead deflected to strike the unfortunate Dion in the eye. Kallisto must have been so shocked at seeing he had struck his comrade that he did not see the wounded tomb robber disappear back down the air shaft that they had created.'

Patroclus shook his head in wonder. 'And did they steal much in these raids?'

Hanufer nodded. 'We found all the gold and treasures that they had stolen from the tombs, both Greek and Egyptian,' he told them.

'And what of the physician who was murdered?' Ptolemy asked.

'I do not believe Galenos was part of the plot, Your Majesty. He was Usermontu's physician and the tomb-robbers coerced him into treating their wounded comrade. They would have told him on pain of death to say nothing about Usermontu if anyone asked, because they could not risk any investigation leading back to Usermontu's villas. He lied to my sergeant about Usermontu, but he was not a good liar and hence he fell under suspicion.'

Ptolemy had ordered that the Necropolis guard Kallisto should be released immediately and that investigations should be made to see which graves had been desecrated. 'The families whose dead relatives were robbed of their possessions must be able to identify their things and have them restored. The expense of re-burials shall be paid by myself.'

The Wepet Renpet Festival began when news of the risen Sothis was spread to all. The Nile duly rose, and the cisterns of Alexandria filled up.

During a meeting with Sergeant Sabu and the two corporals, Hanufer called Cario in.

The young slave feared that he had done something wrong and immediately apologised in advance.

'Say no more, Cario. Today I am taking you to see Hessi the physician, who is skilled in all manner of surgeries. He is going to perform an operation on you.'

Cario started in horror. 'He is going to cut me, my lord?'

Hanufer smiled. 'I have arranged for you to no longer be a *demosios* slave. Hessi is going to obliterate that brand on your shoulder. You are a good man, Cario. I would like you to be a constable under my command, if it is your wish.'

Later that day, Sabu called at the brothel and arranged to take Keket for a walk by Lake Mareotis. He kissed her and she responded willingly.

'Keket, this day I have paid Gorgias and bought your freedom.'

She stared at him in disbelief and beamed. Then her face clouded. 'So, now I am to be your slave instead of anyone who pays, is that what you mean?' she asked with her old defiance.

'No, so you can be free to make your own choices. Perhaps you'll choose me.'

She threw her arms about his neck and kissed him passionately. 'I'll think about it,' she said.

HISTORICAL NOTE

Fall of a Scribe is a work of fiction set in Alexandria, the capital of Ptolemaic Egypt during the reign of Pharaoh Ptolemy II, known as Ptolemy Philadelphus. He was the second pharaoh in the dynasty, having been appointed co-ruler with his father Ptolemy Soter. He then ruled as pharaoh in his own right.

The background to this novel is the fascinatingly complex family history of the Ptolemies and of the dynasties of the other empires that arose after the death of Alexander the Great. He had five generals, known as the *Diadochi*, meaning the successors, who carved up the known world that was his empire. Wars broke out as the power struggle ensued. Ptolemy Soter shrewdly took Egypt as his own and thus established the Ptolemaic dynasty that would last for 275 years, from 305 to 30 BC. The most famous of the Ptolemies was Cleopatra VII, the last ruler of this dynasty, who was immortalised by William Shakespeare in his play *Antony and Cleopatra*.

The city of Alexandria was designed on the Hellenistic model, reputedly on the instructions of Alexander the Great himself. It had a regular grid structure to maximise the cool north winds during the summer, and it was a truly cosmopolitan city. Its main streets were extremely wide, constructed so that a chariot could be turned in them.

Ptolemy Philadelphus oversaw the construction of the famous lighthouse on the nearby Island of Pharos. It was reached by a causeway called the *Heptastadion*, which divided the crescent shape of the coast into two harbours. A scholar himself, he also oversaw the development of the Library of Alexandria and the Musaeum, which was effectively the world's first university. As part of this it had a Medical School, where two famous physicians and anatomists, Herophilus and Erasistratus, carried out ground-breaking research by anatomical dissection. According to the later Roman historian Celsus, they were permitted to use living people, such as condemned criminals, in vivisection.

The mind baulks at this, but whether it is true or not, Herophilus was responsible for many discoveries about anatomy. He described parts of the brain, the intestinal tract, the lymphatic system, liver, genitals and the eye, and amazingly, he described the pump action of the heart, showing that it was responsible for the pulse. He also showed that arteries were six times thicker than veins.

Erasistratus is regarded not only as an anatomist, but also as a physiologist, for he differentiated sensory from motor nerves and he described the anatomy and function of the trachea (the windpipe), the epiglottis (the flap of tissue that prevents food entering the windpipe when one swallows), the heart and the vascular system.

Up to ninety-five per cent of all medical terms are based on Latin and Greek. Most of the anatomical terms and the scientific names of microorganisms are of Latin origin, whereas many of the pathological and medical terms are derived from Greek, or a mixture of the two languages. The reason that Latin became the language of anatomy is because the Romans, who came after the Greeks, translated their medical and scientific works into Latin.

The scholars who flocked to study and work in the Library and the Musaeum under Ptolemy's patronage were legion. Several of them are mentioned in this novel. Callimachus developed a system to catalogue the Library; Posidippus wrote on many subjects, including divination through the observation of birds; and Lycophron was a soothsayer and the inventor of the anagram.

Alexandria was a Greek city in Egypt. The Ptolemies were Macedonian Greeks, but adopted Egyptian ways and did much to integrate the two cultures. Significantly, Ptolemy II married his full sister Arsinoe, having repudiated his first wife, also called Arsinoe. Incestuous marriage was anathema to the Greeks, but perfectly acceptable to the Egyptians. But it divided the opinions of the city, and many Greeks were disparaging about the union. Most notable among these critics was the poet Sotades the Obscene, who was the subject of the first novel in this series, *Death of a Poet*. His infamous poem landed him in trouble with the royal couple and he was thrown in prison. He escaped to the Island of Caunus, but was found by Admiral Patroclus, Ptolemy's vizier, who sealed him in a pithos jar or a lead cage or coffin and tossed him into the sea.

As mentioned in this novel, Ptolemy Soter, the first pharaoh of the dynasty, shrewdly kidnapped the body of Alexander from General Perdiccas, who had been in the process of transferring the corpse in a great gold and crystal sarcophagus from Syria back to Aegia in Macedonia. Having abducted the sarcophagus, Ptolemy had it taken first to Memphis, then to Alexandria, where it was entombed deep beneath the Soma, a specially built temple dedicated to Alexander. This act gave Egypt supremacy over the other *Diadochi*, for they held the mortal remains of the son of Amun.

Where exactly the body was buried in Alexandria is still hotly debated by historians and archaeologists. It may still be somewhere under the modern city.

Finally, as everyone knows, the ancient Egyptians were incredible builders and mathematicians. When one thinks of Egypt one thinks of the pyramids. The accuracy of their construction has amazed travellers throughout the centuries. In order to understand how they worked out the *seked*, or slope of a pyramid, and how it relates to modern trigonometry, I undertook a course in Egyptian mathematics with the Open University. If anything, it increased the awe I have for those scribes of ancient days.

A NOTE TO THE READER

Dear Reader,

If you have enjoyed the novel enough to leave a review on **Amazon** and **Goodreads**, then I would be truly grateful. I love to hear from readers, so if you would like to contact me, please do so through my **Facebook** page or send me a message through **Twitter**. You can also see my latest news on my **Website**.

Keith Moray

keithmorayauthor.com

Sapere Books is an exciting new publisher of brilliant fiction and popular history.

To find out more about our latest releases and our monthly bargain books visit our website: **saperebooks.com**

Printed in Great Britain
by Amazon

44584995R00149